Dustin's Turn

By

June Kramin

Could you win
your true love again
& again?
June Kramin

Dustin's Turn
By June Kramin

...

...

Published by Pau Hana Books
August 2014
Originally published in September, 2012 By Champagne Books, Canada

ISBN: 978-1502359964

Published in the United States of America
Cover Art by Valerie Kramin
Stock images: Dreamstime

Dedication

For Adam & Haggis. Thanks for making me figure out Frank!

And Tiami for wanting more Courtney.

And special thanks to "George" & Danny for the great visit and all your little quirks that made their way into this book. Love you two!

Chapter One

Kaitlyn bolted upright when the phone rang before six o'clock Wednesday morning. She didn't bother to look at the caller ID. Only one person would dare call her before the kids woke up.

"Hey, Court. What the hell is so important that you can't wait for Alexander to start wailing?" She said it with teasing love, not anger. Even after all the years, Kaitlyn and Courtney never lost the banter they'd shared when they were roommates in college.

Through her moving in with Dusty, the marriage, then children, they'd always remained close. Even at that, Kaitlyn had never shared her time traveling experiences with Courtney. Dusty and his sister, Alyson, knew and that was already two too many.

There had been no episodes since Katie last saw Frank, the kind custodian from the library who'd been the one person she could speak to as she went through her time traveling ordeal. He never did much more than lend an ear, but Katie could not have gotten through it without him.

Katie last saw him outside the window the day they arrived home from the hospital with their son, Alexander.

She and Dusty had hardly mentioned Frank since then, wanting to put everything behind them and live a normal life.

That was also the day Dusty opened up the box containing his first novel, *Captain Skinnard's Nebula.* Throughout Katie's trips, one of the constants was convincing Dusty to finish it. With more urging from her, he'd slowly plugged away at its sequel on weekends and an occasional sleepless night.

Kaitlyn was quiet while Courtney explained the reason for the call. The "What?" that she screamed made Dusty shoot awake. "Oh my God, hon. I'll be right there." She hung up before any protests formed on her best friend's lips.

"What's wrong?" Dusty asked. His hands were on his wife's shoulder, he was frantic with worry for her chubby best friend that he'd grown to adore.

"She's sick."

His head slightly tilted in confusion. "And that is going to make you drop everything and fly to Seattle?"

"She's dying, Dusty." Kaitlyn burst into tears after she blurted it out, barely audible. He held her tight, stroking her hair as she sobbed. Her once shoulder-length hair was now half way down her back. Two pregnancies had made her hair grow like wildfire. She let it go rather than fight it, especially after Dusty voiced his love of long hair.

When the sobbing subsided, she sat up and told him what Courtney had shared with her during their brief conversation. "It's AIDS."

"AIDS? Shit, baby." He never stopped with his onslaught of nicknames, but when he wasn't being a tease about it, he still used "baby." "I like 'baby' best. Can we just stick with that?" Kaitlyn had asked him years ago from a hospital bed. "Sure, puddin'. Anything my cupcake wants, my sugar gets."

"She just found out. There aren't any symptoms yet. She's going into the hospital this morning for some tests, so they can see exactly how progressive it is. I think she was just the right amount of drunk to call. It didn't seem as if she really wanted to tell me." Again she rested her head on his shoulder. "I need to go see her."

"Of course you can go. Leave the kids. You don't need to be traveling with them. I can work from home."

"But I'm still nursing."

"You said a few days ago that you've been thinking it's time to wean Alex. He's sixteen months old. I'm more interested in your boobs than he is."

Kaitlyn laughed softly and sat up.

"You've more than done your duty, baby."

"But I nursed Alyson till she was almost two."

"You were also pregnant again. You've done your job, mommy. It's time to claim your body back."

"Are you sure?"

"Of course I'm sure. I'll have him so distracted he won't even miss the evening boobies. I wish I could say the same about me."

She managed a grin. "Always a one track mind."

"And not you? Why do you think I married you, you nympho?"

"You married me because I went through time for you, you bastard."

"That, too." He gave her a gentle kiss. "Start packing. I'll book you flight."

While Katie packed, Dusty took care of the kids. Katie had pumped last night. Now was as good a time as any to try to get Alex to take the milk from him. He hadn't been too successful when he'd tried before, but there was never a reason for him to force the issue. A few minutes proved he wasn't going to be successful now, either. Katie came down the stairs at the fussing. Their daughter, Alyson, was at the table eating waffles, while Dusty sat with a squirming Alex. Immediately the baby reached for her.

"Katie, he has to learn. In a few hours, you won't be here."

"But I am here, Dusty. This will be my last time ever to nurse him."

"But if you don't pump, I'll have nothing to give him when you're gone." Dusty tried to stay firm. But when he saw tears pool in her eyes, he caved. He stood and handed her Alex. "Are those for him or Courtney?"

"Yes," she said, hugging the baby tight.

"He's old enough for whole milk. We don't need to do the crossover to formula. He'll probably take it from a sippy cup better than from a bottle."

"You're probably right. He won't fight you with that from the highchair, I'm sure." She ruffled her daughter's hair. "You'll help Daddy, won't you, honey?" A nod sufficed as an answer.

"Feed him, and then enjoy your freedom." Dusty said. "I suspect you and Courtney will get bombed as soon as she can get out of the hospital."

"There's an idea." She was finally able to force a slight smile. "When's my flight?"

"We need to leave in two hours if I'm going to get you there in time for your security groping."

"Dammit. I should have bought that underwear I saw online."

"What underwear?"

"It makes the people looking at the scanner screens see stars where my girly parts are."

He laughed. "Since when are you shy?"

"Shy has nothing to do with it. I just think the whole new process is disgusting."

"So take the pat down."

"That's so much better."

"Babe, you know you're just being difficult."

Crossing her arms, she said, "I'm crabby. I hate flying these days."

He stepped closer to her. "You go nurse him and I'll ask Mrs. Nelson next door to watch the kids for a couple of hours. I'll say it's so I can take you to the airport. We'll steal the extra time so I can have my way with you."

"I don't know how long I'll be. What makes you think I want to give up any time from my kids to have sex, Dusty?"

"Hello. I'm married to you. Get your time in now. You're not leaving without a proper goodbye."

She smirked. "Didn't fall for that for a second, did you?"

"Nope."

Alex was starting to get impatient, so she sat down on the couch. "Tell Ali she can come eat on the couch so she can sit with me."

"She's probably just about done."

"Even better. Less mess for you to clean up from the couch after I'm gone."

"She had waffles."

"Good. And don't you dare wash that sticky face. Please send her in to me," she pleaded.

Dusty leaned over the couch and kissed her cheek. "You got it."

While Katie nursed, she explained to her daughter that she had to go see Auntie Courtney.

"Is she in a pickle, Mommy?"

Katie smiled at her. It was funny how Ali had adopted the phrase after overhearing Katie use it once when she dared mention Frank.

"No, peanut. She's sick. I'm going to help her with her doctor appointment."

"But she is a doctor."

"Doctors still need to see the doctor sometimes, too, sweetheart."

"Will she get a sucker?"

"Only if she's good." Katie hugged her daughter with her free arm. She'd never been away from her kids for any length of time before. It was hard to fight the tears.

After long rounds of hugs and kisses, Katie walked the kids over to the neighbor's house. Mrs. Nelson loved having the kids at her place rather than going to Dusty and Katie's to watch them. She was a widow, but had a full backyard playground. It was open to any kids wanting to play there. Her grandkids lived far away and didn't visit often enough. All the neighborhood kids called her Grandma.

Although Katie wasn't done with the smothering, the kids were eager to escape it and run to the neighbor's arms.

After loading the bags into his truck, Dusty found Katie upstairs in his favorite nightgown of hers, ready to bid him a proper goodbye.

"How are we going to survive?" he asked as he removed his shirt.

"We've gone weeks before."

"Only the post pregnancy healing weeks and you're the one I had to force to wait until the doctor's okay," Dusty said.

"What can I say? I got spoiled having sex with you. Each one of you," she said with a giggle as she pulled him onto the bed.

"I wish all of those were in my memory as well."

She rolled on top of him. "You should be happy that the only man of my dreams is you."

"Ditto, sugar. Well, you know what I mean."

"There's the writer that I know and love who is always wonderful with words."

"It's a gift."

After a quick non-stop flight and a cab ride, Kaitlyn walked into her best friend's hospital room. Courtney saw her, lit up with a big smile, then immediately burst into tears. Katie rushed over, not hesitating for a moment before crawling in bed with her. They held each other close as they cried together.

"Are you sure?" Kaitlyn said when they finally broke apart.

Courtney nodded. "They've done the test twice."

"But you caught it early. The treatments get better all the time. Right? This can't be as bad as it used to be."

"It's AIDS, hon. I'll be worm food in a matter of years."

"Don't talk like that. You're a fighter."

"I'm also a doctor. Who wants a doctor with AIDS working on them? I might as well just die and get it over with."

"Stop it. Take some time off and come stay with us for a while. You need time for this to sink in."

"It's as sunk as it's getting."

"How…I mean when…who did you get it from? I know you were a little promiscuous in college, but you were careful. Weren't you?"

"I was always protected. I all but made those bastards double wrap the thing."

"So how then? I know you didn't use drugs."

"I slipped once; that's all it took."

"Who was it with?"

"Remember the night I kept you up when I was doin' it with you in the room? You were mad the next morning."

"I do. Ronald? It was him?"

Courtney nodded again. "It was him, but that wasn't the night. It was shortly after you moved in with Dusty. He got in the habit of coming over after his late shift. He ended up falling asleep there once and we were careless the next morning. We had too much to drink and I think I was still drunk. Gotta love the 'morning wood' with the brain of its own." Kaitlyn grasped her hand. "I slipped, Katie. I never dreamed it would come to this."

Katie held her tight. "I'm sorry."

"I know you. You're blaming yourself for moving out." Pushing her back, Courtney said, "Don't go there, hon.

Please. This is a bad enough guilt trip on me. I don't want yours, too."

"I won't do that to you. You said you didn't have symptoms yet. How did you find out?"

"A hospital in Minneapolis called me. Ronald tested positive. They insisted on knowing every lover he'd had for the past seven years." She let out a heavy breath. "Knowing him, it must have been one hell of a list."

"But you've had no symptoms. You've never suspected anything?"

"It stays dormant sometimes for a while. I never thought to have myself tested. I didn't need to. I mean, I guess I should have. Maybe if I were a surgeon, the administration would have done it automatically. I've been straining to remember every procedure I've ever done. I've never bled on anyone or so much as coughed on a patient. I'm certain I haven't given it to anyone else. Can you imagine if I infected a child?" Courtney's voice cracked; once again Katie held her tight.

"But you didn't. Don't think that way."

"How can I not? I've given my notice."

"Hon, no. What are you going to do?"

Courtney shrugged.

"When do you get released?"

"After rounds this afternoon."

"I have an unlimited leave of absence from the house courtesy of Dusty. I'm also officially done nursing. Let's get drunk."

"You're on."

Chapter Two

After Dusty dropped Katie off at the airport, he parked his SUV at home then walked over to the neighbor's. Mrs. Nelson was overjoyed to watch the kids for a few more hours when he asked her. The kids barely acknowledged him with a wave. Ann, another neighbor, was there with her two children. They were busy playing with Ali and Alex. Their children were close in age. Katie often arranged play dates with them, as well as the couples taking turns hosting dinner parties. They were the closest friends Katie and Dusty had. He waved to her, not particularly wanting to go into any details about Katie's trip yet.

"Hey, handsome," Ann hollered back. "Where'd that pretty little wife of yours take off to?"

Shit. Mrs. Nelson had already let the cat out of the bag. "I'll fill you in later, all right? I have to run an errand."

"Sounds good. I'll bring over my Shrimp Alfredo hot dish tonight so you don't have to mess with supper."

"Much appreciated, Ann. I'll pick up some garlic cheese bread and a tackle box of beer while I'm out. Don't drop it off, you and Cal stay."

"He's in Chicago till Wednesday."

"So it'll be just us. I love giving old Greta a rumor to spread."

Ann laughed. "It's a date. I'll be there at six."

On the other side of their house was a vacant home. It had been unoccupied, with a for sale sign in the yard, for over three years. It was huge and gorgeous, but overpriced, especially in the present market. The owners weren't in a rush to sell, so it sat empty. Across from this house, however, lived Greta: the Gladys Kravitz of the neighborhood. She didn't miss a thing that happened in the neighborhood. If by chance she did, she filled in the details herself. Dusty often toyed with her and Katie threw a little fun her way sometimes as well. They'd walked by with the kids one day and heard her say, "Look, there goes God now." Dusty could only laugh and say, "I told you—you were loud, baby."

Dusty thanked Ann again. "I have to split." He said his goodbyes to the kids and Mrs. Nelson. He thought his so-called errand was insane, but he wanted to do it anyway.

About an hour later, he found himself in front of their old college library. He reminisced for a moment before climbing the front stairs. It was here that he'd learned Katie was staying for good and their lives together had officially started. For him anyway. She had almost a year of memories of the two of them under her belt already; he was eager to catch up to her. She wasn't thrilled to live a few years over again, but Dusty vowed to make it worth it for her. Despite the short time they'd had together and the crazy things they went through, he couldn't imagine living another day without her in his life.

Walking through the front door, he smiled at the familiar sights. College kids mingled in the aisles and sat quietly at the tables, studying. It hadn't been that long ago for him, but Dusty thought the kids were awfully young to be in college.

There was a young girl sitting on the couch where Kaitlyn sat years ago when she researched time travel. The scenes of the two of them in here played over in his mind as he wandered over to the sci-fi section were Katie had been searching for answers. A smile spread over his face as he thought back to their college days. Never in his wildest dreams did he imagine that the sex would get better. He attributed it to what he didn't think could be possible—loving her more every day. He thanked the forces of whatever it was that made her time travel. Lost in the memories, he walked right into a man dressed head to toe in olive green. "Frank?"

"Bill," the man said. "I'm sorry. We don't have a Frank here."

"Sorry. You reminded me of someone."

"Can I help you with anything?"

"No. Thanks. I'm just wandering around, reminiscing."

"The school really doesn't take kindly to people other than students using this facility."

"I'm sorry. I'll get going. I was just in the area. I don't want to make any trouble."

"No worries, young man. No offense meant. I'm only doing my job."

"I appreciate it. Thanks."

Dusty drove home, chastising himself for being a fool. What had he expected to do if he found Frank there? He'd probably run screaming at the thought of losing Katie to another time traveling scheme. He didn't want her to go through that again. The last time she'd returned and her memories caught up with their present time, horrible nosebleeds accompanied them. It had scared him bad. He was grateful they were already in a hospital when the final round hit her. No. He didn't want to find Frank again. He drove straight home and picked up the kids from the neighbor's. This time he received a little better greeting than he had earlier. They were ready to come home.

Courtney's mood greatly improved as the day went on. Her posture eventually relaxed, and the scowl on her face was replaced with smiles and occasional laughter as they reminisced over their crazy college stunts.

After Katie had moved in with Dusty, she and Courtney still talked almost every day. Even after Courtney moved to Seattle, the ties between them never loosened.

There wasn't anyone, who wasn't hospital staff, who came to visit; Courtney worked too hard to have much of a social life. Kaitlyn was glad, more than ever, that she'd made the trip.

"You didn't need to rush out here, Katie. I'm not here because I have to be. They just kept me for testing and retesting."

"I don't care. I wanted to be here. That's why I hung up on your ass. I wasn't going to give you the chance to tell me not to come."

"That's why I didn't bother calling you back."

When the doctor finally came in, he spent a lot of time trying to get Courtney to reconsider resigning.

"Thanks for your input, Gene, but my mind is made up."

"Like it or not, doctors are human, Courtney. We're taught to believe we are but the hands of God doing His will, but we are mere humans nonetheless. Accidents happen and we carry on."

"Tell that to a patient I infect."

"We double the precautions we take when helping patients with AIDS. Do you see me afraid of treating you?"

"That's different. It's your job. No one would come to me if given the choice. You know that."

"I don't think—"

"My mind is made up, Gene. I appreciate the sentiment, but this discussion is over."

He closed her medical record. "You take some time off. Come see me when you're ready to take it like a grown up."

"Go to hell and sign my fucking release already!"

He sighed. "Does this mean our date is off for Friday?"

"Good guess, genius."

He rolled his eyes at Kaitlyn, took a step closer, and held Courtney's hand. "I've been tested. I'm fine."

Courtney pulled her hand away. "And we'll keep it that way. Please let me out of here."

He kissed her cheek. As much as he could get of it before she turned away, anyway. He turned back to Katie. "Take care of my girl."

"I'll try." After the doctor walked out, Katie turned to Courtney. "You never said you were dating anyone. I thought you told me everything?"

"We're just banging. Were anyway. Good thing I didn't get attached." She swung her legs off the bed and hopped to the floor.

"He seemed to still want to keep it going. You're the one being pigheaded."

Courtney spun around. "Did you come all this way to tell me how to run my life?"

"Don't you dare!" Katie shouted, now standing as well. "You're killing me, Court."

"No. I'm killing me. Either you're with me or you're against me, hon. I'm not going to spend your entire visit defending myself."

"I didn't come here to fight."

"Good. So let's go get drunk."

Katie walked over and wrapped her arms around her friend. "I love you, you know."

"Love you back. Now come on. We're both overdue for a night on the town. There's a place that totally reminds me of Dicky's. Let's go see if we can get thrown out for old time's sake."

Katie laughed. "You're on."

It was past four when they left the hospital. Courtney admitted that she'd had nothing to eat since she went in that morning. Katie was starving as well, having refused a stale five-dollar airplane sandwich.

They were seated at a high table in the bar area. The waitress came over with menus and Katie turned to Courtney. "How are the burgers?"

"The double bacon is to die for."

Katie refused the menu. "One of those with Swiss and mushrooms please."

"Make it two," Courtney added. "Oh, make mine fries and hers onion rings."

"Got it," the waitress said. "Can I interest you in a draft?"

"Bring out your ten tray sampler thingy," Courtney said. She turned to Katie. "I'll drink the darks and you can decide which light you like. They are really all great."

"Sounds good to me. It's been a while since I've had a drink. I should probably go slowly."

"Bullshit. Cabs are easy to come by here. We'll leave the car parked for the night. I'll spring for it."

Katie took Courtney's hand. "You don't need to twist my arm. Dusty would have our hides if we drove after drinking."

"He hasn't changed, has he?"

"No, and I love it."

Within moments, the waitress was back with a tray of samples. Courtney lined them up darkest to lightest. They each picked one from an end. "Cheers," they said together as they drank their first couple of ounces.

Half a burger later, Courtney ordered another tray of samples for Katie because she couldn't decide which one she liked best. Their waitress brought another batch of light beers. A few had lemon and orange wedges in them. She dropped a large dark beer in front of Courtney.

"I never did understand you and that dark beer. I can't stand a drink you can chew."

Courtney laughed. "I like my beer like I like my men." Her smile quickly faded. "I guess that's what got me in this situation in the first place. How did you put up with such a slut for a roommate?"

"You weren't a slut, Court. Stop talking that way."

"You wanted a revolving door on our dorm room."

Katie giggled. "Okay. You were a little…loose. Don't you dare start wallowing in your choices now. You can't change what happened and I refuse to let you get cranky on me already. I love you, dammit. We'll find a way to fight this."

Courtney was silent and swallowed a big gulp of her beer. "I wish the gods of fate decided I needed a Dusty in my life when I was twenty-five."

"You weren't ready to settle down at twenty-five. If your Prince Charming showed up, you would have only chased him away. I actually sort of liked Ronald, for what little I met of him."

"Liked him? You knew he was literally a 'come and go' kind of guy."

"But you liked him, Court, so I liked him. Don't be so crude and hard on yourself."

"I'm serious, though. I never even had a number for him. He called and I gave him the yea or nay to come over or not. The night he stayed over was really a fluke. I really didn't see him a lot after that, though. I never did know what happened to him. He stopped calling." She started to shred her napkin. "Maybe we should give it a whirl again and I should try to find him. We could have side by side hospital beds in the end and a set of matching bedpans."

Kaitlyn sighed and waved to the waitress. "Some tequila over here, Annabelle. Make it Patron."

Katie knew it was late, but she wanted to talk to Dusty anyway. With the time difference, he would be asleep by now. After she poured Courtney into bed, she called him.

"Hey, babe," he groaned into the phone.

"I'm sorry it's so late."

"I'm fine. You know I'd rather hear from you than sleep. How's it going?"

"So far, she's really wallowing and kicking herself in the ass."

"Can't blame her, I guess. I'm sure you'll see a few stages between anger and fear, too. You sound like you've had a few. How's that going for you?"

"I just had a couple beers and a shot or two. I didn't want to go crazy and be dealing with a hangover on top of everything else. My boobs hurt like hell now."

"I can imagine. I remember you being told to drink beer to help with your production when you were falling short with Alex in the beginning. I bet you're about to burst. I guess if you pumped it would only be a temporary fix."

"It'll keep happening till I dry up. Court is going to write me a script for some pills tomorrow."

"That's convenient, anyway. How are you otherwise?"

"I hate this, Dusty. She had everything going for her. She even had a cute doctor really interested in her."

"Had? This scare him away?"

"No, she's shoving him away."

"She's always shoved everyone away, doll."

"I know, but this is different. We're adults. She had to be thinking about settling down. We're not whoring our way through medical school."

"I can't believe you just said that."

"You know what I mean, dick."

He chuckled. "I love it when you use pet names on me, too." The line was silent. "You okay?"

Her voice cracked. "It's so hard, Dusty. I can't imagine life without her."

"You're a long way from that. You never know what'll happen for treatments over the next few years."

She needed to change the conversation before she started to cry again. "How are the kids?"

"Hardly know you're missing."

"Liar."

"Really. Alex was a dream. He was happy to take milk from a sippy cup. With you not here, he doesn't ask for those great breasts. Ann was here tonight, too. I'm sure her kids helped provide a distraction."

"What was she doing over?"

"I ran into her at Mrs. Nelson's. Cal was out of town. She heard you were gone and wanted to help, so she brought dinner."

"You big baby."

"You know it."

"She bring her Shrimp Alfredo hot dish?" Katie asked.

"Yup."

"Dammit. I'd have sex with her for that recipe."

Dusty laughed. "Her recipe is safe."

"You're not her type."

"Is that a fact?"

"She likes her men with a little more meat on them."

"Did you just call me skinny?"

"You're perfect to me, my love."

"That's not an answer."

"She likes a husky man."

"Cal is not what I would call husky. I'd say his beer belly is perfection."

"If I cooked as great as her, you'd look that way, too."

"You're a wonderful cook."

"Dusty?"

"What, babe?"

"I don't want to talk about food."

"I know. You put up a good front, though. Courtney tell you when it happened? She know who it was?"

"It was someone I'd met. She dated him, or at least…you know…had been together a few times when we were still roommates. Ronald was his name."

"That name doesn't ring a bell for me. Wait. It went back that far?"

"Yeah. She had no clue. Said it happened with him sometime after I moved out."

"Tell me you don't have guilt over that now."

"I promise I don't. I know it would have happened anyway."

"She doing okay, though? I mean other than emotionally?"

"Health-wise she's fine. She didn't even know. Things won't get bad for a while. It's the beating herself up part that's rough right now."

"You take all the time you need. Maybe you can get her to come out here for a while and try to get her mind off it for a bit."

"It'll mean a lot to her that you're offering."

"What else would I do? She's family."

Katie's voice cracked. "I miss you."

"I miss you, too. Call me anytime you want. I don't care what time it is. I love you."

"I love you more."

"Not a chance, cupcake."

After they hung up, it took Dusty a while to fall back asleep. He worried about Courtney wallowing in the "what ifs" and how Katie was going to try to be the voice of reason for only so long before she gave in to the sadness. She was already worn thin and it had only been a day. Again he wished there was something else he could do. Again his thoughts went to Frank.

"Where are you, you damn geezer? Your cupcake needs you."

Chapter Three

The next morning, Dusty accepted Ann's offer to babysit the kids, not wanting to abuse Mrs. Nelson again so soon. The woman was a sweetheart, but his kids could give an Olympic athlete a run for their money energy-wise. He was sure she deserved a break. He called the newspaper where he worked and took a personal day, explaining about Katie having to leave town. They didn't need to know that he had other plans. Voicing it out loud would only reinforce the fact that he'd lost his mind.

As he drove toward their old college town again, his mind wandered to the first time Katie explained her time traveling and how he'd reacted.

"Somehow I came back to my college days. I'm thirty, Dusty. I'm thirty and I have a successful vet practice, wonderful employees, and a beautiful house. I don't know what I'm doing here and it's making me lose my mind."

He'd stared at her blankly as he let her walk away. But something had clicked with him and he had gone after her. He was grateful his younger self had the wisdom to put aside the fact that even though he thought her story was crazy, he needed to find out more.

After her last stay at the hospital, when her memories came flooding back to her, Katie had filled him in here and there on the trips to her altered future and how he was a presence for her there.

Dusty knew it was silly, but he was a little pissed off about how her appointment with her chiropractor, Doctor Wilson Gregory, went. Katie had been more than shocked at his advances that visit, not realizing that in the time she was in, they had dated. Dusty had shared a few beers and Vikings games with him over the years and hated to think of a time when he wasn't around and Wilson had dated his wife. Thinking about alternate lives in parallel universes was not a subject either of them cared for.

Katie was afraid to talk about Frank much, for fear he would reappear. Right now, that was exactly what Dusty wanted to happen. He needed answers. As much as he thought it would never actually happen, his mind would not be at ease until he got it out of his system. He was certain it would be another wasted trip but the way his mind was racing, he would be of no use to anyone at work.

After reaching Dinkytown in record time, he slowly cruised down what the school kids had dubbed "sorority row" long before he and Katie went there. He always admired the architecture of the buildings. He laughed out loud at one strung from top to bottom with toilet paper. Some stunts would remain timeless. This was just one of many reasons he'd rented the small cottage behind an older couple's home just out of town instead of doing the dorm or frat house thing.

Before he knew it, their old coffee shop, Sunriders, was in front of him. He'd left home before making coffee or grabbing a bite to eat, so he pulled in the parking lot. He smiled wide when the same familiar face stared back at him.

"Hello, Art."

"Dustin Andrews! Great to see you!" The owner came around the counter and greeted him with a firm handshake.

"You still with that pretty little fainter that swept you off your feet?"

"Sure am." He quickly pulled out his wallet and produced the latest picture of the kids. "Can you believe she's put up with me enough to give me these two beauties?"

Art gave the photo a good once-over. "Good thing they get their looks from their mother."

"Nice to know some things never change. I missed that droll humor of yours each morning."

"Wish I could say I missed running you a tab longer than my dick each month."

"Hey… I always paid up."

Art grinned. "That you did. Eventually. Double caramel latte?"

"How the hell do you remember that?"

"I forget a name here and there, but never a drink. This one's on me." As Art frothed the milk, Dusty reached in a jar and removed a scone. He glanced around the shop and recalled the many times he and Katie sat here together, studying. Well, she studied while he distracted her. It wasn't long after they moved in together that he'd taken his last class and started full time at the newspaper.

Dusty tried handing Art a five for the scone, but he waved it away.

He thanked Art and dropped the money in the tip jar when his back was turned. The same note was taped on it, just more faded. *Thanks a latte.*

Taking a seat at a tall table by the window, he polished off the scone in a few bites. *What the hell am I doing here?* Again he pondered what Frank's part was in this and why he had showed up for Katie all those years ago. He never seemed to be much more than an ear to bend. Dusty wished he was here for him to talk to now. "Who and what were you, you old codger?"

"You rang?"

Dusty was speechless at the man who stood before him. "I…uh…what?" he said in great shock.

"You rang. Quit your shouting, too. I'm old, not deaf."

"You're…" Dusty was at a loss for words.

"Here. Now what can I help you with?"

"How did you… why… holy shit."

"What's the matter, boy?" Frank asked.

"Am I dreaming?"

"Why? Do I look like I'm the man of your dreams?"

"No…uh… holy crap."

"Look. You're the one that showed up looking for me."

"Yeah, but I didn't think you'd actually show up."

"Are you ever a nut job."

"I think you're right." Dusty sat back and took a deep breath. "Uh…can I get you coffee or something?"

"I'm fine. Thanks."

"This is too weird. We've hardly talked about you since Katie stayed put."

"Afraid I'd show up again?"

"Something like that, I guess."

Frank motioned his head toward the door. "You want me to go?"

"No!" Dusty stood. "I need to talk to you."

"Katie's doing great, isn't she?"

"She's perfect."

"And the kids?"

"You know about…" *Of course he knows, dumbass.* "Um… they're great."

"Your sister Alyson?"

"She's fantastic."

"Then what are you jerkin' my chain for, boy? What's your pickle?"

Dusty had to laugh. "That is little Alyson's favorite saying. Katie said you used to say that all the time." Frank stared back blankly. Dusty finally spoke again. "It's Courtney."

"Oh, yes. They finally discovered that. I'm glad no one else had been infected. Between you, me, and the wall, she was a bit of a loosy-goosy, wasn't she?"

Dusty managed a smile, nodding his head. His eyes widened. "Wait. You know about her health?"

"Everyone in Katie's circle, so to speak, is on my watch."

"Your watch? Then why did it happen?"

Frank sighed. "You're not going to give me that, are you? If I have to do the yin-yang explanation again, I'll grow old before my time."

"Old before your time? But aren't you…" Dusty again was at a loss for words.

"Already dead? Is that what you're thinkin'?"

"Sort of."

"I'm not even addressing that. You going to tell me what it is you want or what, young feller?"

Dusty grew frustrated at Frank's inability to answer anything. He tried to explain it for himself, hoping Frank would hop in and correct him. Avoiding the part about him being dead, Dusty addressed his other comment. "The yin and the yang? Can't have good without evil, can't have happy without sad. That kind of thing?"

"Something like that. In any case, we can't stop what's going to happen."

"You can't say that. What you did kept Alyson alive."

"That was different. It just played out. Katie didn't ask for it. It fell into place. The trips were more about you than her."

"Me? Why me?"

"I don't make up the rules," Frank admitted.

"Who does? God?"

"It's not even that simple."

"Explaining God is what you call simple?"

"In a matter of the whole picture, yes. Look, I broke a rule being there for Katie and things happened to work out.

You were lucky in ways you'll never know, and probably will never fully appreciate."

"If you think for one second I don't know what I have, you couldn't be more wrong. It doesn't make sense that Katie could go back and save Alyson, but she can't do the same for Courtney."

"I don't have the cure for AIDS, boy."

"But you can get her back before it happened. She could prevent it."

"No."

"Why the hell not?"

"Kaitlyn isn't eligible to go back again."

"Why not!" Dusty said again as he banged his fist on the table.

"Don't you lose your temper with me, young man. I'm not even supposed to be here now. You had old Frank curious and I thought I'd pop in. I wasn't going to pop in at the library. The coffee there has always sucked. The stupid mugs are chipped, too. Katie never did complain about them, though. Bless her heart. If you're going to go postal on me, I'll split."

"No! Don't do that." Dusty seized his wrist. "You were at the library when I was there?"

"Yup. Saw you call Bill my name. I can't believe you mistook that codger for me. I'm much better looking. I thought you came to your senses when you changed your mind and left, but here you are hollering for me again."

"I'm sorry. But I need answers. Why can't Katie go back again? Help me make sense of this. The only thing more important to Katie than me or the kids is Courtney. You have to know that. You have to let her help."

"It's simply not allowed. Her chance to change her present is over. Katie didn't have an agenda when she went back. It wasn't of her own free will. If you recall, she didn't want to do it."

"But it still worked. Why can't she go again and save her best friend? You know she'd want to."

"If she went back to the same time, she could risk hurting your present. It would be like an etch-a-sketch erasing. She'd either be her old self and you two would not meet or the trips would play out the same as they did upon her return and nothing would change for Courtney. She can't go back with the memories of her present like before. It just can't be done."

"This isn't fair." Frustrated, Dusty pushed his chair back and stood.

"I never said it was." Frank turned away and tapped his forefinger to his chin. "There is something, though."

"What?"

"You could go."

"Me? I can't leave. What about the kids? I'm watching them while Katie's visiting Courtney."

"Dusty, you of all people should know how this works. They'll never know you've been gone for more than a trip to the library."

"What if this takes a few days?"

"It most certainly will. The outcome here will still be the same."

"Or not. What if I really screw something up?"

"That's the chance you'll have to be willing to take. You were willing to make your wife do it a moment ago."

"Which Katie will she be?"

"I have no way of knowing. You could be winning her over again for the first time or you could meet the Katie trying to convince you she's time traveling."

"Could I tell her what I'm doing if it's the first one?"

"And how well did you take the news when she did that to you?"

Dusty sighed. "I see your point. I guess this is one of your pickles again, isn't it?"

"As pickled as it gets."

Dusty paced the area in front of the tall table. How could he make a decision like this? He wanted to talk to Katie, but he knew he couldn't. She loved Courtney, but she wouldn't risk their lives and especially not their kids. If there was a chance their present would be altered, there was no way Katie would chance it. Not even for Courtney.

Dusty knew he had to make it right, though. He could do this. Katie had risked everything to save his best friend. He had to do the same to save hers.

"I have to do it. When can I go?"

Frank smiled. "I knew you'd see it that way." He rested his hand on Dusty's shoulder and pointed out the window. Dusty saw Kaitlyn jogging toward them.

"Holy crap. I'm there? I went back?" His attention hadn't moved from watching Katie. "So when it's done, how do I—" He turned around, but Frank had already disappeared.

"Well, shit." He took a second to straighten himself up, or rather, grunge himself down. He mussed his hair to be more like his more unruly college hair look, and discovered it was now longer. His dress pants had been replaced with jeans and his dress shirt was now a Vikings sweatshirt. He looked over to Art, who had instantly dropped fifteen pounds. Turning back around, Dusty tried to catch his reflection in the window. He flashed his killer smile at himself, then he saw Katie approaching the door. "Showtime."

Chapter Four

Katie walked in the door and stopped when she saw Dusty. "Fancy meeting you here," he said to her. She promptly fainted. "Oh, crap. I forgot this part." He caught her before she hit the ground, then made his way over to the couch, cradling her in his arms.

Dusty hollered to the owner. "Art, get me a cold washcloth, would ya?"

"What the hell happened to her?"

"Just get it, please."

He settled on the couch at her side while Art rushed over. As he placed the washcloth on her forehead, her eyes fluttered open. She tried to sit up. he promptly pushed her back down.

The words he'd spoken to her came back to him as if he were reading a script. "Just lay back down there, cupcake. Take a few minutes to gather yourself." He turned to Art who, more than likely, was worried there would be a lawsuit coming. Dusty remembered how he and his law school friends always razzed him about one thing or another. He tried to put Art at ease. "You can go. She's fine."

"Was it the shop's fault?"

There was fear in Art's voice. Dusty wished he hadn't teased him so much. *Hot coffee lawsuits.* One of the many things that chased Dusty away from becoming a lawyer.

"She just fainted. I'm a witness. You're in the clear there, Art. Now scram."

"You law boys have me scared to death," he said as he shook his head and walked away.

The dialog played out word for word as it had before. Dusty began to think this was going to be easier than he thought. He turned back to Kaitlyn. *Damn.* His victory was short lived. He couldn't remember what he'd said to her. "Uh…you overdo your run or something?"

"Cupcake?"

He smiled wide. It was coming back to him. "I had to call you something. You blew me off last night outside of Tricky Dicks."

"Last night?" Dusty wasn't ready to re-cap the whole scenario. If things were playing out like this, she had to be the one that went back in time. She'd fainted at the shock of seeing his younger self. She had to know what was going on. He smiled. "I lied to you just now."

"You weren't there last night?"

"No. I was there, but I…uh…I know your name."

"So why did you call me 'cupcake?'"

He flashed his killer grin. This was already fun. "Because you like it when I do that."

"Excuse me?" she said as she sat upright.

"Katie…I need your help here. Courtney is in trouble."

"How do you know my roommate's name? What kind of trouble? Where is she?"

Shit! She wasn't who he thought she'd be. Dusty knew he had to backtrack fast. "Wait a minute… I'm sorry. We're getting off on the wrong foot here. Can I buy you a coffee? A double caramel latte?"

"Caramel is my weakness. But no. Wait. What's this about Courtney?"

"Um…sorry. I...uh…it came out wrong. I meant she must be hurting this morning. You two looked in bad shape last night."

"She was still sleeping when I left."

"Well, there you go. So, can I buy you that coffee?"

"Did I even get your name?"

"Dustin. You can call me Dusty though. I like it when you…I mean…you and my sister are the only ones that…uh…you kinda look like my sister. She calls me Dusty."

"I remind you of your sister?"

"Shit. Sorry…I mean…" Dusty ran his hands down his face in frustration. In all his years, he never stammered as much as he had in the last few minutes. Things were getting destroyed before he even started. He was here five minutes and he'd already pretty much made sure he'd never be having sex with Kaitlyn again in this lifetime. "Can I start this over?"

"Have a little too much last night yourself?"

"Apparently. That and a beautiful woman always leaves my tongue in knots. And I've never met anyone more striking than you." He sat next to her and leaned in for a kiss. What the hell. It had worked the first time.

His kiss had to have taken her by surprise, because she didn't fight him. But when his tongue entered her mouth, she quickly drew back and slapped him.

"What on earth are you doing?"

He grabbed her hands. "I'm so sorry." He tried to kiss them but she pulled them away and stood. He hurried to his feet as well. "Please stop. You're—" he held her arms, supporting her weight as she went slightly limp. "You're not ready to storm out of here. Come sit back down."

Dusty helped her back to the couch and hollered to Art, "Two regulars over here, Art. Stat."

"You're taking law, not medicine. Don't bark at me, law boy."

"Please, Art. Add a scone to that. She looks low on blood sugar." He turned his attention back to Katie whose eyes were still closed. "You shouldn't have gone out running before you ate something."

"How do you know I didn't eat something?"

"You never eat break—" She opened up one eye. "You're shaking. Seems to me you need some food in you. You did pass out. Have you forgotten already?"

"I haven't forgotten that you sent your tongue probing my tonsils without permission."

"I said I'm sorry. I lost my mind." He accepted the coffees from Art and handed her one. A waitress was behind him with a scone for her. "Thanks, Nikki. Can these go on my tab?"

"We need to talk about that tab, Dustin. Art wants you to catch up."

He glanced over at Kaitlyn. She was grinning. Now he was embarrassed. "I told him I get the check from my dad on the first. I'll catch up with interest."

"He's not going to like it."

"It's just a few more days." He reached in his pocket and pulled out a five. "Here's an advance tip. Okay?" He motioned for her to go away. Katie was grinning at him when his attention returned to her.

"So, you're into attacking older women and you have no money. Does this tactic work on many ladies?"

This was not at all going how it should have. "I have plenty of money. I just didn't plan too well this month."

"Let me guess. The heat went out on your car."

"It is you!" he said as he held her face in his hands. "You little minx!" He gave her a hard kiss.

Her knee quickly went to his crotch. He slid off the couch, landing on the ground in a moan. "I asked you to stop doing that!" She ran out of the coffee shop before Dusty could blink.

Dusty lay in a ball on the floor, holding himself in the most dignified manner he could. “That went well,” he groaned with his eyes pinched shut.

Someone stepped over Dusty and sat on the couch. “Well, if she’s not going to drink it.” The cup rattled across the table. Dusty rolled over and opened his eyes. Frank smiled down at him, cup in hand.

“You son of a bitch,” Dusty said as he rapped him in the knee. His finger cracked. He yelped and pulled it back between his legs.

“It ain’t broke, you puss,” Frank said. He sipped Kaitlyn’s coffee. “I told you this wasn’t going to be easy.”

“Well, I thought it was her. She passed out just like before. Last time it was the shock of seeing me.”

“Maybe now it was from overdoing her run. I hear she has a hangover to boot.”

Dusty pulled himself onto the couch. “Look. If you know how this is going to go, can you please give me some pointers? She’ll kill me if I screw this up and something happens to the kids.”

“Not if she doesn’t know you, she won’t.”

Dusty pulled Frank by his shirt. “Look, you old geezer. This isn’t funny! Not only am I not making her fall for me, I’m pretty sure she’s getting a restraining order right now!”

Once again, everyone’s attention turned to Dusty. “Everything here okay, sir?” Dusty looked up. Art was standing there with his shoulders firm. “Mr. Andrews? Do we need a time out?”

Dusty let go of Frank. “We’re fine.”

“Sir?” he asked Frank.

“We’re fine, Arthur. Thank you, though.”

Frank stood. “You got yourself in this pickle. You fix it.”

Dusty reached for the scone. When he leaned back, Frank had disappeared again.

"Ah, hell." Shutting his eyes, Dusty leaned back, wishing he could fall asleep, wake up, and do this all over again. That's what worked for Katie, but somehow he felt those rules were not going to apply this time.

Kaitlyn slammed the dorm room door shut. Courtney promptly threw a pillow at her.

"Damn, Katie. I'm hanging here. Keep it down."

"You're supposed to be in class."

"Well, so much for your early birthday celebration. Could have left the celebrating for today. Happy birthday, by the way. What has you pissed off so early?"

"Some guy I didn't even know tried to cram his tongue down my throat."

"Where?"

"All the way to my tonsils."

Courtney laughed. "Where did this happen? I want to go. Maybe he's still there."

"At the coffee shop and I wouldn't bother. You'd be robbing the cradle. Wait a sec…he said he saw us at Tricky Dick's last night."

"That hottie with the wavy brown hair?" Courtney sat up and lowered her feet to the ground. "You turned that down again?"

"It's not like he asked for a date. He just fucking kissed me."

"Annnnd…"

"And what? That was uncool."

"Katie? It about time someone pops that cherry of yours."

"I'm hardly a virgin, Court."

"So stop acting like it. I swear you haven't gotten laid since second term."

"Just because you keep a revolving door on our dorm room doesn't mean I have to try to keep up. Besides, I have a date with Rex tonight. Remember?"

"You putting out, finally?"

"I don't know. Maybe."

"You've been keeping the poor guy hanging for over a month."

"Since when is that making a guy wait?"

"Since the eighteen hundreds," Courtney said with a laugh. She finally stood. "Well, shit. I'm up. Might as well get to class. Hey, you think this kid has a friend?"

"Where would you fit him in?"

"Har-de-har-har. Have fun with Rex tonight. I want details tomorrow."

"You got it."

"Don't forget to put a sock on the door knob for me."

"I won't come back here," Katie said.

"Good. Because I have a sex date with Ronald tonight."

"Again?"

Courtney shrugged. "He's good. What can I say?"

"Try 'no' once in a while."

"Why would I want to do that?" She quickly dressed and headed for the door. "Ta! Love you!"

After the door closed behind Courtney, Katie flopped on her bed. She wished she knew why thinking about Dustin gave her butterflies in her stomach all of a sudden.

"He called you 'cupcake,' for crying out loud," she argued with herself. "What was he? Eighteen? Get over it, Katie. Think of Rex. Think of hot sex finally with Rex. You have this night coming. Happy birthday, princess." She continued to talk to herself as she got ready for class, then stormed out, hollering at herself for talking to herself.

Dusty waited for Kaitlyn at the bar of the burger joint. He had to try again. He knew she had a date with Rex the day after her birthday, but he had no choice except to look for her tonight. With a little luck, since he wasn't currently in the picture, dates would get screwed up in his favor. He didn't want to have to kill a night here, wasting precious time to set things straight. Katie had admitted to him that in her original past, she had slept with Rex on this night. He had to make sure that didn't happen. He was thrilled to see them walk in together just after six. One thing went in his favor, he hoped his luck would hold out.

Katie was half way through her beer when she finally noticed him. He couldn't text her like he had before and had been subtle about trying to get her attention. He gave her a gentle wave and saw her begin to cough as if she were choking. Rex patted her back. *Shit.* This was not going well already. She pointed to Dusty, Rex walked around her chair and headed over. *Double shit.* Katie stood, blocking him from coming over. She said something to Rex, then made her way over to him. *This was going to be interesting*. Dusty spun around, acting as if he didn't see her coming.

She tapped him on the shoulder. "What do you think you're doing? Are you stalking me?"

"Sort of."

"Sort of? What the hell is that supposed to mean?"

"We're meant to be together, Katie. I can't have you going through with your plans tonight. You can't sleep with him."

Her cheeks flushed and she stepped back. "Excuse me?"

He held her hands. Again he tried to give them a kiss. This time he got away with it. "You're my destiny, cupcake. Please send Rex home."

Dusty saw Rex rushing to the bar. *Oh boy. Here we go again.*

"Look, you!" Rex shouted

Dustin quickly spun Kaitlyn around and pulled her back to him, wrapping his arms around her. "Protect me from your big bad boyfriend, Katie."

"Dustin, stop it. This isn't funny."

"What gives, Kaitlyn? You know this creep or what?"

"Sort of, Rex. I'm sorry." She turned as best as she could with the way Dusty held her. "I don't know what you're trying to pull, Dustin. I'm on a date. Please let us eat. Whatever it is you think you need to tell me, you can do it when I'm not with someone else. I'm not going to ask you again."

"No can do, cupcake. Look, Rex, is it? I'm sorry, but you're messing with my destiny here."

"Your destiny?" Rex said, taking a step closer.

"Yup. Sorry. The lady is mine. You'll have to find another."

"Dustin…" Katie tried squirming out of his hold, but Dusty held her firmly.

"Real tough guy there, using the lady for cover," Rex said as he grasped Katie by the arm, pulling her to him.

Dustin let go of her and stood. He remembered he'd come off as a jerk last time he pulled this, but he didn't see another way to handle the situation. Katie simply could not leave with Rex. He couldn't hang out here and wait a couple of months for her to be done with him. His thoughts trailed to the kids. He wanted to get home. Anger raged inside him for having to fight for the woman he already had.

"Outside!" he shouted to Rex, determined to make it there this time. He was going to win her over with bravery and persistence.

"Stop it! Both of you!" Kaitlyn screamed. She stormed away toward the table. Dustin started to go after her, but Rex planted a solid punch to his chin and sent him flying backward, knocking him down flat.

Dusty's world went black. He heard arguing and felt a crowd gathering around him, but he couldn't shake the cobwebs clear from him head. The words, "I'm not going anywhere with you!" finally sank in. Katie was now fighting with Rex. Maybe this was going to work after all.

His eyes cracked open slightly. "You need help?" the manager asked Katie.

He was standing above Dusty, Katie was on her knees at his side.

"I don't know," she replied, gently shaking Dusty again. "Dusty! Are you with me? Dusty!"

Dusty was still woozy but he could see Rex was now a lovely shade of red. Rex shouted over the commotion. "You leave with me now or you can stay here with that lightweight chicken shit."

"I'm staying, you brute!" she said through bared teeth.

"Have it your way." Rex picked up his coat and stormed out of the restaurant.

"Dusty," she said, shaking him again.

He finally focused on her and managed a smile.

"Welcome back to the living, oh strange one. You sure have a funny idea of how to get a girl to go out with you."

"Not well played, huh?" Dusty rubbed his chin.

Chapter Five

"You have a death wish or something, cowboy?" Katie said as she drove Dusty's car. "You shouldn't start a fight you can't finish."

"Cowboy? You've never called me…uh…I got the girl, didn't I?"

"My, you are an articulate one." She shook her head. "I wouldn't go as far as saying you got the girl." She frowned at him. "I almost kicked your ass myself."

"Yeah, well, almost only counts in horseshoes and hand grenades." *Geez. Is that the best you can do?*

"Good lord. I haven't heard that since grade school."

"Glass chin and a witty little sucker. What more could you want in a guy?" Dusty felt as if he was reading a script from his past.

"You find this amusing?" Katie scolded.

"I'm sorry. I know you're looking for an explanation. I wish I could give you one that you'd understand."

"I'm not an imbecile. At least I wasn't ten minutes ago. I'm not so sure what I'm doing with you now, though."

"You're my lobster, Katie."

That made her laugh out loud. "So you're a *Friends* fan. That still doesn't explain what the hell this is." She pressed and turned several buttons on his dashboard. "Does this thing ever heat up?"

"Only on a good day. That's why I thought you knew me. You made that comment about the heat going out in my car."

"That was just a joke. That's why I don't have a car. All college kids can afford are shitty beaters, but they end up putting more money into them than a car payment. I had no idea I was sitting with the poorest bum in the school."

"You're not even close."

"So enlighten me, Mr. High-Finance-can't-keep-your-tab-current-at-the-coffee-shop-and-drives-a-chariot-like-this."

"I think I need to get you drunk first."

She laughed. "You're not getting into my pants. You owe me a burger."

"Pull up to the Burger King."

"Big spender."

"You're hungry and it's convenient. I promise I'll take you to a nice dinner at *Chez Pauls* some night. I'm really sorry I couldn't come up with a better way to get you out of there."

She pulled in the drive-through and held out her hand. He put a twenty in it.

"I can't tell you how much I despise fighting," she said as she pulled up to the window.

"It's obviously not my sport of choice either."

Dusty carried in the bags of food when they reached his home. After putting them down to take off his coat and help Katie with hers, he longed to press her into the wall and kiss her the way they did last time, as well as have the animal sex that followed, but he didn't think she had warmed up enough to him yet for that. *Bummer.*

He led her to the sofa instead. "Want me to put in a movie?"

"I think I'd rather talk."

Dusty put on MTV for background noise. He really hadn't thought this through. He wasn't sure blurting out the fact that he time traveled to save her roommate was the best way to handle this. She'd probably react the way she would in their present. He'd seen a force five conniption and didn't care to ever see one again.

He sat down but stood right back up. "I'll grab a couple of beers." He came back with two Leinenkugel Honey-Weiss, wishing he'd thought to buy the berry ones she liked. Katie promptly drank almost half of hers without putting it down.

"Do you want something stronger?"

"I have a feeling I'm going to need it," she said, finally putting the beer down. She unwrapped her burger as he stood back up. "You can eat first, Dustin. I'm sure getting knocked out gives you an appetite."

He grinned at her. She was playing tough, but he knew what made her tick. He had no doubt she wouldn't be here if she wasn't interested. They had been through enough together that he could read her every mood. He didn't need time travel and a script on his side. Although it didn't hurt.

"Actually, it doesn't. But thanks for asking. And you call me Dusty, sweetheart. Er… I mean… call me Dusty, okay…Katie." He sat back down and unwrapped his burger. They took a few bites in silence before Kaitlyn started up.

"You mind telling me what I'm doing here with you?"

"I happen to know from a reliable source that you find me charming and irresistible."

In the middle of a bite when he said that, Katie began to cough and had to cover her mouth to keep food from flying out. Dusty stood and patted her on the back. "Shit. Are you okay?"

"I'm fine." She drank another swig of beer to wash it down.

"I have a horrible habit of trying to kill you on our first dates." His eyes went wide. There was no recovering from that one.

"Try to kill me?" Amazingly, there wasn't fear behind her voice. She did reach for her beer and finish what there was of it. He went to get another and returned with a bottle of cherry schnapps, Jagermeister, and the cups to make the specialty shots.

"Cherry bombs? No side of roofie to go with it?"

"I keep putting my foot in my mouth. Maybe this will help untie it. I swear I'm harmless."

"I know you are. I'm not an idiot. Maybe I am for being here, but something tells me I'll make it out alive." She poured them each a drink and they clinked glassed before downing the shots. She reached for her burger again as she asked him, "So, you going to tell me why you keep referring to me in the past tense? You keep talking about things like we've done them before."

"I'm sorry this is…hard to explain."

"You know, that's starting to drive me crazy."

"What is?"

"All your pausing when you're talking to me. I'm not that intimidating to talk to."

"Sorry, I can't help it. I'm nervous. You'll think I'm off my nut when I get around to it."

"Too late. I already think you're off your nut." She poured another round of drinks and promptly downed hers, not waiting for him.

"You don't usually drink like this. What gives?"

She slammed the glass on the table. "See! Dammit! What the hell is this? Are you some kind of freak stalker or what?"

"I once said the same thing to you. Shit. I'm sorry again. This isn't helping." He downed his shot and kneeled in front of her. "Before I tell you, I need something from you."

"What's that?"

"A kiss."

"A kiss? Why do you want a kiss?"

"Because you will probably run out of here screaming and I'll never get to see you again. I'll throw myself off a bridge, never again knowing the softness of your lips, or be able to taste how sweet you are. You're my world, Katie. I'll tell you everything, but I need a kiss first."

She hesitated. He was beginning to feel he really had blown it, but then the unthinkable happened. She leaned into him and pressed her lips to his. All the worry and weight fell from his shoulders. He wrapped his arms around her and kissed her possessively. It was she who parted her lips first, searching for his tongue. Forgetting when and where they were, Dusty leaned her back onto the loveseat where she was sitting and stroked her sides. Her eyes suddenly opened and she put her hands on Dusty's chest.

"Easy, big fella. I agreed to the kiss. I didn't give second base a green light."

"I couldn't help myself."

"And apparently I couldn't either. I'm sorry. I don't want to give you the wrong impression about me."

"You were going to have sex with Rex tonight."

"How do you…why do you think that?"

"Not so easy, is it?" He liked that he now had her stammering for words.

"Rex and I have been dating for a while. Judgmental much? "

"You don't need to defend yourself."

"Why are you making me feel like I do?"

"I promise you, that's not what I'm trying to accomplish."

"Exactly what are you trying to accomplish?" Irritation was flowing in her tone.

"I want you."

"I thought I made myself clear. I'm not sleeping with you. You still kind of creep me out."

"I'm not talking about sex. I want to be a part of your life."

She picked up her now cold burger. With her mouth still full, she said, "Fine. If I ever need a ride in a freezing piece-of-shit Nova, I'll give you a call."

"It's a Chevelle and I need more than that."

She reached for the new beer, but Dusty picked it up first. He opened it and handed it to her.

"Thanks," she said before taking a gulp. He could tell she was trying to think of what to say. "I admit you're a great kisser." Dusty grinned at her words. "But we need to go slow here. You haven't exactly won me over in the charm department. I don't know what makes you think I'm some kind of catch here, but seeing as how Rex will probably never speak to me again…" Katie just let the sentence hang as she played with her fries.

"You want me to heat them up?"

"No. I'm not hungry anymore."

"I'm sorry."

"It's not your fault. I drank too much."

"You gonna hurl?"

"No. Why?"

"It's just that every time…shit. Sorry. I'm doing it again."

She leaned back and crossed her arms. "We never did get to why you do that."

He gently ran the back of his hand over her cheek. "I'm not your stalker, but I have loved you for a few lifetimes, Katie. You love me, too. Give yourself time to figure it out."

She looked deep into his eyes. He could almost see the wheels spinning and expected her to kiss him again. Instead, she reached around him and poured herself another shot. After downing it she said, "That's pretty smooth talking there, law boy. You taking creative writing on the side?"

"How'd you know I was in law school?"

She pointed to the books on his desk. "Real tough one to figure out."

"Ah ha!" Dusty stood and walked over to his desk. "Captain Skinnard to the rescue!"

"Who?"

"My book. You lo…you should read my book."

"You wrote a book?"

"Sort of. It's not done, but I'd love for you to take a look at it." He walked over to his desk and shuffled through it.

"I don't have time for a lot of reading. My school load is pretty heavy."

"That's okay. Just get to what you can."

"You have to know I'm in veterinary medicine and not English. Don't expect much for editing."

"I know you get straight A's, but that's not what I'm after anyway." He thrust the partial manuscript in front of her. She concentrated on the nebula he used as clip art for the cover page.

"I'm not a big sci-fi fan."

"That's okay."

"Well, I'm glad you said 'that's okay' and not 'I know.'"

"I'm getting better at this."

Katie took another sip of her beer, then stood. She faltered a little and Dusty rushed to her side, steadying her. "Where's your *bafroom*?"

Crap. He'd let her get drunk. Now there was no telling how tonight would go. He walked her over to the bathroom, leaving her wobbling by the toilet. "You need help?"

"I can pee by *myshelf*, thankuverymuch."

"If you toss your cookies, there's a spare toothbrush in the second drawer."

"I'm not gonna…aw shit."

Dusty quickly pulled the door closed. He gave her a few minutes before he tapped on the door. The faucet was running, so he gave her another minute. She opened the door and stood there in her t-shirt and underwear. The bottom of the shirt barely covered her up. "I need to lie down."

Dusty scooped her up and carried her to his bed, worried that she wouldn't make it on her own. He remembered what was missing. One small detail from before. "Let me get you a more comfortable shirt." He went to his drawer for his AC/DC shirt and handed it to her. She stared at it blankly. "Want me to turn around?"

"I want help," she said, sitting there with her eyes closed.

"Raise up your arms." Katie did as she was told. Dusty pulled off her tight t-shirt and slipped his on her. Once she was covered he asked, "Bra?"

"Take it off."

He ran his hand across the back, then discovered it was a front latch and quickly popped it free, careful not to brush her breasts too much in the process. After struggling slightly with pulling it through the sleeves, he laid her down and covered her up.

"You warm enough?"

She nodded.

He dared to kiss her forehead. "I'll ride the couch."

"You don't have to. If you were going to attack me, you'd have already done it."

"Want me to get a bucket just in case?"

She shook her head no. "Why are you so good to me?"

"I already told you. I love you."

"That's creepy," she mumbled before falling into a deep sleep.

Chapter Six

Katie woke up with a pounding in her head. Judging by the lack of light, she guessed it was before six. Far too early to be up on a Saturday. A stirring in the bed caught her attention; slowly the previous night came back to her. *What an ass I am!* She opened her eyes and saw Dusty lying next to her.

As if he felt her gaze, Dusty's eyes opened. The warm smile he gave her instantly melted any fear that he judged her for what happened last night. What the hell was she worried about anyway? He was the freaky stalker guy. She lifted up the sheet to look at how she was dressed.

"We didn't have sex, if that's what you're worried about."

"I don't remember changing."

"You ditched the jeans in the bathroom. I helped you with the rest. I swear my eyes were closed when I helped you with your shirt."

"Oddly, I believe you."

Dusty propped his head on his hand. "Do you remember much?"

"I'm pretty sure I yacked. That or you have a cat and it took a shit in my mouth."

"All I smell is cherry schnapps."

"Gross." Katie ran to the bathroom. Finding a toothbrush on the counter, she assumed it was one she'd used by the way it was discarded. She scrubbed vigorously at her teeth and tongue. "You have any aspirin?" she hollered through the door.

"In the kitchen. I'll get it." A moment later there was a gentle knocking. She pulled the door open; Dusty was there with a glass of water. Not being able to help liking what she saw, she allowed her eyes to explore his body. He was shirtless and yummy. She accepted the pills and water from him and closed the door again, hoping to hide the sudden flushing of her cheeks. She wanted to try to recover in case he had noticed.

"You feed me cinnamon or something?"

"Not this time."

"What?"

"Uh…no. It was all booze, sweetheart."

She pulled the door open quickly again. "You got me drunk?"

"You got yourself drunk, cupcake." He stepped closer to her. Katie hated that she suddenly felt weak. "If you wanted to take advantage of me, you already had me," Dusty said as he leaned in for a kiss. Katie wanted to be angry at him, but her pounding heart wouldn't let her. She leaned into his kiss and wrapped her arms around his neck. A moan escaped her throat. She silently cursed herself for letting it out.

Dusty could hardly fight his grin when she moaned. He knew he was winning her over. Scooping her up as they remained locked in a kiss, he walked her to his bed. After placing her on it, he waited for a protest that never voiced itself. His hands slid down her sides and removed her underwear, then he removed his pajama pants.

"You need to get something, Dusty."

"You sure?"

"No glove, no love."

"Give me a second." He ran to the bathroom, returning in record speed with a condom. In another minute, he was inside her. Even though he had made love to his Katie only yesterday, to her this was the first time and that's how it felt for him. He actually felt like he was cheating on his wife and was momentarily guilty. He recalled his fight with her about that subject, but couldn't concentrate on any details of it. The euphoria she put him in let his mind wander to nothing else than what they were doing right then. He took his time pleasing her as he had perfected over the years. He knew every spot that made her gasp, every movement that made her catch her breath.

Dusty knew when she was ready and once again, or for the first time—depending on how you wanted to slice it—they climaxed together.

Katie's legs and arms wrapped around him tight. "Don't move," she whispered before giving his neck a kiss.

"Not on your life," he said, returning the gesture. After his breathing had returned to normal, he slid off to the side and kissed her forehead. "How are you feeling?"

"You asking if I feel like a slut, or about my hangover?"

"Either."

"My head isn't so bad and oddly, I'm okay with this. You're creepy, but damn good in bed."

"Can we go exclusive and stop with the condoms?"

"Exclusive? You work fast, Mister…. what is your last name, anyway?"

"Andrews. Why? You ready to take it already?"

"You sure move fast."

"I know what I want." He couldn't stop from planting kisses where he could reach.

"I could probably go to jail."

"I'm not that much younger than you."

"What are you? Eighteen? I'm insane."

"I'm twenty…one." He had to stop and think for a second exactly "when" he was.

"You sure?"

"I'm sure, babe."

She lifted her head. "Babe?"

"You prefer cupcake?"

"Usually, I prefer romantic dinners, a few dates and maybe meeting your family before sex."

"Okay to the first two, I don't think you're ready for the last one."

"Issues with your parents?"

"You could say that."

"I guess it's a little late for baby steps. I'll cope. For now, though, I need a shower."

"Want company?"

She shrugged. "Why not?"

As Kaitlyn scrubbed Dusty's back with one hand, the other roamed across his body. He heard her giggle softly. Dusty spun around. "Is there something funny back there?"

"You have the cutest birthmark. It looks like the state of Wisconsin."

Facing her, he placed her hands on the subject matter. "Yeah, so you've said." He kissed her before any kind of protest could be voiced over that comment. He'd have to win her over a little more before he filled her in. Maybe he wouldn't have to at all if his luck held out like this.

It suddenly occurred to Dusty that Katie had gotten pregnant somewhere along her time hops. They joked about not being sure which one of him "knocked her ass up." He wasn't usually a praying man, but he prayed like hell that what he was doing wouldn't screw things up. They didn't use a condom the first time they'd had sex in what was now their present timeline. She let him go without one, but of course she had already known he was safe. Dusty worried for a moment that this could have been that time. He would never be able to live with himself for messing that one up. This wasn't the Katie that was traveling, though. Things had to be okay. His mind raced with possibilities. His mood must have changed to her. Katie seemed pulled back.

"Is everything okay?"

He forced a smile for her. "Perfect."

"I was worried you were having second thoughts. I really could have played a little harder to get."

"You don't need to play anything ever with me, puddin' pop."

"Puddin' pop? You going to do this the whole time we date?"

"Pretty much."

"You could have told me that before I slept with you."

"Wouldn't have mattered." Again he covered her lips with his.

After they toweled off, Dusty gave Katie one of his pajama tops to put on. "Don't take this wrong, but you still look a little rough. If you want to hang out here today, that's fine. I have no plans. I could order us a pizza and pick up some movies later."

"That sounds great, but could we squeeze in coffee first?"

"Sorry, I'm getting ahead of myself. Of course. I have eggs, too. I could whip us up something for breakfast."

Katie placed her hand on her stomach at the mention of eggs. "Just coffee for me for now. Thanks."

Dusty busied himself in the kitchen. After a few minutes, Katie joined him. He poured her a cup and slid the flavored creamer in front of her, then returned to the stove. As soon as he picked up the spatula, he dropped it and flew to Katie's side. "Don't!" he shouted as he clutched her hand. She had dropped a heaping spoonful of creamer into her cup.

"What the hell is wrong with you?"

"There's cinnamon in that." He walked the cup over to the sink and washed it out.

"How the hell do you know I'm allergic?"

Dusty thought fast on his feet. "You said something this morning."

"Oh, I guess I did. Thanks." He refilled her cup and dropped it back off. He removed milk from the refrigerator. "This will have to do. I'll get you half and half for next time."

She smiled at him.

"You like the sound of next time?"

"You're burning your eggs."

"Shit!" He rushed over to the stove and turned the burner off. "I really can cook. You're too distracting."

Katie unbuttoned a button on the shirt she was wearing. "I have no idea what you're talking about."

"That's dirty pool."

Dusty walked over and wrapped his arms around her waist. Again they shared a long kiss, but Katie placed both hands on his chest. "I really need to lay down for a bit."

"I'm not really hungry yet, either. Join me on the couch?"

"Sure."

After they were settled, Dusty pulled a crocheted afghan from the back of sofa over them. He turned the TV on softly, but Katie fell asleep right away. Dusty couldn't believe through all his fumbling he had still won her over again. He was surprised when he woke up two hours later, not believing he'd slept that long. Katie was still sound asleep.

As carefully as he could, he climbed over the back of the couch. He got dressed then slipped out to pick up movies and pizza.

When he returned, she was standing in the kitchen, waiting for the microwave.

She smiled at the sight of him. "Just heating up my coffee."

"You feeling better?"

"Almost human again."

He put the pizza down then removed a container of creamer out of the bag. "Got you this while I was out."

"Thanks." She removed the coffee from the microwave and added some creamer. Cup in hand, she lifted the lid to the box and inhaled deeply. "This is perfect. I'm starving." She pulled a piece out of the box and offered him the first bite. He accepted it then gave her a kiss on the cheek with a full mouth. The timing was a little off, but this scene played familiarly in his head.

Katie hopped on the counter to continue eating. "Do you think we're moving a little fast here?"

He picked up his own piece and took his position in front of her, snuggling himself between her legs. "Not at all."

"I was on a date with Rex then somehow ended up in your bed. My first instincts were that you were some kind of crazed stalker lunatic, yet I still slept with you. Have I lost all of my marbles?"

"I'd say you've finally found your senses. You always study too hard, Katie. You were on the verge of a complete meltdown. I was finally able to get you to take a breath and relax."

"How do you know my study habits? We don't have any classes together."

Again Dusty had to think fast. "I've seen you here and there. You've always looked stressed out." He hoped she wouldn't want more of an explanation than that.

She squinted her eyes at him. "I'd know if I saw that baby face of yours before, Dustin."

"Dusty."

"Fine. Dusty. You're fun and all, but I'm not ready to settle down. Sorry if my lack of self-control is giving you the wrong idea. One, I have too much on my study load and B, I'm not a fan of lawyers. I don't see a future with a guy whose profession I'm going to despise."

"Your arguments are invalid, counselor. A, you'll have plenty of time for me and two, I'm not such a fan of lawyers, either. A Minnesota pro bono lawyer died in poverty, and many people donated to a fund for his funeral. The Chief Justice was asked to donate ten dollars. 'Only ten dollars?' said the Justice. 'Only ten to bury an attorney? Here's a hundred. Go and bury ten more of them.'" He waited for her laugh that never came. "No mercy laugh?"

"Sorry. It wasn't funny. Why become something you don't want to be?"

"It's about who's paying the bills but have no fear, I'll get over it soon."

She tilted her head in confusion. "You're dropping out?"

"Sort of."

"How do you 'sort of' drop out of school?"

"I move on to something better."

Katie motioned to the manuscript on the table. "You are going to leave school to become a writer?"

"Not exactly, but something along those lines."

"Man," she said as she took another bite. "I sure can pick 'em."

He snuggled in closer and gave her a quick kiss. "You sure can, darlin'." Returning his attention to the bag, he pulled out several movies. *Somewhere in Time* with Christopher Reeve, *Time after Time* with Mary Steenburgen, and *Time Line* with Paul Walker.

Katie flipped through them. "You into time travel movies or something?"

"It just felt like a theme day."

"You could have picked up all the *Back to the Future* movies while you were at it."

"I never did try turning Dad's Delorean into a time machine for you." Dammit! He'd slipped again. Luckily for him, she missed that.

"Your dad has a Delorean?"

Dusty took another bite and nodded. "He has a thing for cars."

"He has a thing for cars, but you drive a piece of shit?"

"I drive a classic. Don't hurt her feelings like that. If you must know, there's a Beemer in the garage. I just choose not to drive it."

"Let me guess. In your little pea brain somewhere, somehow you think this pisses your dad off."

"Damn, you're good."

Chapter Seven

Dusty became caught up in the familiarity of cuddling on the couch with Katie. While wondering what he would do differently this time around, he suddenly bolted upright, remembering exactly what he was supposed to do differently. It startled Katie.

"What's the matter?"

"Um…nothing. I thought I forgot something."

"What was it?"

"I…uh…forgot."

"You're doing it again."

"Sorry."

"Do you need to be somewhere? I can call for a ride home."

"No, don't do that." He pulled her back to his chest where she'd been nestled before he jerked. "I like this. I promise I don't have to be anywhere right now and if I did, screw 'em." Katie had said that Courtney was dating this Ronald when they shared a dorm room, but she wasn't infected until sometime after Katie moved out. The way he saw it, he had time to find the guy and get him to stay away from her.

Katie hit pause on the remote. "I really should check in with my roommate."

"That's Courtney, right?"

Katie sat up, studying him. "We never did go back to her. Didn't you think she was in trouble or something?"

Dusty tried to word what popped into his head without stammering. "I think it was something I heard. She was dating some jerk friend of a friend. I was hoping she didn't have her heart broken over it."

Katie laughed hard. "Courtney? I love her to pieces, but you should be concerned with other things. She doesn't have a heart to break where men are concerned. She's made no secret about being in it for the fun right now. You must know someone with a bigger ego than yours for them to think she was getting hurt."

"You think I have a big ego?"

"Puh-lease. You carry yourself in a way that screams 'I'm gorgeous look at me, but I don't care if you don't.'"

"Well?"

"Well what?"

"Is that lying?"

She whacked him hard with a throw pillow. He laughed, pulling her to his chest yet again. "I'm kidding. I don't think I'm all that. My track record should prove it."

"I don't know anything about your track record. I saw the condoms in your bathroom."

"So? That's makes me safe, not a player. Have I mentioned the twelve-pack is a year supply?"

She smirked. "What do I see in you?"

"I'm incredibly hot in bed."

"There is that."

"Round two?" he said as he waggled his eyebrows.

"No, freak. I need to call Court."

"You want me to order Chinese for supper?"

"Sure. I like anything." She picked up her cell phone and walked to the window. Dusty grabbed his, going to the kitchen to give her privacy. This was probably the part where he was talked about. He grinned just thinking about it.

"That hottie with the wavy brown hair that we talked about earlier?" Courtney asked.

"Yeah, him."

"How did you end up with him? I thought you were with Rex."

"I was. He and Rex got in a fight."

"No shit? Tell me you're dating hottie now."

"I'm dating hottie now."

"No shit?"

Kaitlyn laughed. "I know. I'm really not sure how it happened."

"He looked a little young."

"Yeah, he is."

"How young, Katie?"

"Twenty-one."

"You cradle robber, you!" Courtney laughed. "You can't be serious."

"I can't believe I am either." She looked around to make sure Dusty wasn't in ear shot, then whispered into the phone, "The sex is incredible."

"O—M—G. You serious? You slept with him already?"

"Don't give me that. You hardly wait till a second date."

"That's me, hon. You're all goodness and purity and shit like that."

"Quit it. I just wanted to let you know where I was. I kind of lost my mind for a bit."

"Don't worry about me. You have some fun. It's nice you are finally letting yourself cut loose. Hey, does he have a friend?"

"Like you're at a loss. I'll find out for you, though. We've never double dated before. This could be fun."

"I have to get running. Ronald is knocking."

"Ronald again? I've never known you to stick to one guy so much."

"Meh. Dry spell. Have fun, hon. Love you."

"Love you back."

Dusty walked back over after he heard her hang up. He wrapped an arm around her waist and gave her neck a kiss. "Not that I was eavesdropping, but did I hear double date?"

"I never know if she's serious but if you know someone that might be interested, I'm sure I could drag her along."

He swayed with her, hip to hip. "I can think of a few guys that like girls with a little meat on them."

She stepped back. "Dustin! That's a horrible thing to say!"

"Shit. I didn't mean anything by it. She's cute, just noticeably a little heavy. That's all. Not enough that anyone would mind."

Her arms were now crossed. He was well familiar with this stance. *Shit.* "So what you're saying is, if I had an extra fifteen or twenty pounds, we wouldn't be here right now?"

"No."

"No?"

"No. Shit. I didn't mean 'no' we wouldn't be…I meant, 'no'—of course we would be. Dammit, baby," he said, wrapping his hands around her waist again. "You're twisting this around. You're more beautiful to me every day. Even after two kids you're…I mean…you'd be that much more gorgeous to me even after you have kids." Her head titled slightly. She seemed more confused than ever, and he couldn't blame her. He'd really stuck his foot in his mouth now. How did he ever survive the first time around? "Can I get a do-over?" he asked.

Her arms were now crossed. "You can try."

"My friend that was with me last night. Dean. Remember him?"

"No."

"Well…we were checking you guys out. I know he'd be into her."

"He the one that thinks she's an easy lay?"

"I never said anyone said that." Her stare told him he must have; he remembered his quick fib. "I knew a guy that knew a guy that did sleep with her and thought he hurt her, but no. Dean doesn't know any of that." He ran his hand down his face. "Maybe I should go lie on the bed and repeat the date over and over like Christopher Reeve. Go back in time to yesterday and start again."

Katie's features softened. "I'm sorry. I'm very protective of Courtney."

"And I'm sorry. I didn't mean to sound like a pig. I really do think she's pretty, just not as pretty as you, of course. No one is as pretty as you. You're perfection, Katie. You know that Plato quote in that Demi Moore movie? You're my split-apart. You're—"

She put her fingers over his mouth. "*The Butcher's Wife* and that wasn't Plato. It was a bad Hollywood misquote. Shut up while you're ahead."

"Bless you."

After putting a healthy dent in the Chinese delivery, they cuddled while they watched another movie. Katie fell asleep before the end of it. When she awoke, the scene played out as it had when she'd previously time traveled to him. She'd insisted she shouldn't sleep with him, he'd placed his hand on her heart and said he knew she really wanted it. They made love and were lying there cuddling when there was a knock at the door.

"This isn't a good time," Dusty hollered, instinctively, then quietly said, "Oh shit." He knew what was coming.

"I pay your rent. You'll make time, young man," a muffled voice answered back.

"Shit. It's my dad."

"Oh my God," said Katie as she quickly stood, scooped up her clothes and purse, and ran for the bathroom.

Dusty knew there was no fighting what would play out next. Again Katie called Courtney and snuck away after a quick, embarrassed hello to his parents. He'd let her go without a fight this time and text her in the morning.

Dusty woke up the next morning, reaching for Katie. When he couldn't feel her, he opened his eyes up and cursed. It hadn't been a bad dream. He was back in his college days and back in his old cottage. Katie hadn't slept over. *Bummer.*

Walking out to the living room, he stared at the four-point buck on the wall. "What are you looking at?" He'd given Katie the story about hunting with his uncle yesterday and as before, she didn't complain about it. Later, when they moved into their first home, she asked that it stay in his office and not go in the living room. She admitted to hating it. If he'd used his brain, he would have figured it out sooner, seeing as how she was going to be a vet. "What a dumbass," he scolded himself. After retrieving a ladder from the garage, he promptly took the deer head down. He wandered back out with it and the ladder and stuck it on a high, empty shelf. Dusty wasn't that big into hunting, it was just something he had done as a teen. He could take or leave venison over beef. Katie always swore she wouldn't "eat Bambi" so he didn't have it much, anyway.

"You whipped bastard." He laughed to himself. The garage was colder than he was dressed for. He removed a sweatshirt out of his closet when he got back in, then sent Katie a text.

Good morning, doll face. Missed you this morning. You awake?

Sort of. Still in bed. Late night gab session with Court.

Sorry about my parents last night. You OK?

Nope. Dead from embarrassment.

I'll make it up to you. Come over?

After no reply he tried again. *Take you to breakfast?*

Coffee. Gimme 20.

He signed off with a heart and his initial *[<3 D],* feeling sappy for doing so, but he didn't care.

She sent him the smiley with its tongue sticking out *[:P],* but it still made him smile.

Dusty pulled up after exactly twenty minutes. Katie was already in the lobby and ran out when she saw him. He hurried around to open the door for her. The gesture earned him a quick kiss. "Worth it," he said as he ran around to his side.

As he sat down, Katie asked, "What was worth it?"

"Freezing my balls off to pretend I'm some kind of gentleman."

She smiled and gave him another kiss. "It is butt cold this morning. I must like you."

Dusty hit a button on the center console. "I just turned your ass on."

"Yes, you did."

"No. I mean literally. Heated seats."

She giggled. "Oh. Thanks for bringing the good car."

He put the car in gear but hit the brakes. "You sure Courtney doesn't want to come along?"

"I asked her. A grunt was all I got as a response. Gee, you this nice to the roommates of all the girls you bang?"

He took her hand and gave it a kiss. "Nope. You're special. And I told you, the list isn't that long. Coffee shop?"

"That's fine. I'm really not a big breakfast person. And I know—you know."

"I promise I wasn't going to say anything. I'm sorry if that creeped you out. I'm just observant. Especially of gorgeous women."

She gave him the look he had dubbed her "stink eye."

"Stop it, Dusty."

"Well, at least you're finally calling me Dusty."

"I still don't know what this is. Let me take baby steps, okay? I really shouldn't have given in already."

"Twice," he said with a grin then kissed her hand again. "Don't try to fight it, sugar."

"Ugh," was the last thing she said before they reached Sunriders.

They sat together on what Dusty called "their" couch after they had their caramel lattes in hand. Dusty bought two croissant egg sandwiches as well. "You want a bite?"

"No, thanks. My metabolism doesn't come to life until later."

He refrained from making any "I know" comments this time. He watched as she blew on her coffee before taking a sip. That never grew old to him.

She looked up at him. "I started your book last night."

"And?"

"I'm amazed how much I'm enjoying it."

"And why is that? You think I'd want you to read it if I thought it was crap?"

"I told you. I'm not a sci-fi fan. Your Captain Skinnard is a great character. He reminds me of you."

She'd said this a dozen times before, but he played dumb. "Me?"

"He's pretty full of himself, too."

"Are we back to that?"

Katie smiled and sipped her coffee. "I had another friend who wrote short stories. She was always afraid they were horrible. Her notebook was titled the 'The You Suck Archives.'"

That made Dusty nearly spit out his food, laughing. "Sorry. But that's part of my point. You seemed pretty sure I'd like it."

"I had already gotten a wonderful review. I was pretty sure you'd like it."

"Why, though? You don't even know me. I like a good book, but reading isn't my passion or anything. I'm too busy right now. Did you think I'd see how wonderfully you wrote and melt into your arms?"

"Is it working?"

"You're certifiable." She leaned over and took a bite of his sandwich.

"Is it a novella?"

He brushed a crumb away from the corner of her mouth. "It'll be a full length novel. It's only about half done."

"Then again, why have me read it? You leave me off at a cliffhanger and I'll kick your ass."

"You'd better stop then. It's a while…I mean, it'll be a while before I perfect it."

"You suck, Andrews. I'm already hooked."

"Maybe it's my ploy to make sure you stick around to the end."

"You are full of all kinds of tricks, aren't you?"

He smirked. "Yup."

After finishing his sandwiches, he picked up one of her feet. He removed her shoe and began to massage it. Most fights ended with one of his foot- or backrubs. It was also the start of sex many a time. Either way, it was a win-win maneuver for him. The only thing she liked better, he couldn't do at the coffee shop.

She moaned as he worked his magic. "You are sure trying hard here."

"Don't talk about what's hard."

She tried to pull her foot away but he held it firm. "I told you, no point in playing tough now. A few more minutes of this and you'll take me before we make it back to my place."

"Keep talkin', law boy."

He grinned at her protests.

Chapter Eight

An hour later, Dusty and Katie were parked in a small nook off an alley, three blocks away from the coffee shop. The windows were fogged up and Katie was straddling Dusty, breathing heavily. Her pants sat without her on the passenger seat, but her coat was long and had her well covered.

"You make me a shameless hussy with no self-control. What the hell is wrong with me?" she asked rhetorically into his neck.

"Not a damn thing."

"How the hell do you keep doing this to me?"

"It's a gift."

"I mean it, Dusty. I'm coming off like a bad Debbie Does Dusty porno. I've never behaved this way."

"I just know how to sweep you off your feet, baby. That and I'm sure the heated seats helped."

She slid back to her side of the car. "I really should get back. I don't see Court a lot. We try to spend Sundays together when we can. I told you I didn't have a lot of free time, Dustin."

"Dusty."

She smiled at him then gave him a gentle kiss. "I don't know why I don't call you that. It does kinda fit you better with that baby face."

"Keep it up, sugar bear, and I'll grow a beard."

"No!" She stroked her hand down his cheek. "Although I am fond of the day-old scruffy look."

Dusty pulled up to her dorm and they shared another lingering kiss. "I'm going to miss you in the morning. I wish you'd stay with me."

She placed her hand on his crotch. "You mean this is going to miss me in the morning."

Dusty removed her hand. He was already getting aroused again by the kiss and didn't want her to think that was all he wanted. "No. I'm going to miss you. You sure I can't get you to stay over? I promise I'll bring you back early so you can get to class."

"I told you. I really want to spend time with Courtney. Besides, I thought we were going to try to slow this down."

"I agreed to no such thing. I don't want to, but I'll let you take the lead here. I don't want to scare you away. Can I take you and Courtney to dinner tomorrow night at least? We'll go to *Chez Pauls*. I'll take you on a proper dinner date."

Katie leaned in for a kiss. "I'm in. I'll text you if Courtney is available so you can call that Dean friend of yours."

"I'll take you both out, even if he isn't available. I'd like to get to know this girl that you care so much for. I have a feeling I'm going to need her approval."

Katie gave him another quick kiss before opening the door. "You're not much for first impressions, but your recovery is nice. See you tomorrow. Six?"

"Sounds good, honey buns." Dusty heard her groan after she closed the door. He chuckled and headed to Dean's. Dean had a two-bed dorm room, but he didn't currently have a roommate. His last one took off for Barbados with his tuition money and hadn't been heard from since. A sock hung on the doorknob, but Dusty ignored it and walked in. Dean was sound asleep and alone. Dusty flew onto his bed.

"You asshole!" Dean shouted as he punched Dusty hard in the arm. "Didn't you see the sock?"

"Yeah. But as I suspected, there's no chick. I knew you weren't getting laid."

"What makes you so sure?"

"Because you're in the middle of a dry spell."

"And I can't break that, why?"

"'Cause I was busy getting some and you had no wing man."

"No shit? You get back into Stacey's pants?"

"Stacey?" Dusty hadn't thought of her in years. "No. Remember the chick you said was out of my league?"

"No fucking way."

"Fucking way. Spent the morning with her, too."

"Gonna make her harder to dump if you let her get attached."

"I'm not going to dump her. This is it."

"You? In love? Get the hell out." Dean pulled the blanket over his head.

Dusty promptly pulled it back down. "I want to take her out to dinner tomorrow night."

"I'm not lending you money."

"I don't need money. I'll use the card."

"Dude, your dad will beat your ass."

"He won't even notice."

"So, what did you wake my ass up for? What do you want from me?"

"A date."

"You're a pretty-boy and all, but I already told you I won't date you."

Dusty gave him a shove. "Come on. She has a cute friend. I want you to come along."

"What the hell for?"

"I'm going to need to win her roommate over if I'm going to make this stick. We kind of jumped right in the sack. I need to go back a few steps and do this right. I want to keep this one, Dean-O."

Dean groaned. "Is her friend really cute, or should I bring milk bones?"

"She's cute. You remember the brunette she was with?"

"The chubby girl?"

"She wasn't that bad."

"I wasn't complaining. I like 'em a little chubby, anyway. More cushion for the pushin' and bigger tits."

Dusty sat on his chest and held the pillow over his face. "You scrodknocker." He let Dean flail for a minute then removed the pillow. "She's a nice girl. You treat her like crap and it's over for me." From what Katie had said, if Dean was half-way human he'd probably get lucky, but he didn't want to use that as part of the bribe. He was hoping they'd hit it off for more than a one night stand. He had to keep Courtney interested long enough for that Ronald to move on.

"Fine. You're buying."

"Deal."

"And we're taking the Beemer, not that piece of shit you call a car."

"Already using it. I don't want Katie to have to go without heat."

"But you have no problem tooling me around in it."

"You're ugly. I don't care."

"Get off me, you homo."

Dusty climbed off him then pelted him with a pillow from the other bed. "Get a haircut tomorrow and be ready at five thirty. Dress nice. We're going to *Chez Pauls*."

Dean finally sat up. "Holy shit. You do mean business."

"I'm not screwing around."

"I'll be your wingman, douche."

"It's Goose." Dusty laughed.

"I know. Get out."

"See you tomorrow at five thirty sharp."

Dusty had forgotten how much he missed Dean. They hadn't kept in touch as well as Katie and Courtney did over the years. Dean accepted a job with a huge law firm in Minneapolis after graduation and was busy more often than not. They shared beers over a summer barbecue here and there, but that was about the extent of it. After all this time, Dean was still single and always had an excuse to avoid a "couples" get together.

Heading for his cottage, Dusty hoped that this date would be the ticket to setting Courtney on a new path. He wouldn't mind falling asleep and waking up in his Katie's arms at any past, present or future, as long as she'd always be there for him. Screwing this up was not an option.

Courtney was climbing out of bed when Katie walked in. "Hey, hon. I didn't think you'd be back till tonight."

"I wanted to come back to you. I never get to see you anymore, Court."

"What really happened? You wear the poor boy out? Did you steal his virginity and he can't keep up?"

Katie laughed. "Stop it. Things are going great. I just don't want to push it. You know I wasn't interested in a relationship. He sure is pushy for such a young thing."

"And you've never glowed so much. I wouldn't have minded if you stayed over again."

"Well, I would have. I want to spend time with you. Sunday is our day when we both don't have so much studying to do." Katie plopped on her bed. "Can I ask you something?"

"Of course. Fire away."

"How much are you into this Ronald guy?"

She shrugged. "You know me. I'm as much into him as I can be. Why?"

"'Cause I want you to double date with Dusty and me. He has a friend he thinks you'd like."

"I don't care, I guess. Ronald and I are kind of just in it for sex. We're not exclusive or anything. I think he calls me when he's bored. I don't need to stick around for that."

"Court…" Katie dragged out her name, clearly showing her disapproval.

"What? I have needs. Batteries cost a fortune."

Katie laughed out loud. "Okay. I'll stop playing mother, but will you give this Dean a chance? For me?"

"I'm in. Hey, he a law boy, too?"

"I didn't ask. Does it matter?"

"I guess not. You know how big his feet are?"

Katie brought her hands to her head with a grunt. "You're hopeless. I love you, but you're hopeless."

Dusty had to try hard not to text or call Katie all day. He went ice skating at the local outdoor rink to kill some time. After a few times around to loosen up, he was happy to have some kids show up in hockey gear, eager to be taught a trick or two when he offered. He couldn't wait for Alex to be old enough to get on the ice. He'd already started watching figure skating with Ali, hoping she'd want to take lessons as well. Dusty caught himself looking over to the bench a lot, waiting to see Frank appear.

After two hours he was ready to go home. He stopped for drive-through tacos for supper and hoped he had enough beer. It sucked that liquor stores were closed on Sunday. He never planned ahead well enough.

After he ate and showered, he sent Katie a text.

How was your day with Courtney?

Nice and mellow. We just hung out.

We good for dinner tomorrow? Dean is game.

She said OK. Hey...What size are Dean's feet?

Dusty laughed hard. *Pervert. Same as me. 13.*

Court just fainted.

You're killin' me, babe. Come over?

Can't. Need to get some sleep. Early class.

:(

You'll live. See you tomorrow at six.

Sleep well, muffin.

Ahhhh...

Again Dusty laughed. He never knew what possessed him to do that to her every time. Her reactions were priceless and he'd learned long ago that she didn't mind as much as she let on.

Seeing as how he was quitting school soon, Dusty skipped class the next day. There was no way he was sitting through the class again that could very well be the one that made him storm away from the whole law school ordeal and finally stand up to his father. He went to the office to try to get information on Ronald, but realized he didn't have a last name. His smile and charm had worked wonders before on Susan, the woman in charge of the records, but even that wouldn't get him a last name. He had no idea what classes this guy was taking, no clue what he looked like.

The weather wasn't too bad. He took the car for a fill up and added a wash since he could. The radio said it would be zero tomorrow. The car washes weren't open when it was below freezing. By the time he purchased some decent dress clothes, he was ready for lunch. He decided to stop for a burger at *Puck You*, one of his favorite sports bars, heavy on the hockey theme.

Dusty enjoyed the fact that his alcohol tolerance was a lot better in his college days. He wouldn't dream of having a beer with lunch in his present, but it sure sounded good now. He sat at the bar and ordered ribs and a Leiney's Dark &

Creamy. He spotted a familiar face across the bar, almost waved hello, but caught himself. Wilson Gregory didn't know him in this time. It was funny to run into him here and now. Even though they were currently friends, thoughts of pummeling him for dating Katie in an alternate time crossed his mind. Realistically, he could hardly beat up a guy for something that didn't happen. Dusty tried to keep to himself and his beer, but every now and then he glanced Wilson's way.

After the third time he caught Dusty looking at him, the soon-to-be chiropractor picked up his beer and walked over. "Do I know you?" he asked Dusty, irritation in his voice.

"Sorry. You just looked familiar. I'm sure we haven't met before. Not unless you come here often. Dammit. Now it sounds like I'm trying to pick you up." Dusty grinned, hoping to ease the tension.

He laughed and outstretched his hand. "Wilson Gregory."

"Dustin Andrews. Nice to meet you. Sorry if you felt I was staring at you. I really don't swing that way."

"No worries. I don't either. Mind if I join you?"

Dusty motioned to the seat next to him. "Please do."

The two men talked over their food, then shot a round of pool. Doctor Gregory had not yet earned the title "Doctor," he still had a year left. Dusty kept his share of the conversation simple. He didn't need to tell a man who was technically a stranger about dropping out. He should have left out the lawyer part altogether, knowing a lawyer joke would be coming.

"A lawyer's dog, running around town unleashed, heads for a butcher shop and steals a roast. The butcher goes to the lawyer's office and asks, 'if a dog running unleashed steals a piece of meat from my store, do I have a right to demand payment for the meat from the dog's owner?' The lawyer answers, 'Absolutely.' 'Then you owe me $8.50. Your dog was loose and stole a roast from me today.' The lawyer, without a word, writes the butcher a check for $8.50. The butcher, having a feeling of satisfaction, leaves. Three days later, the butcher finds a bill from the lawyer: $100 due for a consultation." Wilson laughed heartily at his joke and Dusty, having already heard it, played along for mercy sake.

"You gotta watch us every—"

Wilson interrupted Dusty mid-sentence. "Will you look at the tits on that."

Dusty turned around to see a new waitress standing at the bar, giving the bartender a drink order. "Sorry. I only have eyes for my Katie."

"Come on. You can't tell me you're sticking with just one at your age."

"I'm afraid I can."

Wilson held up his glass in a toast. "Hope that works for you. I'm looking forward to the doctor salary, the fast cars, and all the women I can handle and get away with."

Dusty had to hold back his laugh. In their present time line, Wilson was still single and acting as if he was the town stud. Dusty had overheard one of Wilson's dates say, "It's true what they say about the only difference between porcupines and a Corvette. The pricks are on the outside of a porcupine." Dusty now strained to remember how they met since he wasn't in any of the "married friends circle" things he did with Katie. Was this it? Holy hell, his head was starting to spin.

"You all right?" Wilson asked.

"Yeah. I'm fine. I really need to knock off the beer. I have a date tonight and need to keep my wits about me."

"Not getting her to put out yet, huh?"

"I don't think I need to be sharing that kind of info with you."

Wilson made little whipping motions. "Won't find me tied down. No sirree, Bob."

"Well, good luck with that." Dusty tossed his dad's card on the bar. "I got this." He was going to dent it tonight at dinner. Might as well warm it up.

"Thanks, buddy. I'll catch you next time."

"Sounds fine. I'm not making a date with you, though."

"Fair enough." The men shook hands, then Wilson strolled away to talk to the waitress with big tits.

Dusty's mind went to Katie, once again wondering how she'd hooked up with him. "Baby, you had to have been really, really drunk."

"Did you say something?" the bartender asked when he returned with the tab.

"Nope. Just thinking out loud."

"You okay to drive?"

"I've only had the two beers. I'm good."

"You are old enough to drink, right? My gut told me to card you."

"I'll be twenty-two in a few months." Dusty reached for his wallet and the bartender stopped him.

"No offense. I felt guilty. I don't want to get fired."

Dusty threw a five onto the counter in addition to what he added on the card's tip line. "I'm a regular here. You're the one that's new. No hard feelings." Dusty was beginning think twice about that beard.

Chapter Nine

Cleaned up, sobered up, and dressed to kill, Dusty drove over to Dean's. He sent him a text saying that he was downstairs.

Dean replied: *Gimme five, douche.*

Four, dick.

Love you, too.

Now you have three minutes.

Dean strolled out to the car in no particular rush. After he settled in, Dean pulled out a joint and was about to light it. Dusty whipped it out of his hands.

"What the hell is wrong with you? Don't do that shit in my car."

"You let me in the other one."

"Well, not in this one. I don't want it stinking up for the girls and I don't want you a stoned ass for dinner."

"You're such a pussy." Dean snatched it back and put it in his pocket. "I thought I'd give myself the munchies and eat as much of your money as I could."

"Fine. Just do it without the weed."

Dean pulled a small bottle of Jagger out of his coat pocket. "Is this okay, Dad?"

"Actually—"

"You kidding me? You're going to tell me I can't drink?"

"You can drink. It's just that Katie hurled after doing cherry bombs. I'm sure the smell will make her want to yak. I'll stop and buy you something else, you cryass numbnut."

"So, you did have to get her drunk to pork her."

"No. I *porked* her after she sobered up. Could you kindly not be so crude over dinner? I told you, I really like her."

"I'm not an idiot."

"That has yet to be determined."

Dean huffed and leaned back hard into the seat. "If you don' trust me, why did you ask me?"

"Because I love you, too, snookums." Dusty blew him a kiss and Dean again punched his arm. "Homo."

"Shit for brains."

The insults flew until Dusty ran into the liquor store. He came out with a tray of plastic test tube shooters with mixed shots named "Bahama Mama" and "Sex on the Beach". He also had a bottle of "Hot Sex."

Dean removed one of the tubes. "What's this girly shit?"

"It was at the counter. I don't want to be late."

"You know, you can buy those individually," he said, pointing at the tray of shooters.

"They have a credit card minimum."

"Dude, your dad is totally going to kick your ass."

"I can run faster scared than he can mad."

Dean laughed before taking two of the shots out and handing Dusty one. "Salut!"

"Kanpai!"

The boys had been learning a toast from every foreign student they could find. They could use the internet, but this was more fun. This game was inspired by a few guys they knew, who were on their second year of "the fifty states game." The rules there were simple, but Dusty didn't feel he was man-whore enough to try to bang a girl from every state.

One guy graduated last year on a quest for Maine. He had one girl from Puerto Rico, but he was determined that you couldn't substitute a US territory for a missing state and refused to declare himself the winner.

Dean and Dusty's game was a friendly conversation starter with a new students, guys and gals equally, and the gesture was always appreciated.

Although Dusty didn't need the liquid encouragement like Dean, they had one more shot each before walking up to the girls' dorm room. Dusty wanted to show his gentleman side again. He wasn't going to wait downstairs in the car. Before they climbed out, he reached in the back for a bouquet of flowers for each of the girls.

"You thought of everything, loverboy."

"I mean it. Best behavior." Dean reached for breath spray and gave himself a couple shots. "Hit me, too," Dusty said as he opened his mouth. Dean complied.

Katie opened the door and smiled widely at the two men. Giving her a quick once-over, Dusty admired the dress pants that hugged her perfect body just right and even more so, he admired the low-cut black top that showed off his two favorite curves even better. He longed to run his hands down the neckline as he had done to her so many times, but he had to resist.

"You clean up nice," she said to Dusty.

He handed her the flowers and gave her a kiss on the cheek. "You look great."

"Sorry. I would have worn a dress, but it's too damn cold."

"No worries, sweetness. You're gorgeous."

Katie's attention turned to Dean. "Dean I presume?"

"Yes, ma'am."

Katie turned around to holler for Courtney right as she appeared at her side. She was in a low-cut top as well. Hers was black like Katie's, but her massive cleavage was surrounded by ruffles. Dusty caught himself looking and quickly glanced away. *Damn Dean. Larger women—bigger tits.*

Courtney greeted the two men. “Yummy. Which one of you is mine?”

Dean stepped forward and handed her the flowers. “That would be me.”

She leaned up and kissed him on the cheek. “Thanks. I can’t even say when the last time someone was thoughtful enough to bring me flowers.”

Dusty jabbed Dean’s ribs with an elbow, Dean elbowed him back. She turned her attention to Dusty. “So you’re the guy that has stolen my roomie’s heart.”

“I hope that’s me.”

Courtney leaned up and gave Dusty a kiss on the cheek as well. “Hurt her and I’ll have you killed.”

“Fair enough.” He offered Katie his arm. “Your chariot awaits, ladies.”

“Wait. I want to get these in water. Do we have a minute?”

“Of course.”

“Give us a second.”

Katie closed the door. “So? What do you think?”

“He’s adorable.”

“Puppies are adorable, Court.”

“They are puppies, hon.”

“Dean has a few years on Dusty.” Katie picked up a plastic cup and poured the remainder of a bottle of water in it, adding the flowers as she spoke. “Is that bad? Come on. Dusty’s so much more mature than anyone I’ve dated. Even older guys. If Dean hangs with him, I bet he’s the same.”

“Do we have to stand here whispering and start naming our kids or can we go on a date? I’m starved.”

"Sorry. I was dying to know what you thought. I never met him. He is a cutie."

"Just don't get your hopes up. You know I'm not looking for anything steady."

"Try to get to dessert before you do him in the bathroom."

Courtney pretended to look crushed as she crossed her hands over her heart. "Okay. After dessert, but before coffee."

"Tramp."

"Princess."

Katie gave her friend a hug. "Let's go. We've made them suffer long enough."

As they were on their way to the restaurant, Dusty saw Courtney leaned into Dean when he glanced into the rearview window. He heard her ask him, "You don't smoke by any chance, do you?"

The corner of his mouth turned up in a grin. "Not cigarettes."

"You packin'?"

He pulled the joint out of his pocket, held it up, and motioned to Dusty. "Spoil sport already nixed lighting up in his precious Beemer."

Katie turned around. "Court! I thought you quit that shit."

"I did. Mostly."

Dusty took Katie's hand. "I'm glad you don't partake in that crap."

"I'm too self-centered to not want to be in control of every aspect of my life. And shut up, booze is the one exception and that's rare."

He brought her hand to his lips and gave it a hard kiss. He realized he did that a lot and didn't care. "You're not self-centered." He looked at Dean through the rear view mirror. "I'll stop at the park and give you two stoners five minutes. I don't want to lose our reservation."

"Fat chance with your name, dumbass."

Katie turned to Dusty. "What's he mean by that?"

"Uh…my dad goes there when he's in town for business. I dropped his name to make sure we were treated well." He didn't want to go into the whole "family money" thing with her already. He liked the way things played out before. He was hoping he could get this wrapped up before too much more changed. "Bust out the shots," Dusty said, trying to change the subject.

They pulled over at the park and Courtney and Dean ran into the pavilion. "Must love that crap to go out in this cold," Katie said with a sigh.

"At least they have somewhat hit it off already."

"There is that, I suppose."

"Wanna make out?" Dusty waggled his eyebrows at her.

She scooted over and they shared a lingering kiss. They were interrupted before they expected to be by the door opening. "That was fast," Katie said to them.

"Fucking cold out," Courtney answered.

Dean took a swig from the "Hot Sex" and handed it to her.

"I like how you guys party" Courtney said. "I don't want to get too trashed though. I have a full day tomorrow."

"Me too," Dean admitted.

"Are you in law school, too?"

"Yup. Still want to finish the date?"

"I don't know. My dad's a lawyer. I'd hate to go out with someone he'd actually approve of."

"Don't worry, Courtney. No respectable father has approved of Dean yet," Dusty said, jumping into the conversation. Dean threw a shooter at Dusty and missed.

Katie picked it up and opened it before offering it to Dusty. "You drink it, babe. I have to mind myself if I'm going to be the DD of this crew."

She gave him a kiss on the cheek. Again he thought to himself, *worth it*.

Immediately after everyone was settled at the table of the restaurant, Dusty ordered a bottle of champagne. "That's okay, isn't it?" he asked Katie.

"Sure. I can't tell one from another. Don't go spending a bundle." Everyone was silent as they read the selections the menu offered.

"Either of you been here before?" Dean asked.

"I was once," Katie said. "You haven't though, right Court?"

"Never." She folded her menu. "The name may be French, but it's Greek to me."

Dean took her menu. "Is there anything you absolutely hate?"

"Not really."

"You trust me?"

She pondered it for a second before answering. "Sure."

Dean asked Katie what she was having and then asked Dusty as well. Dusty knew what he was going to pull and had to fight his grin.

A waiter showed up with the bottle of champagne and after a proper presentation, filled everyone's glasses. Another waiter was right behind him, ready to take their food order.

"Are we ready?" the waiter asked in a heavy French accent.

"*Oui*," Dean answered. He proceeded to order for everyone in French. Dusty loved watching the expressions of the girls as he did so. *Oh yeah. Dean's getting laid.*

After the waiter walked away, Courtney said, "Impressive."

"I spent my junior year in Paris. Comes pretty easy when you are forced to use it 24/7."

"I barely made it through Spanish. Long disease names and the bones in the body were a snap compared to another language. What did you order me anyway?"

"Some fancy chicken dish. I ordered a steak for me. You can pick which one you want."

"Nice selection, Dean," Katie said. "I forgot to mention if you ordered veal, you'd be wearing it."

He chuckled. "Dusty told me you were studying to be a vet. I figured that would be on the no-no list. "See," he said turning to Dusty. "I can be trained."

The banter throughout dinner played out as if they had been friends for years. Once the bottle of champagne was gone, the girls switched to a bottle of wine while Dean switched to a fine bourbon. Dusty stuck with a beer, still wanting to take it easy. He might be in his younger body, but his older brain was still in charge.

After the dinner plates were cleared, Dean ordered them four different desserts so they could try them all. "Hey, Dusty." Dean motioned his head to the piano in the corner of the room.

"Dude," he groaned. "No."

"Come on. You know they'll let you."

"I mean it. No." Dusty hadn't played the piano for Katie until he was at his parents' house in his memory of their dating. He didn't know why he hadn't played or sung when they met when they were older, as Katie told him in her original memories of him. But in their present, they had a piano in their living room and he played for her and the kids often. Ali was too little to start lessons officially, but he tinkered away with her on the usual easy children's stuff. Okay, "Requiem for a Dream" wasn't easy, but she loved it and was eager to please her daddy.

"Earth to Andrews…"

"Huh?" Dusty had gotten lost in his thoughts. "I told you no."

"'No' what?" Katie asked.

"You'll see." Dusty tried to grab at Dean's shirt as he stood. He walked right up to the maître d' and handed him some money. He whispered something to him and pointed to the piano. The maître d' nodded and motioned to it, as if to say, "Go ahead."

"Shit," Dusty mumbled.

"What's the matter?" both of the girls asked. Dean walked back over. "Showtime."

"You're a dick."

"Come on, pooky. Show your girl what you got."

"You play?" Katie asked.

"Wasn't planning on it."

"Please?" she begged as she went to his side.

Dusty muttered a "Dammit" and pushed his chair back. Dean took the seat next to Courtney, but Katie walked up with Dusty.

Dusty cracked his knuckles, then turned to Katie. "Don't lecture me on how bad that is."

"You're safe with me. It's Courtney I'd be afraid of." She gave him a kiss. "Play me something."

It only took him a second to think of what to play. "Remember the movie we just watched?"

"*Somewhere in Time*?"

"That's the one. This was one of my mom's favorites." Dusty never liked the attention playing drew. Everyone else in the place was considerably older than their little group. Gray hair and bad toupees filled the tables. He wanted to go with something mellow and that was usually a "geezer crowd pleaser."

When he was done, there were applause from everyone and Dusty tried to get up. He hadn't seen Dean walk over.

"Nice try, now sing for the lady."

"Bite me."

Katie gave him a kiss on the cheek. He let out a heavy sigh as he patted the space next to him so she'd scoot closer. Once again, or for the first time—depending how you looked at it—he played Neil Diamond's "Love on the Rocks."

When he was done, Katie gave him a long, lingering kiss. "You are going to take me to bed now, right?"

"Yes, ma'am."

Chapter Ten

Dusty drove to the girls' dorm first. "I'm going back to Dusty's for a bit, Court," Katie said. "You mind?"

"I'm not your mother," she said as she leaned forward and gave Katie a kiss on the cheek. Next she gave Dusty one. "Thanks for the great night." She turned to Dean. "Walk me to the door?"

"Absolutely."

"Should I wait?" Dusty asked. Dean turned to Courtney, who shook her head. "As much as it pains me to say goodnight, I have a six o'clock lab."

"Gimme ten, buddy."

As Dean walked Courtney to her room, Dusty worried he had been wrong about them and voiced as much to Katie.

"Don't think that way, Dusty. It's a good thing she isn't sleeping with him."

"How do you figure that?"

"Maybe she likes him and wants to not hop in bed right away."

"And make him fight for it? You women think men are deeper than we are. We don't think on those kinds of levels. The fewer games the better."

"Well, I for one I enjoy seeing that she's showing some restraint. It's a new territory for her."

"Or maybe she is really worried about that lab tomorrow."

"Court is damn near straight A's. I bet she didn't do as bad as she said in high school Spanish. I'm telling you, I think she likes him."

Dean had taken Courtney's hand on the way to her dorm room, but they were silent for the short walk. She leaned against it, rather than opening it up. "I really had a great time, Dean. I'm glad we did this."

"Me too." He had to bend down slightly to give her an ever so gentle kiss on the cheek. "Maybe we can do this again sometime."

She gave him a genuine smile. "I'd like that." He turned slightly to walk away, but she reached for his hand. "Please don't get me wrong. I really did have a great time. It's just that damn lab tomorrow."

"I understand completely." He dared leaning in for another kiss, this one on her lips.

She reached up, held onto the back of his neck, keeping him there for a few seconds longer than he'd intended. "I'm really sorry."

"For the kiss?" he asked.

"No," she grinned. "Not for the kiss. I'm sorry we need to call this a night. I can't screw up this lab tomorrow."

"I get it. Really. I'll talk to Dusty. We'll do this again in a few days."

Courtney bit her bottom lip. "Damn school."

Dean smiled at her. "No worries. Soon, okay?" Once again he kissed her goodbye. This time, she pulled his entire body into hers. Her hands held onto his ass as she let out a deep groan. "Screw the lab."

Dusty's cell phone went off.

Scram.

He closed it and smiled.

"What?" Katie asked.

"We've been ordered to leave."

"Really?" He showed her the text.

"I really do think they hit it off."

"Apparently."

"No, I mean really. She at least tried to tell him no when they left the car. That's something."

Dusty shook his head and headed to his place. "You know, I think I'm not going to put out tonight."

"What? Why?"

"Maybe I don't want you thinking I'm so easy."

"Oh right, Andrews. Because you're so hard to figure out and deep."

"I'm serious. You wanted to go slow and we've been anything but that. Maybe we *should* back off."

Katie crossed her arms. "If I knew you were going to do this, I would have gone in with Court."

"Can't spend time with me and keep your hands to yourself?"

"I never said that. I thought you were all about not playing games."

"I'm not. I was teasing you to make a point. It's no fun when you're not true to your feelings. Is it?"

"Point taken. But you didn't need to make that point to me. My mind told me to stay away from you and I did everything but that."

"So you're following your sex drive?" He chuckled that she was getting her feathers ruffled over this, but he knew he'd better back off before she really became upset. Katie never liked to be jabbed at. "I know what you're sayin', babe. I appreciate that you let your defenses down with me. I was a blubbering idiot and I'm lucky to have you."

"That little stunt is going to cost you, you know."

"Foot rub?"

"For starters."

"Bring it on."

Dusty dropped Katie off at seven the next morning. Courtney was gone but Dean was sound asleep in her bed. Katie shook him gently. "Dean. Wake up."

He rolled over on his back and let out a moan. "Hey, Katie. Excuse my nakedness." He pulled the sheet up higher on his chest.

"Dusty is waiting for you downstairs. He thought you'd need a ride. I need to get to class, but you're welcome to stay and sleep if you want."

"No. I shouldn't skip either. What time is it?"

"Seven."

"Crap." He swung his legs off the side of the bed, but kept his mid- section covered. His clothes were spread out everywhere.

"I'll step outside and tell Dusty you're on your way."

"Thanks."

Katie's last class of the day was cancelled. She decided to go to the coffee shop and get a few hours of studying in before she called Dusty. Caramel latte in hand, she made her way to one of the overstuffed chairs in the back. A friend jumped up in front of her.

"Katie!"

"Hello, Adam," she said, accepting the strong hug from him. Everyone called him "Adam the hugger." He was dating a friend of hers. They had a knack for running into each other here and there on campus. He was always in black t-shirts and sported a long beard. Katie often bugged him to trim it.

"Where have you been lately? I missed you at Saturday's kegger," he said.

"Been busy, I guess. I'm only here because Professor Graham had a family emergency. Class was cancelled and I was looking forward to some extra study time."

"Word on the street is you're dating a young hottie with a Beemer."

"Who told you that?"

"A little bird."

"Well, it's nothing serious yet."

"Using him for sex, huh?"

"Stop it," she said as she playfully smacked his arm. "I should introduce you two sometime. He writes, too."

"Any good?"

"Actually…" Katie looked up and saw Dusty walking through the door. She was about to haul Adam over so they could meet, but a girl stood up and flew into Dusty's arms.

"You okay, kitten?" Adam asked.

"Um…sorry. I'm fine. I just realized I don't have the book I need. I have to split." She handed him her drink. "You can have this. I haven't touched it yet." She tried to stay hidden behind him, blocking Dusty's view.

"You know I only drink tea. I'll get you a to-go cup."

He turned to walk to the counter and she shouted, "No!" She quickly turned around, hiding behind a pillar. Adam went to the front of her. "You sure you're okay?"

"I'm fine. I have a big test coming up. I have to go get that book."

She gave him a strong hug. "Great to run into you."

Katie quickly slipped out of the back door and ran the whole way back to her dorm. When she unlocked the door, she threw her books on her bed. "You sonofabitch! How could I fall for you and your shit? Bastard." She kicked at some clothes that were scattered on the floor. She let out another grunt before flopping onto her bed. "Dick." She no longer had studying on her mind. After pulling a pillow over her face, struggling to fight tears, she drifted off to sleep. Anger and the late night caught up with her.

An hour later her phone woke her up. She saw it was Dusty and didn't answer. He didn't leave a message, but he did send a text right away.

Hey, cupcake. You wanna have dinner tonight? I'm cooking.

She didn't reply to that, either. An hour later, Courtney came walking in. "Hey, hon. No Dusty tonight?"

"No," she said as she quickly picked up a book and pretended to be interested in its contents.

"Why not? I thought you two were hitting it off."

"So did I."

Courtney sat next to her. "What happened?"

"Apparently I'm not the only one he's hitting it off with right now."

"You're kidding me. He seemed so—"

"So what? Young and handsome? Yeah, what a turn off. How stupid was I? You know he's beating women away with a stick."

"Hon. He didn't come off like that at all. I think he's really into you."

"Well, I saw it for myself."

"Saw what?"

"Him hugging another chick."

"So."

"What do you mean 'so'?"

"What about Adam the hugger?"

"What about him?" Katie asked, not seeing her point. "I saw him today."

"And if Dusty saw you hugging him, do you think he'd react this way?"

"Don't give me shit, Court. She was very attractive. It didn't look just friendly to me."

Katie's phone went off with another text. Courtney picked it up. "It's him."

"I'm not answering."

"You should give him a chance to explain."

"He'll only lie anyway. I knew this was stupid. I didn't want to get involved with someone anyway. He practically forced himself on me. I should have stuck with my instincts."

"Bullshit. You like him and you know it."

"Maybe I did, but it's better to cut my losses now." She wanted to change the subject. "How are you and Dean by the way? He seemed pretty happy this morning."

Courtney shrugged. "We have a good rhythm."

"You seeing him again?"

"Yeah. He'll be here in a few minutes, actually. It would have been more fun to double date again with you two. I was hoping we could."

"Bull. You enjoy your alone time. You really do like him, don't you?"

"I guess. I'm not pushing it, though. You know how I feel about too many repeat dates right now."

"What about Ronald?"

"I know that's just sex. Dean seems a little…sweet."

"Don't fight it, hon. Ride it out for a bit, anyway. What are you guys doing tonight?"

"He was coming over. I thought you'd be at Dusty's again. I'll cancel and stay with you."

"No. Don't do that. I'm fine. Dusty said Dean doesn't have a roommate. Go to his place. Don't cancel your date because of me."

"You sure, hon?"

"Positive."

Courtney gave her a quick kiss before climbing off her bed. There was a knock at the door. “It’s Dean.”

“I don’t want to see him. Please meet him outside.”

“All right. Love you.”

“Love you, too.”

Courtney didn’t explain about Katie until they were in Dean’s car and on the way to his place.

“There’s no way he’s seeing another chick.”

“Katie said she saw him with her at the coffee shop.”

“He’s into Katie like I’ve never seen him into anyone before. There’s no way this chick is someone he’s seeing.”

“She said they were hugging.”

“Hugging? I’m calling him.”

“Don’t, Dean. Katie will get pissed at me for telling you.”

“And Dusty will have my ass if I don’t tell him.”

She hesitated. “You can tell him but if he admits it, he has to stay away from her. I don’t want him groveling if he’s a cheat and will hurt her again.”

“I can assure you this is a misunderstanding.” Dean dialed, Dusty answered on the first ring.

“Oh, it’s you. I thought you were Katie. You seeing Courtney tonight?”

“I’m with her now.”

“Ask if she has any idea where Katie is.”

“She’s at their dorm not answering your calls.”

“Why not?”

“Were you at the coffee shop today?”

“Yeah. Around three. Why?”

“Katie was there, too.”

“I didn’t see her.”

“Well she saw you. You hugging someone?”

"Aw fuck. That was Alyson, goddammit."

"Shit." Dean held the mouthpiece to his chin and turned to Courtney. "That was his sister."

"I told her not to go crazy," Courtney said. "She must really like him to have gotten so jealous."

Dean returned the phone to his mouth. "That's what she saw, dude. You want us to go back over there? Court can get you in so you can talk to her."

"No," he said with a heavy sigh. "I'll fix this. You two have fun."

"Catch you tomorrow, buddy."

Dusty hung up and dropped his head into his hands. He remembered now how differently this had played out on one of Katie's trips. He was upset with himself for not even wondering if in this time frame, Alyson was alive or not. In one of Katie's time leaps, Dusty had told her about his sister falling through ice and drowning. He'd blamed himself his whole life but in their present time, with what Katie had done with the time traveling, she'd managed to go back and save her. Dusty couldn't keep his promise to not tell Alyson. The girls had been exceptionally close after that. In an alternate future, the baby was named Alyson because of his loss. Now that she was alive, the baby became her namesake.

He was thrilled to see her text message that afternoon and more than happy to meet her for coffee. It hadn't even occurred to him that Katie was there watching, causing her to suspect him of seeing someone else. She wasn't so jealous in their present. They both had friends of the opposite sex. She even kept in touch with that dude from college with the beard, the one that always wore black. He was "the hugger guy" or something like that.

Dusty reached for his phone, but knew it was useless. He decided to drive over to her place instead. He snuck in the dorm with no problem. Now he had to figure out how to get her to open the door.

He knocked on it with no plan in mind.

"Who is it?"

Disguising his voice he called out, "Delivery."

"I didn't order anything."

"It has your number on it. You'll need to sign for it."

As she angrily whipped the door open, he quickly pushed her back in and held her arms at her side. He kicked the door closed with his foot.

"Let me go! Get out of my room."

"No, baby. Listen to me."

"Don't 'baby' me. I'm not listening to you." She continued to struggle, but he held her firmly in his grip.

"Stop squirming and listen. Give me a chance, would you? It wasn't what you thought."

"How do you know what I thought? How did you…" Something sparked in her eyes. "Goddamn Courtney."

"Katie, that girl was my sister."

"Bullshit."

"I swear it. I'd love for you to meet her. It's a long story, but she's also my best friend. I would have had you meet us there, but I thought you were in class."

Katie finally stopped struggling. Dusty let her go and she sat down on her bed in a frustrated plop. "My last class was cancelled. I was trying to show some restraint and stay away from you, so I was going to try to study."

"What did we just talk about? If you wanted to see me, you should have called me."

"This is so fast, Dusty. I don't want you feeling smothered."

"If I recall, I'm the one that started it with the smothering. You can't think I don't want you around every minute. I'd ask you to move in with me if I thought you'd say yes."

"Really?"

"Really."

"Now I really feel like an ass."

He kneeled down in front of her. "Why didn't you come over when you saw me? We could have avoided this."

"I was going to when I saw you walk in, but then she flew into your arms and I…"

"Got jealous," he said with a smirk.

She pushed him away gently. "Yes, I got jealous. Sue me."

"Can I 'do you' instead?"

"You sure you even want a jealous raving lunatic for a girlfriend?"

He leaned in and gave her a kiss. "You going to let me call you my girlfriend?"

"That depends."

"On what?"

"On what you're making me for dinner tonight."

He stood, pulling her to her feet as well. "My 'better than sex' salmon a la Dusty."

"I'll be the judge of that."

"Grab some clothes. Sleep over tonight."

"Do we really want to—"

Dusty cut her off by putting his fingers over her mouth. "What does your heart tell you to do?"

He dropped his hand down and she said, "Stay with you."

"Good. Now pick out some clothes."

Chapter Eleven

They pulled up to Dusty's cottage. After Katie closed her door, Dusty said, "Watch the ice over there it's—" Before he could finish, Katie let out a scream and hit the ground.

"Shit!" Dusty ran to her side. Panic set in when he found her out cold. Again he chastised himself. Katie had told him about this happening once. Why hadn't he done something to prevent it? He alternated between swearing in frustration and calling out her name, trying to get her to respond. Scooping her limp body up, he carried her in and placed her carefully on the couch. He thought about calling an ambulance, then he thought about calling Courtney. Katie had said she was pissed at Dusty when it happened in one of her leaps. She also said Courtney wasn't too fond of him at the time, but he thought they were doing okay this time around. He dialed his phone to call Dean but hit "end." He didn't want to interrupt if they were having sex, but Courtney would want to know. He checked Katie's head for blood, but didn't see any. He hurried to the kitchen for ice for the lump that was coming up in a hurry. He'd start there, then call if he needed to.

Dusty held the ice to her head with one hand and pulled the afghan over her with the other. He sat down and called her name, trying to get her to come to. Slowly her eyes fluttered open.

"Hey, gorgeous. Nice to have you back."

Katie began to cry.

Dusty pulled her to his chest. "Shh… it's okay, babe. Please don't cry. I'm sorry about the ice. I almost called an ambulance. Do you want me to take you in? What can I do for you?"

"Nothing. Take me home please, Dustin."

"Again with the Dustin. Katie, please…" Something finally occurred to him. "Katie?"

"No games. My head is killing me. Just take me to Courtney. She's pre-med. She'll look at it for me."

He leaned her back. "Katie. Courtney is out with Dean."

"Dean? Just take me home. I'm fine. It can wait."

"It's you!" Dusty pulled her tight to his chest and kissed her forehead.

"Stop this. Please take me home. I don't want to be here with you."

"Yes you do, cupcake. It's me."

"Will you stop this! I can't look at you right now. I'll call her myself." She tried to stand up but he pulled her back down.

"You just came from a hospital room. You had a miscarriage. It's not a dream, it happened— happens a few years from now."

She stared at him, no doubt not being able to believe her ears. "How do you know this?"

He held her tight again. "I'm not the 'me' you think I am. That damn geezer did it to me this time, baby."

"Dusty… I don't understand."

He leaned her back. "Do I need to show you my birthmark or make you tell me what Captain Skinnard is about to do to the crew? 'Cause technically I haven't written that part yet, but if I have the 'you' I think you are, you know all about it."

"How can this be?"

"Beats me, but it sure it good to see you." He gave her a gentle kiss. "You really gave me quite a scare again. Do you want me to call Courtney?" Katie shook her head no. "The miscarriage was true. It took us by surprise, but we have two wonderful kids now."

"We do?"

"Yes, we do."

"I'm at the part where I woke up and discovered little Alyson."

"You've told me everything about what's happening to you, but right now we're caught up in some kind of funky time pretzel. Frank sent me back; I hope I'm not making a mess of things."

"If we're together, why are you time traveling?"

"It's not us, it's Courtney."

"Courtney? What's wrong with her?"

"She has an immune deficiency disease. I know what she means to you so I wanted to come back and try to keep it from happening."

"Courtney gets AIDS?" Katie stood up too quickly and swayed. Dusty rushed to be her support and eased her back onto the couch.

"Please lie down, babe. I really am worried about that bump."

"It's okay. I'm sure. Tell me more."

"Do you remember some Ronald she dated for a bit?" Katie closed her eyes, trying to concentrate. "I can see you're hurting. This can wait."

"No. I want to know what I can do to help. My mind is more than scrambled right now."

"And the lump isn't helping. I'm sorry."

"It's not your fault."

"It is. You told me about this and I spaced it. Things are moving a little fast for me here. Can I get you some aspirin?"

"Maybe that's a good start." Dusty got some for her. After Katie took them, he picked her up and carried her to the bed.

"Can I help get you more comfortable?"

"One of your t-shirts would be nice."

He dug through his dresser. The AC/DC shirt was nowhere to be found. It had no doubt already taken a trip to the future and wasn't going to return anytime soon. He dug out one with a Chevelle in much better shape than the one he drove.

Katie managed a smile. "I'll think warm thoughts."

"I've been using the Beemer on you this time around, if that helps."

"The Beemer?"

"Maybe this you doesn't know that much yet. I think I should keep my mouth shut. I'd hate for anything in our present be altered by me screwing this up." He helped her get changed before lying her back in bed.

"You going to join me?"

He took his shirt off. "Absolutely." He stripped down, then cuddled up to her back with his boxers on.

"You never sleep in boxers, Dusty."

"I didn't want to push my luck."

"You're not getting sex with this doozie of a headache, but there's no reason you can't be comfortable."

He kissed the back of her head. "I'm fine."

Katie rolled over to face him. "Where were we?"

"Ronald."

"Right. Yes, I do remember him. He wasn't such a bad guy in all honesty. I don't remember her being into him for anything other than sex. I had to scram quite a bit so they had time alone."

"Why didn't they go to his place?"

"She never said and I never asked."

"Was he pre-med, too?"

"He wasn't in school. I don't remember what he did, but he was older than we were by a few years."

"You have a last name at all?"

Again she squinted as if she were trying to concentrate.

"I'm sorry. I'd say let's do this tomorrow, but I don't know who I'll get."

"I'm okay." Her eyes popped open. "Are you sleeping with me?"

"I want to, but not with your headache, babe."

"No. I mean the 'me' you're seeing now."

He grinned. "Oh. Yes. You're kind of tough to keep away."

"Dustin Charles. That's horrible."

"Hey… I had to win you over. I wasn't going to play nice guy and stay away. What if this is my only chance at having you and the time clock gets re-set again? I need you in my life. Of course I fought for you."

"Why do I feel like you're cheating on me?"

He kissed her nose. "Never. It's you, puddin' pop."

She sighed. "I can't believe I fell for you using all those names again."

"You love me." He held her face and gave her another gentle kiss. "You're a little more jealous this time around than I've ever seen you."

"You give me reason to be?"

"Of course not and I can't explain. I'm not sure this happened yet for you and this is one thing I can't mess up for sure."

Again her eyes closed. "I'm really tired, Dusty."

"Did you think of his last name? Anything else I can use?"

Her eyes were still closed and her voice softened. "It was some restaurant name."

"Denny?"

"No. It was last name sounding."

"Crap. That doesn't narrow it down."

"Poundstone. No, that's not it. It's a P though. I'm sure."

"Perkins?"

"Ummm…that's it." Katie started to breathe heavily after she said that. At least Dusty had something to go on now. He was hoping Courtney and Dean would hit it off and this would be over. If they didn't work out, he'd have to try and hunt this Ronald down. After thinking about it for a while, he decided to try tomorrow anyway. It wouldn't hurt to try to find him rather than sit and wait.

Dusty woke just before Katie. They had slept together facing each other, his arms tight around her. "Hey. How's your head feeling?" he asked when he felt her stir.

Katie sat up, looking confused. She reached behind her head and winced when she touched the bump. "I slipped outside, didn't I?" Her response answered his next question. His Katie was gone. This one was in their present time.

"You did. I'm sorry I wasn't fast enough with my warning. I've been on my landlord about fixing that. You seemed to be sleeping okay so I didn't take you in. We talked for a bit before you settled in bed. I didn't think you were all there. You were pretty adamant, though, about not going to the hospital."

"I don't remember any of this, but it does sound like me."

"I didn't want to have Courtney mad, but I didn't want to interrupt her and Dean if they were, you know, busy. I called another pre-med friend. They weren't worried when everything else was okay and since you were awake for a while. I trusted you. You have enough medical background to not be stubborn about going in."

"Never underestimate my ability to be stubborn. It's almost a superpower with me."

He laughed and gave her a kiss. "I'm finding that out."

"Let's not tell Court. She would probably flip. It's not a big deal."

"I won't. You okay to go to class today?"

"Other than a slight headache, I'm fine. I can't be skipping classes. I have too many finals coming up."

"I'll go start the car."

Dusty dropped Katie off at her dorm. He wondered how much longer he'd have to do this. He was still here, so that meant nothing had changed as far as Courtney's health. She and Dean seemed to be doing great, but somehow Ronald had snuck back into the picture. At least now he had something to go on. He had a last name. Dusty was still uncertain what he was going to do with that information. It was not as if living this double life had no consequences. He couldn't kill the guy and jet back home.

Deciding to cut class was an easy choice again. He had to start looking around for this Ronald. The phone book was an obvious first choice, but a dead end. If he hung around campus girls, maybe he worked in one of the offices. Dusty went to the main office and turned on his smile and charm.

"Sorry, Mr. Andrews. I don't have any teachers by that name," the secretary said.

"How about office help. Maybe a custodian?"

She keyed away at her computer again. "I'm not showing anyone by that name. Are you sure it's this college he's at?"

"No. Actually I'm not. I dropped my girlfriend off and figured this was a place to start."

"If this message is so urgent, why don't you have a location on him?"

"I'm sorry. The last contact my friend had with him was a long time ago. All he knew was that he was in this area. I hope I haven't taken up too much time from your day. I really appreciate it."

"No worries. I wish I could have helped you."

"Thanks again for your time."

Dusty returned to the car, wishing he'd gotten some kind of description out of the other Katie as well as a name. The fact that he was a few years older didn't help. He couldn't come out and ask Courtney anything without her wondering why. After driving to his school and having the same luck with that office, he was at a loss for what to do. There was too much space in between. The guy could work anywhere.

Needing to really kick his brain into gear, he headed to the coffee shop for a strong cup. Art would really flip a lid at the way his tab was growing. There was a person he didn't recognize today at the counter and he was grateful. He paid cash for this round.

He tried thinking about everything Katie said, hoping something would come to him. She said they never went to his place. They always slept together at Katie and Courtney's dorm room. *Why?* It finally hit Dusty like a brick. The son of a bitch was probably married. "That's it," Dusty said out loud. One guy turned his way. Dusty waved. "Sorry. Brain fry." The guy held up his drink in an, "I know how you feel, dude," kind of toast.

Perkins probably wasn't even his real last name. Now he was really back to square one.

Dusty wasn't usually one to wallow, but he was getting increasingly upset and really starting to miss his kids. He wanted this over with. With everything that happened last night, he never got around to making dinner for Katie. He wasn't in the mood for cooking and didn't want to do cheap take out or *Chez Pauls* again. Picking up his phone, he called the one place he could go where he knew he'd get a great meal. If he was when he thought he was, it was time to pay the piper anyway. Might as well get it over with so he could concentrate on his task.

"May? What's for dinner tonight?"

His parent's cook practically squealed at the sound of his voice. "Roast beast if you're coming home, child."

He laughed. Hearing her call it that after all these years still warmed his heart. "Then I'll be there will a date. You guys still eat at six?"

"You know it."

"See you then. Thanks, May."

He couldn't hug his kids, but he'd get some family loving from May and his mother anyway.

"You spoiled baby," Katie teased Dusty on the way to his parents' house. "You call up your old housekeeper and tell her what to make you for dinner?"

"No. I told her I wanted to show up for dinner. She just always makes what I like when I tell her I'm going to show up."

"What's with the change? You said you weren't going to submit me to your parents so soon."

"I needed a change of pace. School has really been bumming me out lately."

"What's the matter? Is it me? Am I keeping you from your studies?"

"Oh, hell no, babe. You are the one thing that makes sense right now." Dusty commended himself inside for that one. He sure remembered a lot of details about their past, even though they seldom talked about it. "It's just…I told you I don't want to be a lawyer anymore. I never did, actually. I need to talk to my dad someday. I was kind of hoping you'd be my wing man."

She giggled. "Your what?"

"You know. Have my back. My dad is going to shit an eggroll. Maybe he'll go easy on me if you're there. Normally I'd bring Dean, but my dad has no problem yelling at me in front of him. I understand if you don't want me to say anything tonight. It can try to wait, but he and Mom sort of have this radar. They'll know something is up."

"I'm not sure what I can do, but I'm with you no matter what you decide to do."

"Thanks."

This time she took his hand and kissed it. "I have never seen you nervous before."

"It shows?"

"More than a little."

"Mind if I get drunk tonight?"

She grinned. "Do what you want. I'll drive home."

Dusty was hoping he planned this right. With a little luck they'd get snowed in and have pretty damn great sex in one of the spare rooms. Even though he had passed out afterward, Katie often teased him about his "rare form" on the 100 proof Captain Morgan that night. They had a bottle of it at their house, but it wasn't touched. It was more of a trophy or a fun reminder for both of them.

Dusty had been so hung up on not getting more information about Ronald from his Katie that it hadn't even occurred to ask this Katie, okay— equally his—about him. He had to figure out a good way to do it, so he didn't come across as if he was doing background work for Dean. Having all night to bring it up, he had time to think on how to carefully word things. For now, he had to warn Katie about his upbringing.

"Don't let the house freak you out, babe."

"Why would it freak me out?"

"It's a little on the big side."

"Our house was no rambler either. My parents did okay for themselves. I assume if your dad is a lawyer, they are doing well for themselves, too."

"That's an understatement." As he said that, Dusty pulled into a driveway and stopped at a large wrought iron gate. He leaned over to an electronic keypad and entered a code.

"You're shitting me."

"Wish I was. Don't let Dad intimidate you. He's sort of rough around the edges. Just be yourself."

"Thanks for giving me warning on this. You could have said something before we made it through the gate."

"You would have only jumped out." He gave her thigh a squeeze before pulling into the last stall of the garage, the one always left available for him and his other sister, Dana. Although Dana and Dusty grew up together with the same parents, he was much closer to and had more in common with Alyson. Alyson had been the result of his father's affair. They were best friends until they discovered at the age of eight that they were siblings. That fact only brought them closer.

When Dusty and Dana were here at the same time, there was a small garage further down the driveway with another empty stall that he used. If he recalled correctly, she was off in Paris with her current fiancé—her third. She would be on number five before she actually married one of them. That would last eight months. Little Alyson loved her and the gifts she brought from all over the world. Alex was still too young to appreciate the collectible cars she brought for him. It was the one thing his sister had in common with her dad. Their love of fine cars. Dusty guessed she was trying to bond with Alex in that same way. Dusty's writing would never get him the lifestyle of a garage full of cars like his father's, nor did he want it. He hoped Alex would be happy with models.

Dana and Katie got along better than he would have expected, but they weren't as close as she and Alyson were.

The bond they shared over what Katie had done for her was beyond measure. Dusty found himself jealous over times when Alyson called wanting to talk to Katie and not him.

Dusty loved Dana a lot, they were just total opposites. She reveled in the glory of the family money, where he had pushed it away his entire life. She thrived on going to different schools, but never did decide on any one major. They never pushed her to get a degree the way they had with him. School and a job were no longer necessities when you had to be "the belle of the ball," perfect hostess, and wife.

The conversation about Alyson being their sister never happened between Dana and Dusty. His father most certainly never brought it up and Dusty wasn't an idiot. Dana would have had one of her award-winning fits, and his dad would have spent a fortune to buy her love back. She liked playing the role of spoiled "only" daughter. Dusty would keep that secret from her for the greater good: peace in the household. Alyson was his and his alone. He liked it that way.

He often wished Dana took more interest in their father's company. Dusty had no desire to take it over in any shape or form. He always hoped Dana would decide she wanted to take it over or at least choose a husband who would do it and remove the burden from him. Things worked out in the end but for now, him taking over the family business was always at the top of his father's priorities; these days still rode hard in his memory.

Even though he had been down this road before, he was not looking forward to a repeat performance of breaking the news to his dad about leaving school.

"Earth to Dusty." Katie waved her hand in front of Dusty's face. They had been parked for over a full minute and he just stared ahead.

"I'm sorry. Coming here always gets my mind wandering. Stay put." Dusty raced around to her side of the car and helped her out.

"I love it when you go gentleman on me."

"This place brings out the worst in me. What can I say?"

Katie scanned the garage, taking in all the amazing vehicles. "Wow. This is some car collection."

Dusty let out a whistle. He had forgotten about the smash on the Aston Martin. "Dad must be pissed about this."

"Holy hell," Katie almost shouted. "That Delorean is impressive."

"Got it up to one-twenty."

"Dusty! You didn't."

"Ticket was three times that. Dad shit a brick."

"I'll bet."

He spun Katie into him and leaned down for a kiss. "I'd rather kiss you than look at cars." She wrapped her arms around his neck; they shared a lingering kiss until someone cleared their throat behind them. They quickly broke apart. Dusty walked Katie over to his mother.

Chapter Twelve

"Hi, Mom." Dusty gave his mother a kiss on the cheek. "You remember Katie, right?"

"Of course. Nice to see you again."

"You, too, Norma," Katie said with a genuine smile.

"Come in. The garage is no place to be hanging out."

They walked in and found Dustin Sr. sitting in a recliner, reading a newspaper. "Nice to see you again, Katie." He stood and walked over to join them. "I don't remember you saying what you're going to school for. Is it law school as well?"

"No. Veterinary medicine."

Norma squealed. "Can you do Princess Sophia's nails for me?"

"That dog ain't dead yet? Isn't she like a hundred?"

"Eighteen. Deaf and blind and still a better child than you."

Dusty grinned. Some things were just always meant to be said.

"Sounds like a Cocker Spaniel," Katie said.

"She is! Could I trouble you?"

"I'd be happy to."

After they left, Dusty went to the bar and removed a beer from the refrigerator. He didn't bother looking at the label this time. He could do without the hundred dollars a bottle conversation again. His dad joined him.

"Dean Hallard called me today."

Shit. It was starting already. Dusty hadn't quit yet, but he knew what it was about. "So he told you I missed the past two days?"

"You mind explaining yourself?"

"Can't this wait until after dinner? I don't think we need to do this right away. Katie doesn't need to see us fighting."

"Are we going to fight? What is so damn detailed about a straight answer that you can't just spill it?"

"Dad, please." Dusty put the beer aside and reached for the 100 proof. *Hell. It worked the first time.* Funny how he still felt he needed the drink to get him through this, even though he had already survived this talk.

Norma walked in declaring Katie was a nail clipping genius and stopped when she found the men were in a serious discussion. "What's wrong?"

"I'm not sure. You try to get out of your son what he's not telling me."

"Oh dear. Can this wait until after dinner?"

Katie went to Dusty's side and watched as he added a dash of coke to his drink. "That bad?" she whispered. Dusty raised the glass to take a drink, but she took the glass from him and poured some out. She added more coke to it. "It'll be okay. I got your back, remember."

May came out of the kitchen and went straight to Katie. "I'm May, dear. Don't you believe a thing this rotten child has told you about me."

"He said you're a wonderful cook."

"Well, you can believe that one. Everyone ready to eat?"

This time they made it through dinner first before the fight broke out. May was serving them drinks when Dusty's father said, "Spill it, Junior."

"I told you to not call me Junior, Dad."

"I'll call you dead meat in a minute if you don't tell me what's going on."

Dusty downed a good portion of his drink. "I'm leaving school."

"You did not just say that."

"I did and I mean it. I'm not cut out to be a lawyer and I never will be. I can give you my reasons, but it won't matter. You'll never see my side of it anyway." He took Katie's hand. "I'd rather not do this now in front of Katie. I wanted you to get to know her, I didn't want to fight."

"Well, we're doing this now, young man."

"No, Dad. We're not." Dusty tried to escape. They were at the door, but this time Katie didn't let him get his coat on before she stopped him.

"We're not going, Dusty. You need to face this. It's better now than later."

"I'm sorry I brought you here."

"I'm not." Katie pointed behind Dusty.

His father was standing there. "Let's sit down and try to be civil. I'm willing to listen, son."

"Holy shit, Dusty. I'm buying a bottle of that stuff if this is what it does to you."

Katie was breathing hard, a completely satisfied puddle in Dusty's arms. He rubbed at his chest where she had bit him, trying to muffle her moans.

The night had played out as it had a few years ago. His father got over it, was giving him his support and paying his rent until the semester was through. Dusty agreed to finish that much. A car for Katie was a part of the deal he managed this time around as well. The BMW was never Dusty's style. He'd traded it in for a VW Beetle for Katie and a simple small model truck for himself. Katie hadn't wanted a car, but she quickly grew used to having one. As soon as she graduated, she picked up the Mini Cooper. After a time travel trek where Dusty broke a leg driving in a snow storm, she'd insisted on the SUVs they currently had. The accident wasn't prevented, but the injury was. *Score one for time travel.*

A storm kept them overnight at his parents' house, as it had before, and once again he snuck into Katie's room after being told he wasn't allowed to share a room under their roof. Dusty hadn't said they were soon to be engaged this time. He thought it might scare this Katie, since they hadn't been dating that long.

"Babe?"

"Hmmm?"

"You know what that Ronald guy that Courtney was dating does? What kind of classes he takes?" Dusty knew he wasn't in school, but Katie didn't know he knew.

"Why?"

"Just curious."

"Is Dean jealous or something?"

"He hasn't mentioned him at all. I don't know what made me think of it." He kissed her, trying to help change the subject. He was sorry he ruined such a perfect moment. "Forget I said anything. Must just be the alcohol talking."

"I don't mind. I hope he's out of the picture now. I really like Dean. It's a bonus that he's your friend. Ronald's not in school. I told you he has a few years on her. You actually probably have seen Ronald around. He works at a sports bar."

"Really? You know which one?"

"I don't know. Court and I usually go to Dicky's. We don't do the sports bar thing and she has said something about him not being allowed visitors when he works. It's some hockey bar, I think."

Dusty tried to keep his excitement down. "Well, I guess it's good to know. Sounds like something Dean and I would do. I guess it's best if we steer away from those bars. You know. Just in case."

"Good idea." Katie yawned and fell asleep. Dusty dropped to his back to think of a game plan, but the booze hit, he was asleep shortly after her.

The next day was once again peaceful in the Andrews household. Dusty played a few songs on the piano when Katie asked him to. He didn't have to be scolded by May this time for never playing for Katie since he had played for her at *Chez Pauls*. He played some cards with his parents, as well as napping with Katie while they waited for the storm to pass. If he had to re-live a few days, these were not bad ones to repeat.

As they drove home, Katie rested her head on Dusty's shoulder. "I'm really glad I was able to spend some time with your parents and May. I don't know why you were so worried about it."

"I can't believe you're saying that. My dad intimidated a lot of my friends. Alyson was about the only one that would come over. He was nicer to her. I learned why later."

"You said that was a long story. You told me she was your sister, but your mom only talked about Dana."

"I'm glad you had the sense not to say anything. My mind was so wrapped up in breaking the news about school, I didn't think to explain it to you and ask you not to mention it."

"I can be a fast thinker when I'm not drinking 100 proof Captain Morgan."

"Yeah, but you did put a dent in that bottle of wine with Mom."

"Don't remind me. I still have a lingering headache. So…you going to tell me?"

Dusty told her again about his father's affair with Alyson's mother and about them moving away years later. He left out the part about her saving Alyson from drowning. Somehow in this mixed up pretzel of a life of theirs, she'd already done it.

"You think your mother doesn't know?"

"I'm pretty sure she does, but it's never been mentioned. Mom has to have her pride and really love Dad to have stayed with him after that."

"She's a bigger woman than I am."

"How so?"

"I wouldn't stay with a guy if he cheated on me. I don't care how much I think I love him. Once trust is gone, there isn't much."

Dusty took her hand. "I'll never give you reason to doubt me. If you ever see me hugging a girl again, you'll know it's a friend. I promise you that much."

"I think I know that now and believe you."

"In fact, the only way I would cheat on you is if I could go back in time and have sex with you all over again." Dusty grinned.

Katie laughed hard. "Would I be aware of this time traveling?"

"I'm not sure. Would it matter?"

"Well, call me stupid, but I think I'd still be jealous of me having to share you with myself."

"Ha!" Dusty blurted out.

"What?"

"Uh…I just think that's funny. I felt the same way once and someone got mad at me."

"You had a conversation with someone about sleeping with them while time traveling?"

"Sort of. Book research, you know. I was talking about throwing in a time traveling girl and some of the things that could happen in my book. The discussion became pretty heated."

Katie shook her head. "I really need to introduce you to Adam the Hugger. You writers and your brains sure go to some strange places."

Dusty had no reply to that. He simply blurted out what he wanted to say. "Move in with me, Katie."

Her head whipped around. "What?"

"Move in with me."

"After a couple of dates and some great sex? I don't think that's a foundation for a step like this so soon."

"Bull, sweetness. We were meant to be together since the night I saw you at Dicky's. I know it and you know it. I don't want to waste time waiting for you to figure it out."

"Dusty. I really do like you, but this is too soon. Please don't start pushing this."

"I know you don't want to leave Courtney, but she'll be fine. She can come over any time."

"It's not only about Courtney. Just because you dropped out of school doesn't mean I don't still have the work load from hell. We can't do this. Don't be angry."

Damn. Maybe he did push it too soon. "I'm not angry, I'm disappointed." He tried hard not to pout about it, but he really hated sleeping without her. As much of a pain in the ass as this time traveling crap was, at least he was still able to be with Katie while she was technically on the west coast. "Are you coming over or am I taking you home?"

"Do you mind taking me home? I have a class to catch up on after losing all that time with the storm."

"I understand." He hated it, but he knew he had to let this Katie finish her schooling.

When they pulled up to Katie's dorm, she turned to him. "You promise you're not upset?"

"I'm not. I promised I would give you your space. I don't have to like it, but I respect the hell out of it, Katie. I'm not going to keep you from your studies. I know how important it is to you. Don't think I take it lightly just because I didn't want to follow in my father's footsteps. I do have goals."

"I know. Don't think I look down on you for your choices either. It's not school, it's …"

"What, baby? Talk to me."

"You're twenty-one, Dusty. How could you have sown your wild oats enough already to know I'm who you really want? How can I disrupt my life to such a degree, worrying you'll change your mind in a few months. Don't be angry with me, but you're too young for this kind of decision."

"This again?" His head dropped back on the seat in frustration. He regretted his reaction immediately.

"What do you mean 'again'? You make a habit of wanting women older than you to move in with you, then get upset when they say you're too young?"

"No. It's not that. I'm sorry. That's not how I meant for that to come out. I get tired of the whole age thing. It's not a big deal, Katie."

"Who else did you love that was older?"

"Don't do this. Please."

"Who, Dusty?"

He sighed, running his hands around the steering wheel. He didn't want to do this, but now he had to come up with something. "I didn't love her. It just happened. That has nothing to do with this."

"I want to hear the story anyway."

"Babe…" She crossed her arms, waiting for him to continue. "The only older woman I was with happened a long time ago. I wasn't in love with her, it was just…"

"Just what?"

"Sex. You happy now? I was young and it wasn't going to go anywhere, she used me for sex."

"Used you for sex? Oh, this I have to hear."

He ran his hand down his face. "I really didn't want to go here. This has nothing to do with anything."

"Will it make me mad?"

"Why would something that happened to me when I was sixteen make you mad?"

"You had sex at sixteen?"

"It was one of the maids. I told you this!" Dusty was getting flustered and forgetting where he was. That was not one of his proudest moments, he didn't care to repeat it. All he needed now was to bring up the incident known as the "Becky Swenson Disaster". He'd told Katie about a date that had gone horribly wrong in his younger days so she could convince the older Dusty, who was giving her a hard time, that she was time traveling. It also was not a proud moment, but the information had worked for her. Thankfully she never brought it up again.

"I think I would have remembered you screwing one of your dad's maids." Katie grabbed the door handle. "I didn't even know you had maids growing up until tonight." She was out before Dusty could stop her. He caught up to her at the door to the dorms.

"Please wait," Dusty said, grabbing her arms. "This is coming out completely wrong. Will you give me a chance to explain?" She only crossed her arms as an answer. "She came on to me. I don't know what she thought she was getting out of it, but she wasn't something I was about to kick out of my bed. Boys will be boys, you know?" He forced a grin but she didn't smile back. "I was sixteen, Katie. It was either sit in the bathroom with a magazine or have sex with the woman who was throwing herself at me. It wasn't serious. I didn't love her and it's not even worth a mention. And to answer your question, my oats are sown enough. I know what I want and it's you. I love you. I'm sorry if that creeps you out. I'll give you all the time you need for that to sink in."

"I appreciate that."

"This may not be the best time to mention it, but you want to go car shopping tomorrow?"

"Car shopping? I can't afford a car."

"Dad and I talked when you were napping. He gave me the okay to trade in the Beemer and get you something, too."

"Dusty!" Katie removed herself from his hold. "I don't want you buying me a car. How crazy are you?"

"Crazy about you, is all. It's not my money. It's my dad's. He said to do it. He also said when you wise up and leave my ass, I need to take it back."

"I don't need or want a car. You've lost your mind. You can't buy me with a car."

"I'm not trying to buy you." Dusty turned around, grunting in frustration. "Why are you being so difficult today?"

"Because you're talking crazy. Please leave before I lose my mind!"

Dusty spun around and stormed back to the car without looking back. When he reached it, he finally looked up, but she was gone. He climbed in the car and smacked at the steering wheel. "Fuckingsonofabitchfuckshit!" He clutched it tight and grunted again. "Way to go, douche bag." Dusty needed to cool off and wanted a beer. He called Dean.

"Wanna hit a sports bar?"

"Can't. Court and I are going to a movie. Why aren't you with Katie?"

"We got snowed in at my parents last night. She wants to catch up on some stuff. I dropped her off at her place." He didn't need to tell him about the fight.

"Sorry, numb nuts. You're on your own."

"Thanks for nothing." Dusty hung up, again sorry for his reaction. He wasn't mad at Dean. He should have been thinking about how thrilled he was that he and Courtney were hitting it off. He sent Dean a text.

Sorry. Shitty day. Have fun.

You need me to cancel?

Naw. Have a good night.

Catch you later.

Dusty headed back to *Puck You*. It was as good a place to start as any.

Chapter Thirteen

Dusty settled at the bar. The bartender recognized him.
"Same draft?"

"Sounds good. Thanks."

The beer was placed in front of him with a coaster. "Sorry again about having to card you."

"No worries. It's your job. Gotta be hard in a college town to be guessing people's ages."

"You got that right. You ordering food?"

"Not tonight. Thanks." The bartender hurried away to help someone else and Dusty scanned the bar. He couldn't ask about Ronald. He'd have no reason to be asking for him. The bartender's nametag read Benji. He doubted that was made up. No one would fake that name in a place like this. Dusty jumped at the sound of plates hitting the floor. Benji hollered to the back, "Hey, Ronald! Clean up in aisle three," as a crowd of tipsy customers applauded the accident.

"Be right there, goddammit."

Dusty took a sip of his beer and waited to see who would come out from the back.

Within a few minutes, a man who appeared to be in his very late twenties or early thirties brought out a mop bucket and a small trash can. He picked up the broken stoneware plates with the help of the young busboy who'd dropped them. "Way to go, dipshit."

"I slipped. Sue me."

Ronald handed him the trashcan. "Take this to the back. I'll get it mopped up. Bring back a wet floor sign."

"Yes, sir," the bus boy said in a mock salute to Ronald. So far, Dusty was not impressed.

Watching Ronald over the next couple of hours, Dusty figured he was the glorified gofer of the place. Through the night, he stocked the bar with supplies and glasses, brought up food orders, helped seat people and bussed tables. No wonder he didn't want Courtney visiting him here. He'd probably told her he was the head bartender or something.

Just before closing, a woman walked through the door and went straight over to him. He quickly held his hand up and said, "Out back," before she could say anything.

Dusty reassured the bartender that he wasn't skating out on his tab and that he would be right back in. He hurried out to the back alley, hoping to catch the story. He hid behind a wooden slatted fence surrounding a dumpster. He couldn't hear any talking, but he did hear moaning. Dusty dared to peek around the wall and saw Ronald with the woman high up on his thighs. She was pressed into the wall and they were kissing like crazy, both equally "handsy." Hurrying back behind cover, Dusty waited it out.

"I told you a hundred times that you can't show up at my bar, Deb."

"But I needed some lovin'," she said with a whiny tone. "You own the place. Why can't I visit?"

Oh boy. This guy was a winner. How many girls was he stringing along?

"It doesn't set a good example. If I allow it, everyone will start doing it."

"I guess it makes sense."

"I'll call you tomorrow, sugar buns."

Sugar Buns? Even Dusty never resorted to that one. He heard what sounded like a smack on her ass. Dusty leaned tight to the wall, hoping to remain out of sight. She and Ronald passed by without spotting him. Dusty went back in, finished his beer, and paid his tab.

The bartender was talking hockey with Dusty when the phone rang. "Hang on a second, buddy. I have to get the phones after nine." After putting the call on hold he called out to Ronald. "Dude. It's your wife. I keep telling you she can't call here unless it's an emergency. Get a frickin' cell phone already like the rest of the planet."

Ronald walked behind the bar and took the call. "Gina. You're going to get my ass fired. What the hell do you want now?"

Gina? Who the hell is Deb? *Duh.* A wife would know he didn't own the place, dumbass.

The bartender walked back over to Dusty and waved him in closer so he could whisper. "That guy isn't that much to look at and I know he ain't got money, but he must be hung like a goddamn walrus."

"Why is that?" Dusty decided it was best to play stupid.

"He gets more pussy in a month than I see in a year."

"No shit?"

"No shit. I wouldn't give a crap except his wife seems like a real sweetheart. He has a little girl, too."

Now Dusty was seeing red. "Makes me want to beat the shit out of him as a matter of principle."

"Well, get in line. He missed work for a few days last month messing with the wrong dude's wife."

"Good."

"My thoughts exactly." Benji knocked on the bar. "Duty calls, my friend. Have a good night."

"You, too. Thanks." Dusty left him an extra five again for the helpful information. There was nothing to do about Ronald tonight. He'd found him, that was a good enough start. Dusty had his share of beers and wasn't going to start a fight with a guy who had a few pounds and inches on him. He didn't need the added bonus of Ronald being the sober one as well. Besides, beating him up wasn't going to solve anything. Dusty needed to find a way to get him to scratch Courtney off his 'people to do' list.

Driving wasn't the smartest choice, but it was side roads for the quick jaunt home. Dusty wasn't going to call a cab after having only a few beers. Again his thoughts went to how he and Katie left things. Already he was thinking about cracking another beer at home, but first he needed to make one stop. Good thing there was a specialty store that had a little bit of everything and was open late on weekends, right across the street.

An hour after Dusty arrived home, there was a knock at his door. He pulled back the door quickly, as if he was bothered by the intrusion.

"I'm sorry if I'm disturbing you," Katie said.

"No. Not at all, babe. You're never a disturbance. I just wasn't expecting anyone. Least of all you, to be honest."

"I felt bad about how we left things."

"Please come in." He took her hand and walked her through the door then took her coat. "How did you get here?"

"I sent Court a text. I have her car. She's still out with Dean."

"I'm glad they are hitting it off…even if you are having second thoughts about me."

"Dusty—"

He cut her off. "Can I get you anything?"

"No. I'm fine. It's late. Can we sit?"

"Of course." They sat on the couch, facing each other. Dusty picked up the half-full bottle of beer from the coffee table, then reconsidered and put it back. He'd probably had more than enough already. "You have something you need to get off your chest?"

"Sort of. I don't think you understand how much I really liked you."

The past tense wasn't missed on him. "Liked?"

"Like, Dusty. I like you a lot. We just need to slow down. I really didn't plan on dating someone, but we really clicked. You have to understand how hard it is for me to try to push you away and get this going at a more reasonable pace."

"Then don't."

"I have to. My studies are going to start hurting. All I want is to spend time with you. You keep talking about things like moving in together and buying vehicles, but it's too soon."

"No, it isn't."

"Maybe not for you, but for me it is."

"No. I mean for both of us it isn't."

"Dusty—"

"Just let me finish. I'm the right amount of drunk to finally tell you this. I can't stand another minute of you trying to break up with me again."

"What do you mean again?"

He knelt down in front of her. "Please let me say this. You are going to think I'm crazy, but let me finish."

"I'll do my best."

"I first met you in St. Paul in an Irish Pub."

"I've never been to a pub in St. Paul."

"You were twenty-nine."

"I'm only twenty-five now."

"I know. I was twenty-five then."

"What in the hell are you talking about? You're not making any sense at all."

"You were there for a baby shower and got pretty trashed."

"I was trashed at a baby shower?"

"It was the after-shower party. You and a few single girls went out afterward. I finally got brave enough to approach you. We kind of hit it off and we went back to your place."

"So, I'm still a slut when I'm twenty-nine?"

"You weren't a slut. I was the smooth talker back then that I am now or vice-versa. However this messed-up shit works. Wait, I don't mean that. I love every minute that I remember with you. You have more memories than I do, though. You don't only stick to our past. You meet me in a different future and I win you over in that timeline, too."

Still looking confused, she crossed her arms. "Okay. I'll play. So what does this older you and me do?"

"You have a successful vet practice and I work at a newspaper doing a few columns."

"So why do I time travel? We seem to be doing what we said we wanted to do."

"You tried to dump me on your thirtieth birthday. You thought I was too young for you, just like you thought tonight."

"This is one hell of a tactic you are trying to pull over one comment I made. Now you're talking crazy." She tried to stand but he held her back. "You said you'd let me finish." She relaxed again to keep true to her word.

"You time traveled, Katie. Fate, or whatever it was, sent you back to me. We met again at the ages we are now and I won you over. We're married and we have a wonderful family."

She looked deep into his eyes. For a minute, he thought she believed him, at least until she spoke.

"You're drunker than you look and you're an idiot for thinking I'd buy this. For God's sake, Dusty. I only asked to slow down a little. I never said I wanted to break up, but now you're talking crazy." She crawled over the back of the couch to escape. He rushed over and took her by the arms again.

"You're the love of my life, Katie. I know everything about you. I love how you blow on your coffee before you drink it. I love the little moans that escape your throat when we kiss. How you squeal just right when I 'jumper cable' you like this." He touched her sides in a way he usually did when he snuck up behind her. He had dubbed it 'jumper cabling' her because of the way she reacted. She jumped and squealed then covered her mouth with her hand. "I know every spot on your body that makes you gasp for breath when I touch you just right. I know you had a belly ring when you were eighteen and your mother made you take it out. Your parents call you on your birthday every year at the time you were born, and they are always each on a phone extension. Tom Petty is on your ipod and "Breakdown" is one of your favorite songs. You lost your virginity when you were nineteen, and it kills me that it wasn't me that took it. It was another year before you had sex again and that was only because you thought the guy looked like Hugh Jackman. Lucky for me the guy was a dick and it didn't last long, but I wish you would get rid of the ID bracelet from him that you keep hidden in the false bottom of your jewelry box." He stopped talking when she stood there with her mouth wide open. Her eyes fluttered. "Please sit back down before I lose you." He took her by the arm and sat her back down on the couch. She was still speechless.

"How do you know those things?"

"I told you. We're together now. We have been for a long time. There isn't a thing we don't know about each other or a secret we keep. I meant it when I said you were my destiny that night in the bar. My world would have ended if you were successful in breaking up with me. Something brought you back and put us together earlier. I couldn't be more grateful for whatever or whoever is responsible."

"So, I time travel?"

"Yes."

"Am I time traveling now?"

"No. I am this time. You actually came back the other night, though."

"What do you mean?"

"After you hit your head on the ice. The 'you' that came to was *my* you."

"*Your* me?"

"The you from…actually, it was a you from before. You slipped on the ice in our past but when you came to, it was you that was traveling back. Somehow I got that you." Her look told him she was as confused as hell.

"I'm sorry. I know I've had a few too many beers, but there isn't a better way to explain it. It seems our lives are twisted together like a pretzel and we are destined to be together at every section, no matter what. I don't know why I got so upset tonight. I should have known everything would be okay. It always is."

"So if we're together, why are you back again? Why risk not getting me to fall for you? Did something happen?"

"We're fine. It's someone else."

"Who?"

"I don't want to upset you. This is already too much to sink in for one night. I'm sorry. I was really trying to get through this without having to tell you. After I left you tonight, I found what I was looking for. I'm sure I can find a way to fix things."

"Fix what? Tell me, Dusty."

"Babe, please." He held her hands. "Can we just leave it at this for now?" He pulled her to his chest and held her tight. She was putty in his arms, no doubt still letting things sink in. "I really do love you more than life. I'm sorry I've put you on a rollercoaster these past couple of days. I really don't know what I'm doing. I always get crazy around you. I can't believe I ever found the courage to speak to you that first night."

Katie released the hug and looked up at him. "What did you do?"

He grinned. "I waited for you outside of the girl's bathroom and pretended to not see you and bumped into you."

“Smooth.”

“I was, wasn’t I? Anyway, I apologized and introduced myself. You went straight to turning my name into Dusty. You put your hand on my cheek and said, “You’re cute and all, but you’re a little young to be in here, aren’t you?”

“Did I really?”

“Those exact words. I walked you back to your friends, but they made me pull up a chair. You were getting razzed a lot for not dating much. They made up excuses and left so we could be alone.”

“Then we went to my place?”

“Yup. Your friends picked you up, so I drove you home. I really didn’t want to blow it and push for sex, but one last drink turned into…you know.” Again he moved his eyebrows up and down. “You were kind of an animal.”

Katie blushed and he chuckled. He brought his hand to her cheek.

“Don’t be embarrassed. Being shy about sex is never who we were. We clicked from the get-go. You asked me to stay the night and I was more than happy to. We spent Sunday between the bedroom, the shower, and occasional food breaks. The rest is history. Of course I have to go by what you told me. My memories of you are from our days now. After you were sent back, you stayed and the clock re-set.”

“So, why did I try to dump you when I turned thirty?”

“You thought I wouldn’t be ready for kids. You couldn’t have been more wrong. Birthdays are not your favorite time and you were handing me out an extra dose of cranky.”

“Did I take you back after I time traveled and discovered differently?”

“Yes, but I thought I had won you over with the key chains.”

“Key chains?”

Dusty pulled one out of his pocket. It was almost identical in style to the one that he had made her before. It read *Dusty Loves Katie*. "They only had the one so I made this for me. I really thought I screwed up tonight. It's all I could do to keep a hold of our present."

Katie kissed him. Gently at first, but then she needed more. They leaned back on the couch together and shared a long kiss of tongues, ravenous for more with each touch. Katie's hands went to the elastic of Dusty's boxers, but he stopped her and held her hands in place.

"I don't want this, babe. Knowing I have you again is all I want. I didn't spill my guts out so we would have sex."

"Since when is this about you?" She playfully bit at his bottom lip then removed her shirt.

Dusty cuddled into Katie's back the next morning. Although he had played it tough, he was more than happy she'd stayed over. He would have been happy to have just "slept" together, but this was Katie. He knew better. She suddenly bolted up and shouted, "Courtney!"

"Babe? What is it?"

She turned to him with a look of pure fear. "It's Courtney, isn't it? She's why you came back this time. You said something the first time we met."

He let out a heavy breath. "Yes. I'll have it taken care of, though. I promise. We can't tell her about this. There's no way she'd believe us. We have no idea what it'll do to her. She could end up pissed off at you for making up such a crazy story and never speak to you again or something."

"She'd never do that. I have to help. What is it you're trying to do?"

"I promise I have it taken care of. If I didn't, I'd be begging you for your help now. I finally pieced things together."

"Is this why you set her up with Dean? You trying to keep her from someone?"

"Damn your female intuition. I never do get away with anything our whole lives." He gave her a gentle kiss on the lips.

"Is it Ronald?" His head dropped. "I knew it. What happens? Does he beat her up or something? That asshole."

Dusty jumped out of bed and whipped the covers off. "Go to school, Columbo."

"I don't want to go to school. I want to help you."

"You can help me by doing what you're supposed to be doing. Get to class before you get an A minus, cupcake."

"Dusty…this isn't fair. I want—" Her protests were interrupted by her phone.

Dusty picked it up and read the text. "Courtney is looking for her car."

"Shit. Tell her I'll be right there. We're not done, though."

Chapter Fourteen

Dusty started coffee after Katie left. He would have been thrilled to have had her help a couple of days ago but now that he thought he had a game plan, he'd rather Katie not be involved. He hoped she could keep her promise and not say anything to her best friend.

He'd found the guy, now the question was what to do about him. Thinking about beating him up last night was a passing thought he was glad he let leave as quickly as it came. It wouldn't have solved anything, especially with Dusty out cold on the ground.

The words the bartender said to him played out in his mind again. *He gets more pussy in a month than I see in a year.* Suddenly Dusty wondered how many other women were infected along with Courtney. If he was that much of a player, the numbers were sure to be high. Countless lives ruined by the act of one careless man. He had to try to do more than keep Courtney away from him. But what could he do?

"There's always a hunting accident."

The voice startled Dusty so badly, he dropped his coffee cup. He spun to find Frank in his home. "Jesus, old man."

"Not even close."

"Very funny. You scared the shit out of me."

"Good thing you're wearing the brown pants."

Dusty wouldn't give him the satisfaction of a laugh. "How do you know where I live?"

"You're kidding me, right?"

"I should start locking my door."

"Is that anyway to treat a friend? How about a cup of coffee?"

"As soon as I get this mess cleaned up I'll get right on that."

As Dusty picked up the pieces of the shattered cup, Frank hopped on a stool at the counter. "A lawyer opened the door of his BMW when suddenly a car came along and hit the door, ripping it off completely. When the police arrived at the scene, the lawyer was complaining bitterly about the damage to his precious BMW. 'Officer, look what they've done to my Beeeemer!' he whined. 'You lawyers are so materialistic, you make me sick!' retorted the officer. 'You're so worried about your stupid BMW, you didn't even notice that your left arm was ripped off.' 'Oh my gaaad...' replied the lawyer, finally noticing the bloody left shoulder where his arm once was, 'Where's my Rolex?'"

Dusty removed a rag from the sink and wiped up the spilled coffee. "Like I didn't hear that one the day Dad gave me the Beemer." He tossed the rag back in the sink, removed two cups from the cabinet and poured fresh coffee. "Besides, you'd think you of all people would know I'm not going to be a lawyer, anymore."

"Of course I do, you shithead. I just like that one."

"Shithead? You sure have the wool pulled over my wife's eyes. What little she said about you was always nice. In fact, she mentioned a few times how bad she felt for swearing in front of you."

"That girl's a keeper. Why she kept getting sent back to your ass is one of those things you'll have to ask the big guy when you get there."

"God?"

"No. Phil from the butcher shop. What do you think?"

"Geez. Someone took their cranky pill today."

"I'm not cranky. I'm wondering how long you're going to masturbate on an idea about how to help Courtney before you actually do something."

"Hey, I found the guy with no help from you, so you can keep your teeth in, you geezer."

"You don't have forever, you know. This isn't a second chance like Katie had. There is no staying here again. You two have lived your lives. Fix this and get out. You do have your kids to consider this time around."

"So, I'm not messing that up while I'm here? That's a load off my mind."

"Light load."

"Look—"

"You look. I wasn't about to let you jeopardize those babies. I broke the rules before, letting Katie stay with the younger you last time. You're lucky I'm not already hung out to dry over that and able to help you now."

"She wasn't supposed to stay last time?"

"Who wants to live their college years again? You were selfish for wanting her to stay. You're damn lucky she loved you enough to be willing to go through with it."

"I think we had a great life. I wouldn't have wanted anything that would hurt her."

"I know. She wanted it, too, or it wouldn't have happened. Enough of that. You need to go take care of this Ronald character. And no, you can't take him hunting and pull 'two go out but only one comes back.'"

"Like I could kill the guy."

"Certainly couldn't take him in a fist fight."

"You are a witty old fart, aren't ya?"

Frank slid off the stool. "Figure it out, Dusty. Time's running out."

He walked to the door and turned back around with his hand on the doorknob. "A man walked into a bar with his alligator and asked the bartender, 'Do you serve lawyers here?' 'Sure do,' replied the bartender. 'Good,' said the man. 'Give me a beer, and I'll have a lawyer for my 'gator.'"

Dusty went to two classes that day. He made the deal with his dad and he wanted his younger self to at least pretend to be respectful and keep up his end of the bargain. The sports bar didn't open up until later, anyway. Despite the scolding from Frank, his hands were tied. At four o'clock, Dusty again went to *Puck You*, hoping to find Ronald. What he found instead was Katie siting on the half wall outside the door. His mind was wandering since he still didn't have a plan; he didn't see her until she was right in front of him.

"Katie? What are you doing here?"

"Same as you."

Dusty took her by the hand and walked them away from the doorway. "You shouldn't be here. I told you I have to do this."

"She's my best friend, Dusty."

"I know, but it's something *I* need to do."

"Why? Why can't I help?"

"Because I don't know what I'm going to do yet."

She crossed her arms. "Good thing it's in your hands then."

"Don't you give me grief, too. I've already had my ass handed to me today."

"By who?"

"Just… someone. I don't want to explain it, not that I can anyway."

"Well, it doesn't matter."

Dusty was confused. "What doesn't matter?"

"He's not here today. I already asked. The bartender kind of had an attitude about it, too."

"Like how?"

"Like I wasn't the only one asking for him today. I thought maybe you came and went already, but then I saw you walking over."

"Come on. Let's get out of here and talk about this somewhere else. I can fill you in on a thing or two. I skipped lunch. You hungry?"

"Starved. I haven't had time for anything all day. Those burgers smelled good in there."

"I don't want to eat here. I'll take us somewhere else."

They sat in *Chez Pauls* again, much to Katie's dismay. She didn't want to go somewhere so elegant, but Dusty insisted it was this for privacy or their place and pizza again. She gave in pretty easily. Dusty ordered for her this time, since she knew he'd know her favorites.

"So, what have you learned about him so far?" Katie asked once they were settled.

"That he's the biggest asshole on the planet. He seems to be stringing a few other ladies along besides Courtney."

"That prick."

"Well, it gets worse. He's married."

"Married?"

"And has a kid."

"I can't believe he's doing that to her."

"Courtney or his wife?"

"Both, I guess. That's horrible. I don't know what gets into you men that you never get enough."

"Hey. Don't lump me in with that asshole. I've never strayed from you. Besides, you're all the sex machine I can handle."

She swatted him with her napkin. "So if I held back now and then, you'd go looking for it elsewhere?"

"Of course not. I love you and you know it. I don't need you looking for a fight."

"I don't want to fight. I'm just trying to figure out how someone could be so intentionally cruel."

"Again, not trying to fight, but maybe his wife is sleeping around, too. Not everyone has eyes for only one person through the time space continuum."

Leaning back, obviously frustrated, Katie said, "It doesn't make either one of them right."

"Absolutely not. We can sit here and decide how wrong it is, or we can try to come up with a plan together. What were you doing there?"

"I went there mostly looking for you. I was hoping you weren't going to do anything too stupid."

"Like attack him with my glass chin?"

Katie laughed hard. "No. I suppose you wouldn't start a fight."

"A fight wouldn't do anything but piss him off. He wouldn't stray from Courtney at the sight of me unless he thought I was her husband and he already knows better."

"I don't know that we have to really do much. I think Courtney is really into Dean."

"We do know it's not over."

"How do you figure that?"

"I wouldn't still be here if that was the case."

"Oh. Good point."

The food showed up and they put the serious talking aside while they ate. They became lost in conversation as Dusty told her more about them. He was careful not to tell her certain things that might alter her decisions in the future.

They didn't return to the subject of Ronald until they were walking back out to the car.

"I'll go check in again tomorrow," Dusty said. "If you want to come with me you can, but I'd rather you didn't. And before you protest, I'm not trying to shut you out. I just think I can say more to him 'man to man' than I can with you there. He knows you. He's not about to start talking about banging everything that moves with you around."

"Good point, I guess. So what do you want to do now?"

"Go car shopping."

"Car shopping? Really? I told you how I feel about that."

"Yes, but you also know you can't change our fates. You've already accepted the car."

"What did I get?"

"I'm not telling you. I want you to at least think you have a chance at a free will."

"What are you going to do with the Chevelle?"

"I already gave it to a kid at school. He's here on a scholarship and could use it."

"You're sweet."

He shrugged. "Kid has to live off campus. He needed it."

"Maybe you're not so sweet. I forgot about your heat."

"He's taking auto shop as an elective. He can fix it."

Katie laughed hard.

Even though Dusty knew what car Katie wanted, he drove to two lots before he took her to the one where he'd seen the little yellow VW Beetle earlier that week. When he saw it, his memory flashed back to him and Katie buying it all those years ago. She put up a good fight about a car, but once she saw that one, he could hardly pry her out of it. Something about having a Barbie car that looked just like it and it was always her favorite accessory. "Why is Divorce Barbie so expensive?" Dusty had said to her. The punch line, "Because she comes with all of Ken's things," earned him a hearty laugh. He pulled his arm to his side in a victory move. He'd finally gotten her to laugh at one of his jokes.

Dusty sat in the finance office while Katie browsed around the showroom floor. She didn't want to be there for the "gory details" as she called it. The car and truck they looked at came in just over the trade in amount for the BMW, but the salesman assured Dusty they could 'fudge' the numbers. "Just for you," the salesman said. Dusty smiled, but inside he was thinking the guy was pond scum. He knew the cars were overpriced. If the salesman didn't drop the prices they'd walk out, but he already knew they didn't have to do that.

While the paperwork was being filled out, Dusty turned around and saw Katie running for the bathroom. He quickly ran after her. He didn't heed the sign on the door that said "women" and walked in. Katie was throwing up in the handicap stall.

"Shit, sweetie. What happened?"

"You mention one food name and I swear I'll kill you." She flushed the toilet and slid to the floor.

"Can I come in?"

"Yeah," she said with a groan.

He opened the door and sat next to her. "What did you eat?"

"I didn't eat anything. I drank some cider."

"Cider? That shouldn't set you off."

"They were kind enough to add cinnamon to the mix. I was cold and it sounded good. I didn't think to stop and smell it first."

Dusty grinned. "You know, for as bad as your allergy is, you think you'd be more careful about this. You are a doctor."

"Shut up. It shouldn't have had it. Someone probably dropped a couple of cinnamon sticks in there, thinking they were doing everyone a favor. That's all it takes to set me off."

He pulled her head to his chest. "I'm so sorry. That didn't happen last time or I would have warned you. Well, you did yak a lot when we first met, but those were my fault. You didn't do it here. I guess a certain amount of history does have to repeat itself."

"Don't say repeat itself. That's what the meal did and trust me, it isn't as good the second time around."

Her eyes remained closed, she felt clammy to his touch. "I don't think you're in any shape to drive home." She shook her head no. "We'll get the car tomorrow. You want me to take you back to the dorm or you want to come home with me?"

"I want to spoon with you," she whispered.

He kissed her forehead. "I'll be right back." When Dusty walked out, there were two salesmen waiting outside of the door for him.

"Is she okay?" The one asked that had helped him.

"Yeah. Your cider made her sick."

"I'm sorry. I assure you it was made fresh not too long ago."

"It's not that. She has an allergy to cinnamon and drank it before she gave it a sniff test, I suppose. She's usually more careful. It's not your fault." Dusty shook their hands and returned to the finance office. He grinned while walking there. The expression on the salesmen's faces showed they were worried there would be a lawsuit. If his mind weren't so preoccupied with Katie, he would have played with them for a bit.

When the deal was done and he walked back to the bathroom to carry her out, the salesman came over to him.

"Here's a year's worth of free oil changes for both of the vehicles. It's the least I can do. I also had our secretary print a sign to make sure no one adds the sticks again."

Dusty shook his hand. "I appreciate it. Thanks."

Katie was right where he'd left her. He put one hand behind her back and another under her legs. "You ready, babe?" She put her arms around his neck and nodded. His new truck was waiting out front. He slid her in, then walked around to the driver side. She scooted up until her head was on his lap. "The bench seat is the best bonus to this thing already." He ran his fingers through her hair. "Thanks for letting me get you a car."

"I should be thanking you, you nut job."

He patted her shoulder. "When you feel better, snookums."

"If I had the strength, I'd hit you."

He laughed. "I'll try not to jostle you too much." After a pause he added, "I love you." She opened her eyes. "I know. That's still weird for you, but I have to say it." Katie smiled and closed her eyes again.

Dusty carried her into his cottage and again helped her get changed into his pajamas. He wasn't ready for bed, but Katie didn't want to sleep alone. She joined him on the couch while he watched a football game. Dusty sprawled out while Katie cuddled up close to him, resting her head on his chest. She let out a final sigh, wrapped an arm tight around him and whispered, "I love you, too," before falling asleep.

The next morning brought the usual hurried chaos to get to class. Dusty was grateful that she seemed to accept his explanations of their situation. She agreed to try to live life as normally as possible. Katie told Dusty that Courtney had an errand close to his neighborhood today after classes, so she would get dropped off and save him the drive to get her.

"Sounds good. We'll go get your car when I get home."

After he dropped her off at her dorm, Dusty went to talk to the Dean of Students to arrange a compromise.

"I have a lot of things on my plate right now. My father doesn't understand. I promised him I'd finish this semester and I planned on it, but something came up."

"A girl?"

"No. Of course not. It's just…stuff. I promise I'll take the finals and pass with flying colors. Give me this, please. I don't want to disrespect him or you, but I know I can ace this without taking the time you're asking me to in class."

"You know you're one of our finer students. I've never been unhappy with your work and honestly, I had high hopes for you. It pains me to no end that you are dropping out."

"It's hardly dropping out. I'm finishing with a decent amount of credits for any job. I just can't do the lawyer thing. Dad understands. You have to, too."

"You're throwing away a terrific career."

"I'm not throwing away anything. I need to do what is right for me."

Dean Hallard toyed with the pen in his hand for a few moments. "But you're asking me to lie to your father. His company is one of our biggest contributors. If I upset him—"

"He's not going to find out. We've made an arrangement and I'll be fulfilling my part. I'll talk to him about that library fund and get him to kick in some more if that'll help sweeten the deal."

"Now you're trying to bribe me."

"Absolutely."

Dean Hallard laughed. "All right. I'll look the other way, but you have to show up for finals and get nothing less than eighty percent."

"Piece of cake. Thanks." Dusty stood and extended his hand. The man shook it firmly.

"You spread a word of this to anyone and the deal is off."

"My lips are sealed," Dusty said while pretending to lock his lips with a key. After he walked out of the office, Dusty commended himself. Although he didn't like to think he and his father were anything alike, they both had their negotiating skills. Now he was free to concentrate on his task: Ronald.

Chapter Fifteen

Dusty lucked out that day, catching Ronald starting his shift at ten o'clock. He hung out, watched TV, drank a few beers, and had lunch while he killed his day observing Ronald. Having had the foresight to bring his laptop, at least he appeared to be a student hard at work. He chuckled to himself. *Sans beers of course.* His father hated when he used "sans." Dusty, of course, used it whenever he could fit it in.

Before he realized the time, it was six o'clock. Ronald was walking to the bar and Dusty called him over to his table. "You've busted your ass all afternoon. Let me buy you a drink."

"I appreciate it." He outstretched his hand to Dusty. "Name's Ronald."

"I heard that a time or two. I've been here a while. They kind of run your ass ragged. Nice to officially meet you."

Ronald hollered to the bar from the table, ordering a beer. "Come get it, asswipe," the bartender shouted back. With nothing but men currently in there, Dusty guessed there wasn't anyone to get offended.

"On my tab," Dusty told the bartender.

Ronald returned with his beer and continued their conversation. "Yeah, I noticed you here since we opened. Must be nice being on the other end of this restaurant thing."

"I try not to make it a habit, but I had to skip class today. I had a lot of catching up to do."

"Thought I saw you the other night, too."

"Yeah, well, my girl has been busy studying, so I guess I am guilty of coming down here to catch a game or two."

"She's not into sports, huh?"

"Not really. She'll tolerate a Vikings game now and then, but she'd rather partake in sports of our own doing. If you know what I mean." Dusty gave him a wink and Ronald chuckled.

"Hell, yeah. Best sport there is. Wish I could convince my wife of that."

"Ouch. Sorry I said anything."

"Naw. It's all good. It's not like I'm not getting it elsewhere." Dusty was appalled that he was openly admitting his affairs to a total stranger. "She was an animal when we were dating, but she got pregnant. Now everything is about the baby."

"I'm sure you just need to give her time."

"Kid's almost two."

"Oh. Well… then I can't really say. I know there's all kinds of help out there."

"The 'give a shit' boat left long ago. Like I said, I'm getting it elsewhere."

"She know?"

"Don't think she cares."

"Not to keep prying here, but why do you stay with her if you don't love her?"

"Never said I didn't love her, I just have needs. I'm a guy after all. Besides, I can't afford her and the house now. I certainly can't afford a divorce, child support, and two house payments."

It took everything Dusty had to continue to bite his tongue. Okay, he couldn't for a second longer. "Look, I'm not just a nobody sparking a conversation."

"You're not? What gives?" Dusty could tell that made him nervous. *Good.*

"No. I know a little about you and I needed to talk to you."

Ronald slid out of the booth. "You a goddamn bill collector?"

"No. I'm not after anything. You can sit back down." Hesitantly, Ronald sat back down. "I've seen you around. You are seeing a friend of my girl's."

"What's her name?"

"Courtney."

"Brunette or redhead?"

"Jesus. What is it with you?"

He downed a long draw of his beer. "I have a way with the ladies." He cupped his crotch and laughed. "They always come back for more."

Dusty had to hold back his look of disgust. He hated to think of Courtney ever having been with this jerk. He had to have some kind of switch to turn his personality off when he was around women. "She's a brunette."

"Kinda heavy?"

"She's a sweetheart. I don't think I like this already."

"What? You want a go at her? I'm sure she'd take a pretty boy like you. She'll come back to me when you're done."

Dusty reached across the table and grabbed him by his shirt. "Knock the shit talk. She's a friend."

Ronald didn't flinch at all. "I assume you're going to make a point here sooner or later."

Letting go of his shirt, Dusty leaned back. "You obviously have enough on your plate. Leave that one alone."

"Why should I?"

"Because I asked you to."

Laughing hard, Ronald stood and picked up his beer. "I don't think I know you well enough to go doing you any favors, kid."

"How would you like it if word got to your wife about your extracurricular activities?"

Ronald leaned down, now nose to nose with Dusty. "You ain't got the balls." He turned away and took a step then spun back around and punched Dusty in the eye. "There's more where that came from if you even think about upsetting my wife again."

Katie was waiting for Dusty when he walked into his cottage, holding a bag of ice on his eye. She hurried over the back of the couch when she saw him. "What happened?"

"I'll give you three guesses and the first two don't count."

"I guess the meeting went well." She took the bag down and examined his eye. "It doesn't look too bad."

"Go ahead and say it."

She grinned. "At least he didn't get you in the chin."

He returned the bag to his eye. "I meant 'I told you so.'"

She covered her mouth with her hand, fighting laughter. "I'm sorry."

She tiptoed up and gave him a kiss as close as she could to his hurt eye, then she took his hand and walked him over to the couch. He slid down the back and flopped into it. "Can I get you anything?"

"No. I'm just going to pout here for a while."

"I would have taken you for more of a fighter, seeing as how you were a hockey player and all."

"The dude sucker punched me. It wasn't much of a fight. Hockey wasn't that bad in school. Things aren't always what they look like on TV. I liked the skating more than the game.

I used to score the most points because I was faster than everyone else. I didn't stand there and shove 'em to start a fight."

"You think we can go skating someday? I'd love to see your moves."

He perked right up. "You want to go now?"

"Really? You feel up to it?"

"I'm always up to it. You have skates at your dorm, right?"

"Yup."

"Let's go, muffin top."

"Muffin top? You do realize that's what they call the fat that hangs over your jeans, don't you?"

"You're shitting me? Never heard that. It's the best part of a muffin. Ewww… thanks for putting that into my head."

"It's your fault."

"You need to get something to eat first?"

"Not now, after that comment."

"Stop it. You're a twig."

She laughed. "No. I actually had a late lunch. I'm fine."

Katie and Dusty spent a lot of time together on the ice. As much as Dusty liked to goof off and get fancy, he wanted to be close to Katie. Shortly before the rink's closing time, Katie said she was "done for" and said she'd be waiting on the bench.

"I know you're dying to go play with those boys, Dusty."

"Not at all. I'm enjoying my time with you."

"I like that you can't lie to me. Go have fun." She kissed him and patted his behind, sending him on his way.

After a half hour of hockey slides and slap shots, Dusty noticed an elderly man approach Katie. He moaned a "crap" under his breath, said goodbye to the boys, and hurried over. He slid to a stop at the wall by the bench.

"Hey, old timer. You trying to make time with my girl?" Dusty didn't want to let on that he knew Frank. He hoped Frank had planned on playing along.

"Wouldn't dream of it. Just out for a stroll and couldn't leave this beauty here alone." He extended his hand. "Frank. Frank Collins. Pleased to meet you both. You sure know your stuff out there."

Dusty shrugged. "It's all in fun."

"You look familiar," Katie said to Frank. "Have I seen you around somewhere?"

"Don't think so."

"Hmm… I'm pretty sure I've seen you. Where do you work? Or are you retired?"

"Wish I could say I was. I do clean up duty at the pickle factory these days."

Dusty covered up his laugh with a cough and looked away. Katie returned her attention to Frank. "I didn't know there was a pickle factory around here."

"Just a little west of town. Keeps me busy."

"I guess that beats being a greeter at WalMart."

"Yes, I suppose it does." He took a deep breath and glanced between the two of them, then slapped his hands to his knees. "Well, I guess I'd best get going. Thanks for sharing your bench with me, little lady." He tipped his hat to Dusty. "Nice meeting you, young fella. Take care of this one."

"I plan on it," Dusty said with a wide smile. He slowly skated to the opening while Frank walked along the wall with him. "So what gives? Why are you here?"

"Nothing. I miss talking to the pretty little thing. You don't deserve her, you know."

"Yeah, I know. But thanks for making me feel special, you old coot."

Frank laughed. "A man died and was taken to his place of eternal torment by the devil. As he passed sulfurous pits and shrieking sinners, he saw a man he recognized as a lawyer snuggling up to a beautiful woman. 'That's unfair!' he cried. 'I have to roast for eternity, and that lawyer gets to spend it with a gorgeous woman.' 'Shut up!' barked the devil, jabbing him with his pitchfork. 'Who are you to question that woman's punishment?'"

"So now you're telling me I'm her punishment?"

"No punishment for the self-inflicted. She loves you, boy. She practically went through hell for you once and would do it again. I stopped by to say watch yourself. That shiner there isn't very becoming. On the bright side, at least he didn't get you in the chin." Frank chuckled and strolled out of sight. Dusty walked over to the bench and sat down to take his skates off.

"What was he saying to you?" Katie asked.

"Just told me you were a beauty and I'd better treat you right."

"That seems awfully 'off' conversation for a stranger. Don't you think?"

"I don't know. Most of the old people in my family always speak their mind. Maybe I look like trouble."

"Hardly, Dusty."

"Well, he's a guy and he was young once." Dusty's skates were off and his shoes now in their place. He stood, took a hold of the bench, and leaned Katie backward until it lay on the ground. Katie squealed as she wrapped her hands around his neck. Leaning in close he said, "And he knows the only thing that is on our minds at all times."

"Hockey?"

He grinned. "Yeah. That." He gave her a kiss then stood the bench back up. "Something tells me you're in the mood for some apple pie a la mode."

Katie put her hands on her hips. "You know, this really isn't fair. It's worse than if you could read my mind. You already know everything we've done and everything we're going to do for years."

He cupped her face in his hands and gave her another kiss. "Admittedly, yes. Most things are playing out somewhat the same, but we need to make some changes and wing it now. I thought we'd have some memories together of what we did since we couldn't do anything about Ronald right now. If you don't want to go for pie, we don't have to. We can seek out your comfort food."

"Of course I want to. You know all food…" he joined her as she said, "is my comfort food."

She slapped him on the arm. "Dammit. That isn't fair."

He wrapped his arms around her and pulled her close. "Don't think you didn't mess with my brain every chance you could, too."

"Like what?"

"Let's talk over some pie." He picked up their skates, then they walked arm in arm to his truck.

"No, I didn't," Katie said with a laugh over her generous serving of pie and ice cream.

"Yes, you did. From the minute we met you threw that at me. Just like that you said it. 'My guess would be you are a writer.' I thought you were psychic."

Katie laughed harder. "I can imagine we laugh a lot together."

"That we do," he said as he took her hand. "We've had our doozies, too."

"What did you do?"

"See. There you go. Assuming it's my fault already." She sat there with her arms crossed, waiting for the story. "Okay. You're right. Once I came home with a puppy."

"A puppy? Why would I get so upset over that?"

"The kids were little and you already had your hands full."

"Still, though. That doesn't sound like a doozie of a fight starter."

"It was an Irish Setter."

She chuckled. "They are very handsome and sweet, but admittedly that isn't my favorite breed. It's been said that those dogs can't find the end of a leash."

It was Dusty's turn to laugh. "That's exactly what you said. You were willing to give it a chance, but then it ate one of about every pair of your shoes."

"I'm not so materialistic."

"And the couch." Katie had to cover her mouth to keep food from flying out.

"Blue never took to him either."

"Blue?"

"Our cat. I came home with her, too. You didn't mind her too much. I did that to you twice."

"We have two cats?"

"No. I showed up with her on two different time trips. She apparently was meant to be ours."

"Interesting. So, you found the puppy a home?"

"A nice farm right outside of the cities. An elderly couple lost theirs a few months back and were eager to have the same kind of dog again. They agreed that theirs wasn't the brightest light bulb in the box, but it made up for it in loyalty and love."

"Were the kids upset?"

"He ate enough of Ali's toys, she was okay. Alex was too young to care."

Katie leaned back. "What kind of vet am I if I can't even handle a puppy?"

"You're a wonderful vet, Katie, and an even better mother. You actually take a break from your practice to stay home with the kids."

"I do? Do I close it?"

"You have a friend fill in."

"Who?"

"I don't want to tell you an influence your decision."

She stared at him. "Fine. Play that way." Returning to her pie she added, "If that's the extent of our spats, I think we're okay."

"Oh, there's more. Half of the fun is making up, so I'm not giving anything else away. I'm still not sure on the order of things here. I'm not giving up any of those times with you and chancing missing out on the make-up sex."

"So, if you were given the chance to go back and set things straight, you wouldn't?"

"Well…most of them." He innocently sipped his coffee.

"And how many strippers and bachelor parties do these involve?"

Now it was Dusty's turn to choke on his coffee. "Dammit. You are psychic."

After Dusty's coughing spell from choking on the coffee stopped, he cried out, "Shit!"

"Shit what?"

"We still have to get your car."

"Then double shit," Katie said.

"Why's that?"

"I didn't get a campus parking pass. I totally spaced it."

"So stay at my place again."

"I already talked to Court. We were going to stay in tonight."

"Really?"

"Don't give me the wounded puppy look, Dusty. I know we're supposed to end up together and all, but I have to live somewhat of my normal life now until we get this figured out. Especially if what you say about Courtney is true."

"If? I thought you believed me."

"I do. What I meant was, if she's going to die in my future, I want to see her as much as I can in my present. That's all."

"She and Dean doing okay?"

"It sounded like it. She just wanted girl time."

Dusty remembered a text he'd received while he was at the bar. Dean said there was a party at one of the frat houses. Courtney must not have wanted to go. He told Dean no but if he couldn't have Katie tonight, maybe he'd go after all.

"All right. We'll get it and park it at my place. The garage is two stall. I'll call Freeman and tell him to get off his ass and come pick up the Chevelle tonight."

"You sure?"

"Of course. You know…."

"What?"

"You don't have to get a parking pass at all. Just move in with me."

"Are you going to bring this up every day?"

He shrugged. "Probably."

"Well, unless you're trying to pre-plan make-up sex for tomorrow, don't."

"Why not, baby? Come on. I love when you wake up next to me. I don't want to wait."

"Give me a little more time. Okay?"

"If I'm remembering correctly, you moved in with me by now last time."

"Well, that *me* had a year with you already."

"But I only knew you for a few days and I knew what I wanted."

"Dusty, please. Just a couple of days. I know I'm not seeing that much of you so you can't possibly understand how much this situation with Court is killing me."

"Trust me. I know you; I get it."

"Do you? In between the sex, the food, me throwing up, and you fighting with your dad, that doesn't really leave a lot of time for shit to sink in. Within days you've convinced me you're from"—she lowered her voice and looked around—"the future and told me more than I should have probably heard about my life. You have to give me a couple of days or you can forget about me moving in with you. You'll be checking me into a padded room." Her voice cracked and her eyes filled with tears.

Dusty rushed to the other side of the table and held her tight.

"Hey…shhhh. I'm sorry. Of course you can take all the time you need." He let up only enough to kiss the top of her head, then pulled her tight to his chest again. "I'm sorry. I suppose I'm not thinking straight."

"Because you're spending your days and nights in a beer-induced stupor watching this Ronald. Maybe you can lay off the drinking and get busy, Dusty." She leaned back and gently stroked by his eye. "You didn't win him with booze. Now you have to figure it out. Now that I know about Courtney, I can't live with myself if we don't do something about it."

"You have to promise me you won't tell her."

"But why not? Don't you think if she knew she would never sleep with him again?"

"Let's reverse this, shall we? Tonight Courtney says to you, 'I just met a guy. He's young and a little bit crazy, but I believed him when he told me he's from the future. He told me to tell you not to sleep with Dusty again 'cause you're going to catch something from him and die.' What do you think you would do?"

She sighed. "Check to see what kind of drugs she was on."

"Exactly."

"Well then, Andrews. You'd better do something and you'd better do it quick."

"I'm working on it. You're with her tonight so we're okay there. I have tomorrow to start another plan of attack. I'm not going to let you down, babe. I swear."

They didn't talk much more after that. After picking up her car and driving it to Dusty's, he took her back to her dorm then went home. He stood in his driveway waiting for

Dean to show up with their friend, Freeman, who was picking up the Chevelle.

It was in the high forties that night, but he wore only a heavy sweatshirt. By Minnesota winter standards, forty was warm. Dusty wanted some fresh air, hoping to clear his head and have an idea pop into his mind about what to do. He was drawing a blank just staring at his fireplace. Within ten minutes, the unmistakable rumble of Dean's engine approached. He had a huge diesel truck with oversized tires. Dean had been a farm boy and the master of farm equipment. He said he needed the truck so he didn't get homesick for a tractor. Dusty bought him a huge stuffed pig for it and said its name was "Bacon" like the one in the movie *Varsity Blues*. The pig remained in the truck ever since as their mascot. Over the years they'd added to it. It now sported a Viking's jersey, a Twins hat, and the latest addition, a brandy keg around its neck, like those found on a St. Bernard in cartoons.

The rumble of the diesel engine was now masked by AC/DC's "Highway to Hell." After pulling to a stop on the street, Dean turned the music down. Dusty's landlords were nice enough; Dean was always careful to be respectful of them when he showed up. He spent too many drunken nights on Dusty's couch not to be friendly to the old people as he dragged his ass to school the next morning.

The men shook hands and exchanged the usual pleasantries, guy style, and Dusty took a razzing for the black eye. After a few "ugly bastards" and "dickheads," Dusty handed Freeman the keys. "The pink slip is in the glove box. Take good care of her, friend. She's been good to me. I really hate to give her up."

"I would have thought your old man would have wanted to fix her up for his collection."

"Dad doesn't mess with any of that. He likes to buy 'em already restored."

"Well, you keep your eye on Hot Rod Magazine. She'll be in there someday."

"I thought you were broke."

"I didn't say anytime soon," he said with a laugh. "Shop class is kind of excited to have her there, though. We'll get her guts purring great for starters."

"Glad to hear it." After shaking hands again, Freeman was on his way.

"We hitting '*I Felta Thigh*?'" Dean asked with a nudge to Dusty. Dusty laughed. Dean always found a way to mess up a sorority name. His favorite was "*Kappa Tappa Kegga*."

"You're not on a hunt, are you? Aren't things going good with Court?"

"They're fine. She wanted to stay in so, I figured we'd have guy time. I'm not looking for a girl, just a night out. Court has me covered in the sex department. As a matter of fact, and if you tell anyone this I'll kill you, I needed a night off. So does the Major," he said as he pretended to adjust himself. "Besides, we're too young and handsome to get tied down every night already."

"I don't know. I kinda like it."

"Geez, Dust. You seriously ready to cash it in at your age?"

"My age? You have three years on me, assface. And what's wrong with being happy?"

"I don't know, man. I feel like there's more to be had before I call it quits."

"You stringing Katie's friend along? She's going to have my balls if you piss off Courtney."

"She's not looking to settle down, either. She's the one making that clear. We're having fun and that's it. She lets me know every time we're together that I should keep my options open."

"Maybe she's trying to make sure she doesn't get hurt."

"I don't know. I think she means it. She keeps going on about this internship in Seattle coming up. I'm not going to follow her there. Especially not at this stage in the game."

"But wouldn't you—"

"We going to stand in your driveway and write up my wedding invitations or are we going to '*I Eta Pi*?'"

"I don't know. I've done more than my share of drinking this week already."

"Come on, you pussy. Afraid your vet school girlfriend will neuter you? Or has she already?"

Dusty gave him a shove. "Eat me. Let me go grab my wallet."

"Get a jacket too, dickweed. It's supposed to chill off here soon."

"Well, that was a nice few minutes of weather."

"More than we usually get this time of year. Now hurry up."

The night went pretty much as every frat kegger party went. Dusty might have his current time memories, but apparently there was no convincing his younger body to behave. He cursed the fact that he couldn't turn down the egging on and partook in the beer bong that was passed around.

They stumbled back to his place well after midnight. Dean claimed the bed and Dusty took the couch. He stared at the ceiling and wondered how he'd fare in tomorrow's adventure with Ronald with a black eye and a headache. He thought about getting up to take aspirin as a precaution, but couldn't drag his ass to the bathroom. Putting his thoughts to his happy place, Katie, he finally fell asleep.

Chapter Sixteen

Dusty woke up to the phone ringing. He slapped around on the nightstand until his hand found it. He lay back flat on his pillow and mumbled a groggy hello. His eyes opened suddenly when he realized where he was. He wasn't on the couch in his cottage. He was back home.

"Dusty!" His wife's hysterical voice caused him to care about nothing else.

"Babe! What's wrong?"

"She's gone!"

Who's gone? Is what he wanted to say, but he was sure he should know this if she was this upset. He quickly stood, wanting to check on the kids. He knew he had to say something before he reached their rooms.

"Honey, I'm so sorry."

"She wasn't supposed to go yet. Dammit! We had years left."

"Shhhh. I'm here, babe. Talk to me." He had gotten Ali's door opened, and was relieved to see she was sound asleep. Ali was the same age. Katie was calling from Seattle. *What happened now?*

"She OD'd last night. She…" Katie's sobs took over and she could no longer speak.

Dusty waited until she gathered herself. While he waited, he went to Alex's room. He was sleeping as he always did. Sprawled out with his arms over his head. Even with the sadness in Katie's voice, he took comfort in the fact that his kids were here and safe. His mind raced to what happened. How could he have traveled back to his present when he didn't get a chance to fix things yet? Everything had been moving along nicely, or so he thought. He wasn't screwing things up so badly that he was forced to be done without being given the chance to make it right. *Was he?* He rushed back into their bedroom and looked in the mirror. *No black eye.*

"I can't believe she's gone," Katie finally continued. "We had such a good couple of days. I really thought I was getting her to come around."

"Do you know what happened? What set her off?"

"I don't think you should have told Dean for starters."

"Dean? What does that have to…" Dusty's mind was racing. Had he told Dean in "this" time? He had to cover fast. "Um…sorry, babe. I thought he'd want to know. We talked and he asked about her."

"I'm not going into how furious I am with you about this. You should have known she'd be sensitive about it. I trusted you to keep this between us."

"Babe—"

"I'm angry, but I still need you." She started to cry again.

"I'll get the kids to Mom and Dad's. You know May will be thrilled. I'll get out there as soon as I can."

"They're taking her away. I have to go."

"I love you." She hung up without another word. "Fuck." Dusty hung up, then called Dean.

"Hey, asshole. What are you doing calling me so early?"

Dusty ran his hand down his face. He didn't even know where to begin. "What did you and Courtney talk about?"

"Just the good old days. Told her I wish we had a real shot at things. You know…crap chicks like to hear. I thought she was down and could use some cheering up. Why?"

"I just hung up with Katie. Courtney OD'd last night."

Now Dean sounded wide awake. "You're shitting me!"

"Wish I was. Katie's pretty messed up. I'm going to fly out there on the next available flight."

"You need me to watch the kids?"

"No. I'm going to call May."

"Then I'm going with you."

"I'm not so sure that's such a good idea. Katie's pretty upset."

"Tough shit. I'll be there in thirty minutes, ready to go. I'll get the company car to drop us off at the airport. As a matter of fact. I'll get my secretary to make the reservations. You deal with calling May."

Dusty was too upset to fight with him. *What had he done wrong?* "I'm not going to fight you. See you in a bit."

When Dean arrived, Dusty was still hurrying around the house, trying to gather what he thought the kids would need to get by for a few days. He still wasn't exactly sure how long they would be. Dean caught up to him in Ali's room, stuffing a bag with Barbie and Polly Pocket toys.

"Hey, buddy. Can I help?"

"I think I have everything. Her suitcase of clothes is packed. I thought she'd want some toys."

"Dude. I've been to your parents' place. They have a friggin' Toys- R-Us there. She'll be fine."

"I know. Ali likes to sleep with this one rabbit; I can't find it."

"The white one with the pink ribbon on its neck?"

"Yeah."

"She was holding it when I walked in."

"Shit." Dusty sat down on the bed and lowered his head to his knees.

Dean took a seat next to him. "What gives? You're taking this harder than I thought you would. I know she was your wife's best friend and all, but still, Dust. You're more off than usual."

"I feel like I missed something. Like…you know. This could have been prevented."

"What could you have done? I had a cousin do the same thing. He had cancer and got sick of being told he was going to die. They didn't even give him a year, but the wait must have been driving him crazy. Every visit they gave him a couple more months. Somewhere into his third year he blew his brains out. He was sick of waiting to die."

"This is helping me how?"

"I'm just sayin'. Court was a strong person, but knowing you're going to die is enough to send the strongest person in the world over the edge. I'm sure she was too damn proud for her own good and refused to watch herself go downhill."

"But she had so much time."

Dean slumped his shoulders down. He pinched at the bridge of his nose as if he were fighting tears, swallowing hard before he spoke. "Her mind worked differently. She was stubborn in many ways. Remember the ride she had me on when we were dating? I loved her, man, but she never would commit and decide to stay with me."

Dusty knew he must be missing something from his memories. Other than them going to the frat party, he and Courtney seemed to be doing great. "Refresh my memory. What happened with you two? I remember things going so well there for a while."

"I honestly think she kept trying to beat me to the punch."

"What punch?"

"You know. Dump me before I could dump her. I really was more attached than I wanted to be, but I could only fight her for so long. She kept shoving me away and I finally let her go. I never wanted to…" His voiced trailed away and he cleared his throat then slapped Dusty's knee. "Come on. We gotta go. Our plane leaves in four hours. That gives us enough time to get the kids to your folks and just enough to get to the airport for our groping by TSA."

"Thanks for coming along. I don't know how Katie will be, but I'm glad to have you."

Dean stood, then pulled Dusty to his feet as well. They shared a quick "man-hug" then Dean walked him to the window. He pointed out to the limo. "Fully stocked bar. Should have stayed in law school, dude."

Things moved quickly at Dusty's parents'. His mother was excited to have the kids for an extended stay. She was waiting on the front steps and clapped her hands together when she saw the limo. It barely came to a stop before she came rushing over to it.

"Gramma!" Ali shouted before climbing over her father to get out of the car. Dusty allowed her to be out of her booster chair since it was a limo, as long as she didn't rat him out to her mother.

Dusty was right behind her, accepting a long hug from his mom when Ali ran over to May, who had joined them. In her embrace, Dusty couldn't fight the tears that had been building since he took Katie's call. Now that they were here, leaving them was even harder than he'd anticipated. All he wanted while he was trying to help Courtney was to return to his children. Leaving them now because he didn't succeed weighed heavy on him.

"It's okay," Norma said as she rocked with him. "Go to your wife, son. She needs you. The kids can stay as long as you need them to. They'll be fine."

"Thanks." Dusty cleared his throat and ran the palm of his hands over his eyes. "I hope Dad doesn't mind the chaos." He and his father butted heads on a regular basis when he was younger, but he had done a complete turnaround with the grandkids. Dusty hardly recognized the man who played with his children.

"Are you kidding? He's leaving work early today. Should be here any minute. Took the next two days off, too."

"Tell him I'm sorry we couldn't stick around to see him." The last thing Dusty wanted was for his father to see he'd been crying.

Dean climbed out of the car with Alex asleep on his shoulder.

"Where do you want him?" he asked Norma.

May barged over. "Right here in my arms. You two boys bring in their things."

Once they were back in the limo, Dean poured them each a drink. Dusty protested. "Dude, it's not even eleven."

"It's for your nerves. You look like hell, man."

Dusty accepted the cup and downed the shot. "Great. Booze for breakfast. Just like the good old days."

"I'll buy you something to eat at the airport."

"I'm not broke, y'know."

"I know. It feels good to be helping. Shitty excuse to get some guy time."

Dusty held out his glass again for Dean to fill. "I don't know how I'm going to get Katie through this. They were closer than sisters."

"Speaking of sisters, did you call Alyson?"

"Not yet. There wasn't time this morning. I'll wait until we're home. She'll probably want to stay with Katie for a few days. She'd met Courtney a few times, but it's not like they were friends on their own."

"It's a shame dudes have that 'no banging your best friend's sister' rule. I would have loved a piece of that."

Dusty managed a laugh and returned the glass to its holder. "This fucking sucks, but I'm glad you're with me, asswipe." He closed his eyes and again chastised himself for not being able to do anything about it. *What the hell went wrong?*

Dean shook Dusty awake. "Come on, sleeping beauty. We're here."

It took Dusty a second to get oriented. He'd fallen asleep in the limo. The booze knocked him out cold for the hour ride. The driver gave them their bags from the back and they used curbside check-in. The line for security was faster than usual. Amazingly, they had all the lanes opened up over the lunch hour.

They found an empty table at *Wolfgang Pucks* and ordered some food. Dusty declined a beer, but Dean overruled him with the waitress. "Make it two," he told her. "The big baby can take it."

Despite his growling stomach, Dusty only managed about half of the enormous burger.

"Who's Frank?" Dean asked, causing Dusty to choke on a French fry.

"Huh?" he said, stalling while he could think of an answer.

"Frank. You mumbled his name in your sleep."

"Just a dude. Kinda pissing me off right now."

"Guy from work?"

"Yeah. I guess you could say that."

"Want me to get a hit out on him?"

Damn Dean. Only he could make Dusty laugh when he felt like this. "If I could send you to him, I'd consider the shit out of that."

"Anything I can do?"

"Guess not. Not anymore anyway."

"You want to talk about it?"

"Naw. You'd only lock me up in the closest looney bin."

"I'm here when you're ready."

“I know. Thanks.”

Dusty walked into Courtney’s house without knocking. Katie caught sight of him from the living room, immediately ran over, and flew into his arms. He held her tight as she sobbed into his shoulder. Katie’s crying was inconsolable, as if she’d held back her tears until he showed up. He picked her up; she wrapped her legs around him. As he rocked with her, Dusty glanced around the room. Most were faces he didn’t know. Wanting to give Katie some privacy, he took off down the hall. Having visited Courtney with Katie a few times, he knew his way around the house. He walked them to Courtney’s room and closed the door.

Sitting down on the bed, he continued to hold her tight. “It’s okay, baby. I’m here.” Her violent sobs finally started to settle down. He sat with her, stroking her back.

“I found her,” she said, wiping at her eyes with her sleeve. “Damn her for putting me through that.”

“Shhhh…it’s over, baby.”

“Far from it.” She sniffed and leaned back, reaching for a tissue on the nightstand. “Her parents, aunts, and uncles just showed up. I’m a mess.”

He held her face in his hands. “You’re beautiful.”

She pushed his hands away. “I don’t give a shit what I look like. I don’t know what to say to these people. They look at me funny, Dusty. I show up and all of a sudden she kills herself. I can’t imagine what’s going through their minds.”

“Did they know about her diagnosis?”

“As far as I know, no. I was the first one she called.”

“Did she leave a note at all?”

“No.” She flopped into his chest again. “This is so unfair.”

"There you are."

Katie turned to the sound of the familiar voice. "What are you doing here?" she said harshly.

"Your old man was in rough shape. I thought I should come along. How are you, darlin'?"

"How am I?" She quickly climbed off Dusty's lap and took the distance to Dean in two strides. "How am I? I just found my best friend dead in her bathtub. The last person she talked to was you. What the hell did you say to her?" Katie pounded her fists into Dean's chest. He quickly grabbed her wrists after she hit him again. "What did you do, Dean?"

"Hey. You're not going to do this to me, Katie. Don't put this on me. You're ripping my heart out here. You know I wouldn't say anything to hurt her. I loved her, dammit. She's the one that always pushed me away."

Katie leaned into his chest. "I'm sorry. I'm so angry with her. She didn't have to do this."

He released his hold on her arms and wrapped his around her. "Did she tell you I was out here a few months ago?"

She leaned back. "You were?" Dusty said it at the same time. Dean had never told him that, either.

"I wanted to get back together. And for good this time. I was tired of this on again, off again, long distance crap. I wanted her to move home."

"What happened?" Katie asked.

"She obviously turned me down. I thought about moving out here. I can't stand this damn gloom, but I would have done it for her. She told me she was over me and doing some doctor, but I knew it wasn't serious. I think she was doing what she always did. Act like sex was just sex and she didn't want or need love. She did a number on my heart over the years, Katie. Lord knows I tried to make it work."

"Oh, Dean. I'm so sorry." Katie continued to hug him.

"I need to sit down." She walked him over to the bed and sat between the men.

Dean started to explain. "I called last night to talk to her again. I didn't care that she was sick. I wanted to move here anyway." Dusty saw a tear fall from his eye. "She said she'd think about it and call me today. I guess I did kill her."

Katie stood, wrapped her arms around his head and pulled him to her chest as he cried. Dusty left the room to give his friend some dignity. He had been mingling with everyone, trying to figure out who was who, when Katie called him back into the room a while later. When he walked in, they were sitting on the bed, holding hands.

"Hell of a set of pillows your wife has, dude," Dean said with a grin.

"Keep your face outta her tits, butt munch."

"Hey. I would've found a reason to cry when Ali was little had I known the reward."

Dusty gave him a playful smack on the back of his head. He was glad things were getting back to normal.

"I hate to interrupt this pitiful attempt at manly emotion," Katie said, "but we need to talk. If it can be avoided, I don't want to tell her family about her disease. I don't want her to be the butt of rumors and speculations. This happened years ago and isn't going to be fair to her memory. Do we have a deal?"

"Of course, babe."

"Definitely," Dean added. "I'd like to talk to the medical examiner and get a hold of him before anything is released. I'm officially her lawyer, anyway."

"You are?" Dusty said with great surprise.

"Yeah. She wanted a lawyer she knew she could trust. Imagine that."

"I'll introduce you to her mother. She can let you know where to go."

"I'd appreciate if you only let her know of my professional connection with Court, Katie. She never let me meet her family. It was another way of denying we were ever in a relationship. At least, that's what she seemed to be doing."

"Of course," Katie agreed. "I think the less complicated we make this, the better."

After Katie introduced Dean to Courtney's mother, she lit up. "My Courtney's Dean? It's so nice to finally meet you. I wish it was under better circumstances."

Dean was confused. "She mentioned me?"

"Of course she mentioned you, dear. She talked of you often. You were a dear friend to her for many years. I always thought you two would hook up someday." She dabbed at her eyes with her handkerchief. "You'll take care of the details of her will and such for me, won't you?"

"Of course. It's my job."

"I know it has to be hard for you."

"That's an understatement, but I'll get it done."

"Bless you." She gave him a kiss on the cheek. "I'll get you the name of the funeral home where they took her."

Dusty cuddled up tight to Katie when they finally crawled in bed that night. He knew she would be out in seconds. The crying had to exhaust her. Sleep wouldn't come so easily for him. He had many days, if not years, of torturing himself over not having been able to change Courtney's fate. Now he had the added guilt of sending her to her grave earlier for hooking her up with Dean.

Even though Dean had confessed that he loved her more than he ever let on, Dusty hadn't owned up to the fact that he pushed them together all those years ago, trying to prevent her prematurely dying because of hooking up with Ronald. He didn't know he'd fail and send her to the grave even sooner for loving Dean. He didn't know if Katie would be able to forgive him for that.

He was miserable that Katie was so grief stricken, but grateful that her thoughts were preoccupied, otherwise she would have sensed something was up with him. He kissed the back of her head and hoped sleep would overtake him soon.

Chapter Seventeen

The next morning, Dusty didn't feel nearly ready to get out of bed but the sun was blazing through the window, hollering at him to get up and get the day going. He couldn't even pry his eyes open yet. They had a lot to do with funeral plans with Courtney's mother; he was going to lie there until Katie gave the command to wake up. He cuddled up to the body next to him and gave the back of her head a kiss.

She let out a gentle moan and shifted a bit. Dusty jumped when he felt a hand on his crotch. "How's my Cookie Monster this morning?" the voice asked sleepily. *Shit. That wasn't Katie.*

Dusty bolted upright. "Stacey?"

She rolled to her back. "You were expecting someone else?"

Dusty looked around the room. He was in her dorm room. *What the hell?* He hadn't been with Stacey for at least two months before he met Katie. She was enough to just about make him swear off women altogether. *When the hell was he now?*

He quickly slid out of her bed, wrapping the sheet around his waist.

"Uh…no. I remembered I have to pick up a friend. Sorry." He quickly found his pants and pulled them on. *Katie's going to kill me! What the hell is going on?*

Stacey sat up angrily, crossing her arms under her bare breasts. "You going to call me later?"

"Yes. Um, no. I'm sorry, Stacey. I can't. I'm sorry I let whatever happened last night happen, but I can't see you anymore."

"Whatever happened last night? That just happened to be—"

He put his hand up. "Please don't say it. Look, I'm sorry." He scrambled around the room looking for his shirt and socks. "It's not you— it's me."

"That old line? I thought you were different, Dusty."

"I can't, okay? I'm sorry. School is hell and my dad is on my ass. I don't have time to treat you the way you deserve to be treated. Okay?"

"You'll be sorry, Dustin Andrews."

"I already am," he mumbled under his breath.

"What was that?"

"Nothing. I can't find my right boot."

Stacey climbed out of bed and strolled to the closet, flaunting her naked body. She pushed the door closed and found the boot against the wall. She walked over to him slowly with it, waving it back and forth. "You liked that corner. Are you sure I can't get one more ride out of you and get you to change your mind?"

He swiped the boot from her hand. "I'm sorry. I really have to go." He pulled his other boot on and hurried to the door. He said goodbye, but before he closed the door something she said made him step back in. "What was that?"

"Is your friend Dean seeing anyone?"

"No. I mean, yes. He has a pretty steady girl. Why?"

"I thought if you weren't interested, I'd try him."

Dusty stepped back in the room. The memories of her came back to him more clearly. He did have a hard time breaking up with her. She never would let it stick. He blamed himself since he gave in too many times after too many drinks. *Boys will be boys.*

"Look. I know we keep doing this, but I mean it this time." He hoped he was at a place where that statement made sense. "Don't go messing with Dean. He has a good thing going."

She strolled up to him and ran her hand down his chest. "How else can I prove to you what a good thing you've let get away if I'm not as close as I can be to you and rub it in?"

He held her hand. "Look. I'm trying to be civil. I'm sorry if I'm coming across like a jerk. Don't mess with Dean. I mean it. If you're looking to dig your nails into a law student, there are plenty of us out there."

"Like who?"

Dusty had to think fast. "Freeman."

"Freeman? He's on a scholarship."

"Yeah, but he's a good guy."

She scoffed. "Nice try."

"He got it on his grades; he has some money. And rumor has it he's hung like a horse."

"Really?"

Dusty shook his head in disgust at her reaction to his made up comment. "I have to split. I'm really sorry. You deserve better than me."

"Ain't that the truth."

Dusty hurried out, realizing he had no idea if he drove here or what. After a brief walk down a few side streets, he found his car. It wasn't locked and his keys were in the visor. *Gotta love having a piece of shit that no one would even steal.* He started it up and took off without waiting for the heat to kick on. *What would be the point?*

He dug his watch out of the glove box as he drove. It was almost exactly two months earlier than his previous visit.

Why the switch? He knew he had time to save Courtney, yet he was sent back to the present. Was that to show him what happened if he failed? "Nice of you to wrench my heart, asshole."

"Anytime, puddin'."

Dusty stomped on the brakes and spun around to the voice in the back of the seat. "I ought to beat the shit out of you!"

"I'd like to see you try."

Dusty stormed out of the car and slammed the door. Frank followed. Dusty caught him by the shirt and pressed him to the car. He was pissed, but the guy was old. Going easier than he wanted to, he instantly regretted the light hold he had on him.

Frank now had Dusty by the shirt and spun him around so he was now pinned at the vehicle. "You're farting around and it ain't helping."

"I didn't put me in bed with an ex-girlfriend. What if Katie finds out about it? She'll have my dick in a jar."

"Ms. A cups? Please. I have to say that psycho was about the lowest you ever sunk. And F—Y—I, you didn't cheat on Katie. You haven't technically met her yet."

"Yeah, right. Like that's going to matter."

"So you saw another woman naked. You didn't do anything. Hmm… you're right. You're screwed, Andrews." Frank let go of his hold and straightened Dusty's shirt. "You have a lot of balls grabbin' a helpless old man like that."

"Helpless my ass. What gym do you go to?"

"The gym of the love of a good woman."

Dusty winced at the thought of the geezer having sex. "Too much info, pal."

"I'm through screwing around with you. Get your shit together. I just gave you a head start."

"You mean you just screwed up everything I had going."

"Really? You want me to punch you in the face so you can get caught up with Ronald?"

"I meant Katie. I'm before I ever met her. I finally won her ass over and spilled the beans, now she has no clue who I am or what I'm doing."

"Do you remember how many times she had to go back to your sorry ass?"

"That was different."

"Hardly. I think it's payback time."

"You're doing this to punish me?"

"No. I think we needed the clock rewound a smidge. You saw how well your interfering thus far got you."

He lowered his head to his chest. "Yeah. It made her die even sooner."

"Right. Try again, numb nuts."

"You know, I have half a mind to tell Katie how you treated me when this is over."

"You wouldn't do that."

"Why wouldn't I?"

"'Cause that would leave you with nothing." Frank walked away and Dusty flipped him the bird with both hands. "I know what you're doing," Frank said without even turning around.

Dusty decided not to send another retort his way. He got back in his car and headed for home.

As he showered, he cursed for being sent this far back. He hoped he wouldn't have to deal with his father a third time on the same subject. For now, he had two choices. Skip classes again and either approach the Dean of Students in advance or wait for the wrath of being busted after skipping a few days. He decided to skip a few first. Maybe he could wrap this up quickly, now that he was ahead of the game. He knew where Ronald worked and he knew he had a nice left hook. Dusty needed to come up with another tactic.

His mind roamed to Katie's stories of all the times she'd met him and had to convince him that she was leaping through time. He was a hard sell, but she eventually convinced him. She had the unfair advantage of being a female. Men generally listened to anything if they had a goal in mind. Listen now, act on the information, sort out the details later. If he blurted out the things she had, there's no way he would be allowed within fifty feet from her. He wished she had a hidden birthmark to use as leverage, like the one she had used on him, but she didn't. He could only try a few quirks and facts when the time came. For now, he wanted to try the old fashioned way and "woo" her for a date. As always, wanting to see Katie was on the top of his list in any date and time. He headed over to the coffee shop, hoping to get lucky.

His thoughts went to what Frank had said. He quickly convinced himself that he wasn't wasting time. With Ronald's schedule, he had to wait until at least ten to catch him. That was if he had the early shift. Depending on the day, he may not show up till four. "Can't just sit around with my dick in my hands," he said, quoting his father. *Wise man indeed.*

Dusty couldn't believe his luck in finding Katie and Courtney sitting in the coffee shop. In his and Katie's original present, they hadn't met until they were older. It was funny how through all her time leaps and now his, they always ran into each other. Someone or something was really determined to get them together.

After pouring Dusty's coffee, Art once again gave him hell about his tab. "After this, you're not getting another damn thing until you pay up, Andrews."

"I told you, I'd pay you Friday." He kept his voice low, hoping to lower Art's. That was his usual line; he hoped it was fitting now. He turned around and saw Katie and Courtney look his way. *Crap.*

"Today is Friday, butt munch."

"Oh. Gimme a second." Dusty walked over to the ATM and checked his balance. He saw that a check had been deposited from his father, so he pulled out enough cash to cover the bill and a nice tip.

"You know," Art said when he placed his drink in front of him. "You're the poster child for why I don't like to run tabs."

"You love me." Dusty blew Art a kiss then sat in a chair across from where Katie and Courtney were on the couch. The girls looked his way, he raised his large coffee up in a greeting. They smiled a pleasant hello, but didn't say anything. He pretended to be interested in his phone. Out of the corner of his eye he caught Katie glance back over at him. She whispered something to Courtney and they laughed. When Courtney walked to the bathroom, Dusty stole the chance to go over and sit next to Katie.

"Good morning. Come here often?"

She at least smiled pleasantly at him. It wasn't a crash and burn yet.

"Is that really the best you can do?"

"Sorry. I get tongue-tied when I see a strikingly gorgeous woman."

She shook her head then blew on her coffee before sipping it. He had to hold back from commenting on it. Katie tucked her hair behind her ears. "Look, you're positively adorable, but I don't really want to be picked up."

"I wouldn't just pick you up. I'd carry you all the way back to my place." She laughed with a snort then covered her mouth. "I'll give you points for originality there."

"Can I trade in those points for a date?"

"Sorry. No."

"Why not?"

"Honestly, you're a little younger than anyone I've ever dated. I'm pretty sure that includes when I was in high school."

"I'm not as young as I look."

"How old are you?"

"Just a few years younger than you."

"And how do you know how old I am?"

"I'm good as guessing these things."

"Really? Well, you are aware that you'll piss off a woman if you guess older than she is, right?"

"Yup. She's even more pissed if you guess her weight wrong."

"You're not stupid enough to try and guess someone's weight, are you?"

"How about this. I guess your age, height, and weight and you go out with me."

"Are you crazy?"

"About you, the second I saw you."

Katie held her face in a serious stare before she took a sip of her coffee. "I overheard your conversation with Art. We go on a date and I have to buy?"

"Hell no. I'll take you to *Chez Pauls*. I have money. It's just a game I like to play with Art. He loves the banter as much as I do. Honest."

Dusty glanced up. Courtney had returned and was standing behind the couch. Her arms were crossed. "What do we have here?" she asked.

"I'm trying to get a little wager out of your friend." He turned back to Katie. "I'll up the stakes. I'm right and you bring your friend along, too. We'll make it a double date with my best friend."

"What are you getting me into, Katie?"

"A dinner at *Chez Pauls* if he guesses my height, age and weight."

"What? Is he with the traveling circus? I didn't know there was one in town."

"Tell you what," Dusty said. "You both get a shot at my age first. If you aren't within two years, the deal's off."

"You're on," Katie said, finally getting interested. "If you are a day over seventeen, I'll eat escargot while we're there."

Courtney let out a chuckle. "That was my vote but since you stole it, I'll go eighteen."

Dusty stood up, pretending to be defeated. He turned to walk away then quickly spun back around and pointed at Katie. "You're one hundred and eight pounds, five foot three, and twenty-five. I'd say you were a Scorpio, even though you probably don't get into the whole Zodiac thing. And for the record," he pulled out his wallet and held it up. "I'm twenty-one."

Katie snatched the license from his hand. "And a half. Shit."

He took his license back, then bent down and kissed Katie on the cheek. "I'll pick you two up at six. I assume you're roommates. What dorm are you at?"

Katie's mouth was wide open so Courtney answered. "Gunther Hall."

"It's cold. Don't worry about fancy dresses. Wear something comfortable." He walked over to the bar and picked up a to-go cup then walked out before they had a chance to come up with a reason to cancel.

"Just what the hell was that?" Courtney asked Katie. "I thought you were dating Rex."

"Well… I sort of am. It's not a big deal. We're not even sleeping together. It's only been a few dates."

"I've never seen you so smitten. What's with this kid?"

"Honesty? I don't know. I was curious about him from the second he sat down."

"Do you know what he does? Is he in school?"

"I don't have a clue."

"Way to go, hon. You set me up with a friend of his that's probably a troll."

"Oh, come on. He wouldn't do that. It's probably someone his age or younger. You'll be in luck. You'll be with a boy hitting his sexual peak and actually be able to keep up with you."

Courtney mussed Katie's hair.

"Witch," Katie said with a giggle.

"Dog poop analyzer."

"Human wiz sniffer."

Courtney flopped over the back of the couch, laughing hard. Katie plopped her with the pillow in the stomach. "So you'll go with me?"

"Sure. I guess I can tell Ronald I made other plans if he calls. It's not like we do anything but boink, anyway. I'll ride bitch for you and your date."

"Love you."

"You'd better."

Chapter Eighteen

From the coffee shop, Dusty went to Dean's dorm. They both had late Friday morning classes in college. Once again, Dusty removed a sock that wasn't necessary and woke him up. "I don't want a dinner date, Dust. There's that kegger at '*I Eta Epsilon*'. I thought you were going with me."

"We can do a kegger any time. These look like some nice girls. Come on…I need my wing-man, man."

"What do they do?"

Dusty thought for a second. He technically didn't know yet. "Do you care? They're breathing and they have legs."

"*Chez Pauls*?"

"Yup."

Dean finally gave in. "All right. But only if you get the good looking one and I get the basket case."

Dusty laughed. "I swear yours is all right, too. I know you'll hit it off."

"You're buyin', and use the Beemer, not that piece of shit you call a car."

"Deal. Dress nice. Try not to look like a lawyer."

From there, Dusty went to *Puck You* to look for Ronald. He hated to admit he was actually getting sick of beer. He ordered an appetizer and a coke from the bartender, who now had no recollection of him. After almost an hour, Dusty knew Ronald must have the later afternoon shift. Thinking he was in the clear, he asked the bartender about him.

"Ronald doesn't come in till later today, huh?"

"He's on at four today. Can I help you with something?"

"I was supposed to get something from him. Must have gotten the days mixed up. I'll swing by his place. He still over on Grant?"

"Not unless he moved. He's on Roosevelt, I'm pretty sure. Had that yellow Victorian in a need of a paint job."

"Shit," Dusty laughed. "All these damn president streets around here. I'm sure I would have ended up in the right place. Just got the street name wrong. That sounds like the house."

The bartender leaned on the bar in front of Dusty. "Look. If you're trying to score weed, I have a buddy with a lot better shit than he's got."

"Weed?" Dusty sat upright then quickly tried to cover his shock. "No. It's not that at all."

"Owes you money for the horses, doesn't he? Aren't you a little young to be a bookie?"

Dusty wasn't sure whether to look upset or not. He opted for a forced chuckle. "I'm not after him for anything. He's an old friend." Dusty reached for his wallet and paid his tab. "Thanks."

"Any time."

As Dusty left the bar, he was again amazed at the willingness of a stranger to blurt out info like that. He could have been a cop for all the bartender knew. Dusty caught his reflection in the window. "Cop my ass." He decided to cruise down Roosevelt and look for Ronald's house. He knew it was a long street and had an East and West to it. From what Dusty learned about him, he aimed for the west section, since that was the poorer area. He found the house after two blocks.

Just to be sure, he drove down the whole length of the street. There was only one other Victorian and it was nicely painted in a neutral tone and trimmed in blues, oranges, and greens. He went back to the yellow Victorian and paid more attention to details. There was an old red Ford F-250 in the driveway. Dusty was sure he saw it in the parking lot behind the bar one of the times he was there.

He still didn't have a game plan, especially one that involved approaching Ronald in his own home. Feeling a little worthless right now, he continued to cruise past, hoping Frank didn't show up any time soon and get on his case. He decided to go home and call Alyson. He needed a little female advice.

"Hey, bro," Alyson answered. "What are you calling for out of the blue?"

"Is this a good time?" Again he was relieved she was around. He couldn't handle knowing a time when she wasn't. He was grateful he didn't have any memories of living through her accident and death.

"Hell, yeah. I'm at Mom's. We're snowed in."

"You guys are in a storm?"

"Didn't you hear about the fifty car pile-up?"

"You're shitting me."

"Nope. Glad I didn't try to go out today. I would have probably been in it. You guys don't have anything?"

"Nope. I don't think we're due anything for a couple of weeks."

"Shitty. I should move back."

"You say that every winter."

"Well, I'm still planning on opening a business there when I'm done with school. What's up? You didn't call to talk weather."

"Can't I just want to tell you how much I love you?"

"I love you, too, but nice try. Your dad up your ass again?"

"No. Things are fine with him," *for now*, Dusty thought to himself. "I have a question about a woman's perspective."

"Fire away."

"Say you're married—"

"I'm married."

"No. Suppose you were married—"

"Is he good looking and rich?"

"Alyson!"

"Okay. I'm sorry. Fire away."

"If you found out your husband was sleeping around, how would you take it?"

"Easy," she said with no hesitation. "I'd leave him."

"But you have a small child."

"Can I have twins?"

"Stop it!"

She laughed again. "Sorry. I'm getting cabin fever and I have the willies. I'd leave, Dusty. I don't care if I'd be on my own with a kid. I don't tolerate that crap. He'd probably not be much of a father, anyway. Remember Bobbie Schelten? I caught wind of him cheating and—"

"Can we focus on me again?"

"Sorry. You screwing around with a married woman?"

"Hell, no. I know a guy."

"Oh. The old 'I know a guy.' Dammit, Dusty. What are you in the middle of?"

"I swear! It's not me. I actually know one of the girls he's messing with. I found out he's married and there are a few others he messing with, too."

"And he has a kid? Asshole. You still have that .22?"

"Yeah."

"So, shoot the bastard."

"There's a helpful thought."

"Have you told your friend?" she asked.

"Not yet. I'm afraid she'll get pissed off at me."

"I don't see why. You're trying to help her. I'd want to know."

"What about the wife?"

"If it were me, I'd find a way to tell her."

"Do you think she'd clobber the messenger?"

"Hard to say. I'd want to know, though. Find a way to do it. You have a girl you can take with you and maybe soften the blow?"

"Maybe."

"Maybe? Do tell."

"I think I've met 'the one,' oh dear sister of mine."

"Puh-lease, Dusty. You're barely twenty-one."

"I mean it." Dusty remembered about the hugging incident. He knew that was going to happen soon. "Hey, you're coming down in a couple of weeks, right?"

"Did I tell you that? I made the plans a couple days ago."

"I…uh…thought so. Maybe I dreamt it. Anyway, I'll have you meet her then."

"Sounds good. Good luck with your friend."

"Thanks. I need it."

After Dusty hung up with Alyson, he called Freeman. He knew he was going to give him the car, there was no point in making the kid wait for it. This would also be the perfect time to talk to him about Stacey. If he could get the ball rolling, maybe he wouldn't have to deal with any of her episodes of showing up and wanting him to take her back. He couldn't remember exactly how long she was out of the picture before he met Katie. This could have been the last he had to see of her, anyway. Dusty almost felt bad for sending her to Freeman, but his friend could have a few months of great sex before she turned on him. Even if he threw in that she was a little crazy, after he said "great sex" Freeman was bound to go deaf to anything else.

After the quick exchange of the car and title was done, Dusty got ready for his date. The night panned out pretty much as it had the last time the four of them went out. Dean ordered in French and made Dusty play the piano. This time though, they covered more school topics since neither of them knew anything about each other. Courtney also talked about her internship offer in Seattle. She hadn't brought that up last time. Dusty didn't remember hearing about that until months after Katie moved in. He thought her decision to go there had something to do with losing Katie as a roommate. He was glad now for this insight. It was one less guilt he could carry around.

Courtney didn't have the excuse of class the next morning so she stalled considerably less before inviting Dean into her room. Less meaning she pulled him after her from the car, not giving Katie a chance to protest going with him to his place.

"Well," Katie said with a sigh. "That's just dandy. I don't know why I didn't see it coming. I guess we get to kill some time."

"We'll go back to my cottage. I don't have a roommate and I promise to behave."

"You have any good movies?"

"Good *guy* movies. If you don't want stuff blowing up, I'll swing into the video store."

"I'm not picky."

Having a few selections in mind he said, "I'll stop anyway."

They wandered through the video store and Dusty was elated when Katie picked up *Somewhere in Time* then put it back. He really wasn't in the mood to watch it again. She picked up *Timeline* though, which threw him for a loop. He decided to play it safe. "If you're a Paul Walker fan, I do have the *Fast and the Furious* movies."

She smiled and said, "Maybe after this and after I have my way with you."

"Pardon?"

"Did I say that out loud?" She grinned and pulled him to her by his shirt. She gave him a quick kiss. "I don't know what it is about you, but I'm afraid you bring out the devil in me, Andrews."

Unfortunately for Dusty, he was preoccupied with the DVD player while Katie poured her coffee and added the creamer. He wouldn't get the chance to make her toes tingle tonight. *Damn fate*. Once again she slept on his chest after throwing up, while he watched a movie alone.

Katie was a little more reserved the next morning, but he was able to coax her again after a brief shower. Dusty thought he could get used to winning Katie over throughout eternity. Each trip was a challenge and he thoroughly enjoyed it. He felt indestructible; knew he could win Katie over again and again no matter what that old coot, Frank, threw at him. He'd love to continue this game, but he missed the kids. He wanted to get back to his normal life.

After he and Katie ate breakfast, he decided to jump right into talking about Courtney. He wasn't going to waste any time like his last trek. There was no way he wanted to live through seeing his wife's heart break like that again.

"I know yesterday was the first time I saw you, but I know I've seen Courtney around before."

"Really? Where?"

"I don't remember exactly, but she was with a guy I know. He's bad news."

"Who?"

"Ronald Perkins. He works at a sports bar. I know for a fact he's married and has a kid. Courtney isn't the only chick he's doing on the side either. Sorry to be so crude."

"Are you serious?"

"I wouldn't make this up, Katie. I really like Courtney and I think Dean really does, too. I don't want to see her involved with someone like him."

"Honestly, I don't think she'll be too heartbroken over it. I think it was just a sex thing. I'm surprised you saw them together. I don't know that they've been on a formal date. They pretty much just…y'know. Don't get me wrong. I don't want to paint a bad picture of her. She doesn't make a lot of time to date, but still says she needs…y'know."

Dusty wrapped his arms around her. “Yeah. I know.” After a long kiss he tried to get back into the conversation. “Well… maybe Dean can help her out there and she can stop seeing him.”

“Again, I don’t want to paint a bad picture here, but she’s not really looking to settle down. I hope Dean isn’t getting his hopes up. I’d feel horrible if he gets hurt.”

“Don’t worry about him. He’s a good guy, but our workload is pretty rough, too. I’ve never seen him get ga-ga over someone. I’m sure he’ll be happy to take it slow.”

“So we agree then?”

“Absolutely. Dean will be shopping for wedding invitations in a week.” They shared a laugh. “Seriously, though. Do you think you should tell her about the guy’s wife?”

Katie took some time to ponder her response. Dusty didn’t expect that. “I’m really not sure how to handle this.”

“Huh?”

“My, my, you’re articulate for a lawyer.”

“Law school student. Not lawyer.”

“Still. Don’t get me wrong, I’m furious at this guy. I want him nowhere near her again, but I don’t know what she’d do if she found out about it.”

“You don’t think she’d get pissed and dump him?”

“She’s a tough one to read. She’ll get mad all right, but what she’ll do scares me.”

“How so?”

“She could take a bat to the guy’s vehicle, not to mention his head, or it could totally go the other way. She could decide the wife is probably cheating, too, or treating the guy like crap and think he deserves the sex.”

This really threw him for a loop. “Seriously?”

“She’s going to be a doctor, Dusty. Healing the world is what she wants to do. I really don’t know how into the guy she is. Maybe he’s given her this sob story of ‘my bridezilla’ and she's into it for the sympathy. If that's the case, she'll get pissed off that I found out."

"Holy crap."

"What?"

"You should be a trial lawyer, not a vet."

She laughed. "My favorite animals are those that are monogamous."

"I've heard orcas are."

"No doubt you got that from a movie."

"I guess I did."

"Well, that was false. Lots of other animals are, though. Beavers, bald eagles, even some voles."

"You're learning this in Veterinary Love School?"

"No, goofball. I've been fascinated with animals my whole life. I've always wanted to know everything that I could. That was one thing I found endearing. Animals that stay, for the most part, with one mate. Don't take my reaction the wrong way. Of course this makes me angry, Dusty. I feel sorry for the woman and by no means want Court anywhere near him, but if I've learned anything in my years with her, I have to let her do what she wants. I can't have her upset at me."

"But you guys seem so close. How could she get mad at you for looking out for her?"

Katie shrugged. "I'm a mother hen with her and she hates it. She's defied me before just to prove she could do what I said she shouldn't. She ended up with a broken arm once, pulling a stunt I begged her not to do." She caressed his chest. "I love that you care so much, but I have to let her ride this out. That being said, if you tell Dean and the two of you decide to go beat the shit out of this man and tell his wife, I promise to play stupid."

Dusty silently sighed in relief. He was worried he was seeing a side of Katie he never had before. She was Courtney's mother hen the whole time he knew her. He was more than shocked at her responses, but was glad she made a comeback at the end.

"We'll give them a few days. Maybe she won't be interested in him anymore and be into Dean and this whole conversation will have been for nothing."

That would be great, but Dusty knew he didn't have a few days. Especially not if Frank had anything to say about it.

Katie and Dusty spent a lazy Saturday together again. It never got old for Dusty to lounge around with Katie. Lately so much of their days were spent chasing the kids around—this was nice. He felt guilty for enjoying her all to himself. He'd almost forgotten what spontaneous couch sex was like. Just thinking about the kids not being around made him miss them again. He saw Ali in Katie's eyes and longed for his children. Again he hoped this would be over soon.

As much as he wanted to spend the rest of night like this, he thought he should go do something about Ronald. He finally thought of a way to justify to Katie that he had to do something. He sat her up and handed her a shirt to cover herself.

"What's wrong?" she asked.

"I've been thinking about our talk and I don't think I can live with doing nothing."

"I understand how you feel about Dean and not wanting to hurt him, Dusty, but I don't think I can get involved with this. I'm sorry if that makes me sound horrible."

"It doesn't. I understand your reasons, but I think I need to go talk to his wife."

"Why do you have to get involved?"

"It hits me at a personal level, I guess. Before I was born, my dad had an affair. I found out when I was eight that I have a sister as a result of it."

"I'm sorry. Was that really hard on you?"

"Actually, she was already my best friend so it only made us closer. I want you to meet her in a few weeks."

"You already want to subject your family to me?"

"More like the other way around, and yes. I'll give you a couple of weeks, though, before I'll have you meet my parents. They don't live too far away. Anyway, Mom never let on that she knew, but it came out years later that she knew all along."

"But she stayed with your dad anyway?"

"She said she loved him and had to work through it for herself. And before you ask, Mom came from money so staying with him for stability wasn't even an issue. I was surprised how I felt when I found out that she knew. I'd wanted to tell her for years, but didn't know how to do it. I was so afraid to hurt her as well as afraid she would leave Dad."

"So you wouldn't do it for your own family, but you'll mess up a total stranger's life?"

"At least I knew Dad never did it again. This guy keeps doing it. What if he bangs the wrong girl someday and brings a nice STD home to his wife, or AIDS even? You want the guilt of that child growing up an orphan on your conscience?"

"Boy, you sure are focusing on the big picture here."

"I can't help it. Guys that treat women like this bother me. What if something happened to your best friend? Could you live with that?"

Her hand rested on his cheek as she started intently into his eyes. "You really are serious about this, aren't you?"

"Very. But I understand if you don't want to come along."

"Come along? Where? What are you planning, Dusty?"

"I know for a fact that the dude is working right now."

"How do you know that?"

"I hang out at the bar where he works."

"And you're going to go talk to him?"

"No. I want to go talk to his wife. I want you to come with me."

"You have the dandiest ideas for a second date, pal."

"I'll take you out for a burger afterward. All this sex has me craving rare meat."

She laughed then gave him a gentle kiss. "If you insist, I'll go with you. Maybe a woman being there will help soften the blow."

"That's what I was thinking."

"I still don't like it."

"I know. I'm sorry, but I really feel I need to do this."

"I suppose I'll admire you for this someday."

"You'll reward me, too. I'm sure of it." He gave her a quick kiss before he stood. "Shower before we go?"

"You mean sex."

"Only if you insist."

She stood and joined him. "Let's get this out of the way first. I'll stay here again tonight, if you don't mind another sleepover."

He pulled her close and growled playfully. "Are you kidding? I'd ask you to move in if I thought you would." She leaned back and stared hard into his eyes. "Does that scare you?"

"A little. We've known each other less than twenty four hours."

"A guy just knows these things. No worries. I'll wait until you come around." He kissed her cheek then turned to walk away. Katie squealed. "What?"

"You have the cutest birthmark!"

"Ha! Caught you looking at my ass."

Chapter Nineteen

Dusty drove to Ronald's house, Katie sitting as close to him as she could. Remembering how much he loved driving around with her, he made a mental note to do it again soon when he got back to their normal timeframe. He gave the back of her hand a kiss.

"Let me guess," Katie said. "You asked around until you found out where he lives. You really are on a mission."

"Getting his address wasn't tough. Turns out this winner sells weed."

"Crap."

"What?"

"That's why Court is smoking again. She hadn't done it for a long time. It's a shame Dean smokes; they'll never knock it off." That part of the night had played out as before. Dusty never ceased to be amazed at the things that were determined to repeat themselves.

"He's not that bad, though. But you're right, it would be nice if one of them didn't and tried to get the other to quit. It surprises me with her studying to be a doctor."

"Oh, trust me. I've heard every medicinal use excuse there is. She actually claims to need it sometimes after a bad day and getting brain fry. I shut up long ago."

Dusty had no more comments on the subject, having had the same arguments with Dean. He gave her hand a squeeze. "Are you ready?"

"I guess so."

They climbed the poorly shoveled stairs and let themselves in the door to the all-season porch. Things were a complete mess. Boxes were thrown everywhere, toys were scattered in with broken furniture. Katie scrunched up her nose. "I smell tomcat."

"I don't even need a vet degree for that one." He took her hand in one of his and knocked with the other.

After a minute, a woman answered the door with a toddler on her hip. "Can I help you?"

"Are you Gina? I mean, Mrs. Perkins?" Dusty asked.

"Depends. Are you a bill collector?"

"No. I'm not. I'm sorry for the intrusion. I needed to speak to you about your husband."

"He get hurt?" There wasn't a lot of concern behind her voice.

"No, ma'am. I'm sorry. This is difficult, but I felt I had to speak with you."

Her eyes went from his to Katie and back again. "He get this whore pregnant or something?"

"Excuse me?" Katie said, releasing Dusty's hand and placing it on her hip.

"I assure you, Ms. Barrow is not involved with your husband. I take it by your reaction, though, that you are aware of his…extracurricular activities."

"Is that what this is about? What are you? A boy scout? I know that two-bit loser sleeps around."

"Um. Sorry if I'm out of line here, but don't you want to put your daughter somewhere so we can talk?"

"She knows her daddy is worthless."

Disgusted, Katie started to turn around, but Dusty caught her by the hand. "Well, then, I guess we'd better leave you to your evening." He wrapped an arm around Katie and they hurried back to the car. Dusty started it up but before he could pull forward, he saw Gina standing by his window. She had a light jacket wrapped around her shoulders. He rolled the window down and waited for her to speak.

"I'm sorry."

"No. I'm sorry to be butting in where I'm obviously not needed."

"I found out he was sleeping around long ago. Not a whole lot I can do about it. My parents kicked me out when they found out I was pregnant. I have nowhere else to go."

"There's lots of help out there for single mothers."

"He'd kill me if I left him."

"Gina…Does he beat you?"

She looked away, giving Dusty his answer. After a minute she spoke again. "Not a lot and not bad. Just mostly when he's drinkin'."

"Which is a lot of the time," Dusty said as if he knew the answer. She couldn't return her attention to him. "I know some people. I'll find you some help."

"Why do you care what happens to me?"

"Because he's involved with a friend and he could end up hurting her someday, too. What he's doing—all the different partners—it isn't safe."

"I know. We only…when he…" she bit her bottom lip.

Dusty held his hand up. "You don't need to tell me. I'll be back. I'm going to help you. You have my word on that."

Gina addressed Katie. "I'm especially sorry for what I said to you. You look like a really nice lady."

"That's okay. You seem to have more than your share of reasons."

"It's just…this isn't the first time one of his whores have come looking for him. Not that you're…"

Dusty could see Katie fighting tears. Gina had placed her hand on the door. Dusty placed his hand on hers. "We'll be back soon."

"I appreciate the sentiment, but I won't be holding my breath." She walked away, brushing tears from her cheek.

As Dusty pulled away, Katie went into a tirade. "That fucking asshole! She barely looked eighteen! He beats her and probably rapes her? Go to the police station, Dusty. This Ronald is going down."

"Hold on. We can't go in there and make accusations. She's so afraid of him, she'll deny every one of them and that will only get her in more trouble with him later."

"Then what now? You get me involved in this and then you tell me I can't do anything?"

"I didn't say that. We need to figure out what to do."

"Can't we get her to a women's shelter?"

"She already said she's afraid of him finding her."

"Then what?"

"Can I break our deal?" he asked.

"What deal?"

"I want to involve my mother. If you're going to ride this out with me, you'll have to meet them sooner than I planned."

"Is it really that bad?"

"Mom and May are great. Dad and I don't always see eye to eye."

"Who's May?"

"The housekeeper."

"You have a housekeeper?"

"Um, yeah. Sorry. My family is kinda loaded. I was going to get around to that later, too."

"The BMW kind of gave you away, law-boy. Sorry to burst your bubble."

"So, will you only love me for my money now?"

Her eyebrows raised as if he was crazy. "I never said I loved you."

"Yet," he said with a grin.

"You're certifiable."

"Crazy for you, cupcake."

"Oh geez."

"Don't worry. It'll grow on you, sweetness."

Dusty called his mother, but she was out of town until tomorrow afternoon. He and Katie made a plan to drive out and talk to her then. He didn't want to give her any details over the phone. She was about to give a lecture at what he called her "Estrogen Fests"; he didn't want anything else on her mind. Not having a better plan at the moment, they decided to go out for the burger they discussed earlier.

After Dusty paid the check, someone by the bar shouted. "Katie? What the hell?"

Katie mumbled, "Crap."

Dusty said, "Oh shit," under his breath as Rex rushed over to their table.

"We had a date. Thanks for calling me."

"I'm so sorry, Rex. We got busy. I completely forgot."

"Who's this clown?"

"This is my friend, Dustin. We had an errand today, trying to help a girl."

"Help a girl, huh? By the looks of you, I'd say you just crawled off the couch with this asshole."

"Hey. Knock that shit off. Don't talk to her like that," Dusty said. He stood and gave Rex a shove.

"Make me," he said, shoving back.

Dusty knew how this was likely to end, but he had to play somewhat dumb. "Is this your boyfriend, Katie? I'm sorry if I created a problem."

"Boyfriend? She ain't spreading them for me if that's what you mean. Congratulations, asshole."

"That's it!" Dusty shouted, shoving Rex again. "Outside!"

"Why wait?"

Rex punched Dusty again, but this time it landed on his cheek. The force of it sent Dusty back a few steps, but he wasn't knocked out. Other patrons were there to break it up quickly. Katie continued to voice her anger at Rex and pound at his chest, while strange men held him back.

Dusty took Katie by the arm and led her out of the bar. When they were outside, she stopped him. "I'm so sorry, Dusty. He's never been so angry like that. We've only had a few dates and he was always so sweet." She touched the small cut and he winced. "I want to take you to see Court."

"I'll be fine."

"I want her to look at it, Dusty."

"What if she and Dean are busy…y'know," he said as he made a cup out of one hand and poked his index finger in and out of it.

Katie laughed at him. "I'll call her first."

"You want to tell her about Ronald right away, don't you?"

"Yes, I do."

"I appreciate your restraint in at least getting through the meal before bolting over there."

"You're the one that wanted me to do it."

"I know. I'm glad, really. We'll do it together."

Dusty and Katie showed up at Dean's. He and Courtney were doing pretty much what the two of them would be doing later. Movies and sex. They happened to catch them on a break; Courtney was happy to look at his cut.

"Hell of a shiner," she said as she examined it. "I didn't think Rex had it in him."

"I don't know why he flipped out so bad," Katie said.

"'Cause you have 'fucking hair,' hon. Mother Teresa would think you just had sex, seeing you from a mile away."

Self-consciously, Katie ran her fingers through her hair. Courtney laughed at her. "You know that guy has been wanting in your pants."

"I wasn't ready," she said, putting her hands on her hips. Dusty fought his grin. She always did look cute when she got pissed.

"So. Do tell. What does wonder-boy bring to the table that Rex didn't?"

"Courtney!"

The men laughed at Courtney's boldness.

She gave a final glance at the butterfly bandage she put on Dusty and stood up straight. "You'll live."

"Thanks. I owe you a big favor, but I'm afraid all I have is some bad news instead."

"What bad news?"

"Dusty, let me," Katie said, stepping forward.

"Be my guest." He made a sweeping motion with his hand, as if giving her the floor to speak. He went over and sat with Dean on the couch.

"There's no easy way to say this." She motioned her head in Dean's direction. "Should we really do this in front of him?"

"Dean's a big boy. I'll only tell him later anyway."

Katie rolled her eyes. "Jackass."

"See. I knew you'd start using pet names soon, too, pumpkin."

She ignored him and returned her attention to her best friend. "Ronald is married."

"He is?"

"Yes. His wife is barely old enough to drive, she has a small child, and we're sure he's abusive."

"What? How do you know this?"

"We talked to her today."

"You talked to her? How did you find out?"

"Dusty knew the guy. He did some background checking on him. He'd seen you with him and knew the guy was bad news. We did it for you, Court. Don't be mad. You're not the only one he's sleeping with and that came straight from his mouth. He's a man whore. He has no decency and deserves to be shot."

"So let's go shoot him," Courtney said with a shrug.

"Really? That's it?"

"What did you want from me? I love him? I don't care what he's done? He has a dick the size of King Kong and you gotta take the bad with the good?"

"I…I guess I didn't know how you'd take it."

"I'll go to his work right now and send his nuts into next Tuesday and tell him to stay away from me."

Dusty stood. "As much as I'd like to see that, I want his wife to be free and clear of him first. He has an angry streak in him and I don't want her catching the brunt of it. This will have to wait a day or two until we get this sorted out."

"What's with you taking this on, Dusty?" Courtney asked as she walked over to him.

"You're important to Katie, so you're important to me."

"Really?"

"Of course." He shrugged as if it were no big deal. "My mom has always done charity work for single mothers and such. It got ingrained in my head. It will be right up her alley to hop in and help this girl."

"And what about Ronald?"

"I imagine after she's gone, it'll only make things easier on him. He can bring chicks back to his place now," Dean said.

"That's not good enough," Dusty replied. His thought went to Courtney getting the disease again. She might be saved now, but there would be other girls. This wasn't over.

"What are you thinking?" Katie asked.

"I'm not sure. We'll take this one step at a time." He turned to Courtney. "If he calls you, please blow him off. Don't say anything about this. Just make an excuse to not see him, okay?"

"Make up your mind, Dusty. You want me to blow him off or not see him?"

He dropped his head to his chest with a chuckle. He forgot how he had to watch his mouth around Courtney. Everything he said, she could and would turn into a dirty phrase when given the chance.

Dean reached for her and pulled her on his lap. She squealed as he did so. Dusty took that as their cue to leave. "Thanks for looking at my cheek."

"You two stay out of trouble. You hear?" Courtney scolded.

"We'll try." Dusty counted out the score so far. One chin shot, one eye, and one cheek. He was pretty well rounded. He hoped this was over. Maybe he ought to take a boxing lesson or two when this was all said and done.

Katie and Dusty were once again in a tangled mess of sheets, pillows, and comforter a while later. Katie was lying on top of Dusty and rested her chin in her hands. "Why am I so comfortable with you?"

"My relentless charm and good looks?" She kissed over to one of his nipples then gave it a playful bite. "Ouch!" he half laughed, half screamed. He rubbed it for a second then flipped her to her back as she squealed. "Foul, missy."

"I was serious, Dusty. I've pretty much pushed everyone away most of my life. I had a lot of boyfriends, but nothing I let get very serious. I've certainly never gone to bed with someone so soon before."

"You were just saving yourself for me."

"You're awfully sure of yourself."

"I knew we were meant to be when I saw you. The fact that Courtney and Dean get along so well is a bonus."

"You really seem intent on keeping an eye on her."

He grinned. “Jealous?”

“No. It just seems like there is something more I should know about this.”

“There is nothing else you need to know, sweet cheeks. I hate any guy that treats a girl like that. I don’t know if I could look the other way, even if Courtney wasn’t involved. Like I said to her, I guess it was my mom rubbing off on me. She dragged me to enough black tie fundraising events; that stuff starts to sink in.”

“I suppose.”

“You’re just as kind-hearted. You can’t tell me when you’re a successful vet that you won’t volunteer your time at a local animal hospital and do spay and neuter clinics.”

Her eyes went wide. “I always planned on doing that. How would you know that?”

“I told you. I can tell.” He gave her a gentle kiss that turned into something that lasted much longer. Their tongues intertwined and low growls escaped their throats. The lovemaking began again with Dusty still only feeling a little guilty for cheating on his wife with herself.

Chapter Twenty

Katie shook Dusty out of a sound sleep. "Dusty, wake up." He sat up quickly. "What's the matter?"

"It's time."

"Time?" He was confused. It was pitch black. He was waking up enough to realize he wasn't *when* he just was. *Which Katie was this?* A realization hit him as she placed his hand on her large, pregnant stomach.

"It's time to go. I've been lying here watching the clock. They're coming every seven minutes."

"Shit! Seven minutes, Katie? Why didn't you wake me sooner?" If there was one thing Dusty didn't want to live again, it was this.

"They were kind of wonky for a while. They were twelve, then six, then fifteen. I didn't think it was happening."

He threw the sheets off and hit the floor, running to the dresser. Maybe if he moved faster this time, they'd make it to the hospital. She let out a loud moan, and he rushed to her side. "You okay?"

"That one friggin' hurt!"

"Come on, babe. Let's get you going." She cried out again as he stood her up. "Jesus, Katie. I don't know. Let me call an ambulance if you're that bad."

"No. I'm fine. What if it's a false labor? I'm not going through the embarrassment. I'm not due for another nine days."

"This has to be it with the way they're hitting you. Let me call."

"No! Please, Dusty." She placed her hand on his face. "I want you to take me. I'm fine."

"Okay. But will you please put a comfy maternity dress on this time?"

"This time? I like my jeans. They're comfy and it has to be ten degrees outside."

She let go of him and walked to the closet to pull her jeans on. He sighed and pulled a sweatshirt off his closet shelf. "I'm going to pull the car up. I'll come back up and get you. I don't want you taking the stairs on your own."

"Yes, Daddy."

When Dusty ran back up the stairs, she was waiting for him with her overnight bag. He took the bag then her arm and slowly walked down the stairs with her. A strong contraction hit as they were halfway down. Her nails dug into his arms as she let out a scream. *Crap!* It's happening just as it did before.

"Babe. Please. Let me call an ambulance."

"No, Dusty." Tears began to stream from her face. He never could stand to see her cry. "Please, no. First babies take forever. I'm just some kind of weakling that can't take the pain. What kind of mother will I be? What was I thinking? Maybe we shouldn't do this."

He couldn't hold back his laugh. "It's a little late for that, sweetness. This kid is coming out. He or she is excited to meet their beautiful mama."

She sat down. "I can't do this."

"Babe, please. We don't have time to mess around here."

"Oh, so you sit with me for some Lamaze classes and now you're a professional on childbirth?"

"Come on, Mommy. You can call me every name in the book, but I'd like to get going."

"Kiss me." He gave her a quick kiss and tried to stand her up. "No. Kiss me right."

"Baby, come on."

"Not until you kiss me. If I ever needed to get lost in you, Dusty, it's right now. Please kiss me."

He didn't want to stall, but he knew there was no changing their history. He sat next to her on the stair and brought her to him, both hands holding her face. His gentle kiss quickly turned into one of entwined tongues that made him forget for a second what was going on.

When they finally broke apart she said, "You know, Dusty. If we have sex, maybe the kid will want to stay put for a while."

"Nice try, cupcake. Let's go." He helped her to her feet and made it out the door and in the car without any more incidents.

"Are we in a storm watch?" she asked.

"I haven't heard anything other than we're getting eight to ten inches." He grinned at her. "Of snow between now and noon."

"I'm about to pass a watermelon from my crotch and you're making sex jokes?"

"You just…never mind." He gave her hand a squeeze. "Sorry, babe."

She shook his hand free. "Both hands on the wheel, Dusty. This shit looks nasty."

Oh, how he loved these hormone swings. *Not.* After they drove for a while, he realized the radio was off. What they both needed was a good distraction. "I'll see what we can get on the radio for an update." After a few channels, he caught one that said the winds were picking up and they were indeed in a weather advisory and unnecessary travel was discouraged. "I think we qualify as necessary travel. At least the plows have been out. The roads are fine." Katie hadn't said anything for a while. "Babe? You okay?"

She had both hands on the sides of her stomach and was panting in quick breaths. "Bad one?"

After a few more breaths she said, "They're all bad." She then let out a scream that made Dusty hit the brakes. The road was slick enough to send them sliding a little.

"Shit! What was that?"

"This kid isn't waiting!" She screamed and threw herself back. She grunted hard through more breaths and reclined the seat back. "Oh God, Dusty. Do something! Make it stop!"

He flung his car door open and tried to stand. A curse escaped him after he got hung up on the seatbelt. *You think I'd remember it this time!* He ran around the front of the car. His feet slipped on the icy road but he caught himself on the hood before he fell.

"Dusty! Where are you?" Katie screamed.

He reached the door and flung it open. He saw her scrunch up and squint her eyes shut. She looked like she was bearing down. It was then that he remembered the jeans. Quickly leaning in, he grabbed hold of them and pulled them down to her knees. A scream came out of her that ripped him in two. He placed his hands down just in time to play the first game of catch with his daughter. Only her head was out and she wasn't crying. Even though he had been through this before, he was scared at the silent infant. Katie's water never even broke, but it wasn't something he realized the first time. He had remembered an old Rescue 911 about a couple having a baby at home and it wasn't crying either. The guy said, "I wanted my son to cry, so I knew I needed to make him mad."

Dusty wanted to do the same. He'd taken his finger to the baby's lips and flicked at them. A hangnail caught the water sack and broke it. He did the same again. Another scream escaped Katie as the rest of the baby's body came rushing out.

He always remembered the way Katie sat up after that like nothing had happened. She reached for the baby and held her close. "Just what was your hurry, little one?" Dusty opened up the back door and removed Katie's robe from her overnight bag. He came back beside her and quickly wrapped up the baby. "We gotta hit the road, babe."

She couldn't take her gaze away from the baby. "Umm hmm."

Dusty hurried, but drove carefully, to the hospital. They were only another five minutes away. The scenario played in his head a few times over the years; he always wondered if he could have gotten there sooner by another route. The answer was no. He tried this time; they had only gotten a few blocks closer. Although he knew it would be a girl, in the past they hadn't known until the doctor asked once they got there. In Dusty's haste to get her covered and warm, they hadn't even looked. He didn't want to give it away and spoil the surprise for Katie.

Everything from here on out played like a movie for him. They insisted Dusty cut the cord and finish the job. They filled out the birth certificate with a "guesstimate" of time of birth and wrote "Daddy en route" as delivering physician.

"I want to name her Alyson, Dusty," Katie said as she held the baby, still unable to take her eyes off her.

"I'd like that a lot. So will Alyson."

Katie's head dropped to her pillow and her eyes finally closed. "I'm so tired."

"Can't blame you for that." Dusty turned off the light and crawled in bed with her, wrapping his arms for the first time,again, around both his girls. "If I live to be a hundred, I don't ever want to hear you scream like that again."

He pulled her close and gave a strong kiss to the back of her head.

He almost fell asleep but opened his eyes at a strange feeling. Startled by a body by the window, he tried to focus in the dark room and make out the silhouette. He swore it was Frank but after he blinked, the figure was gone. Dusty wrote it off as fatigue. The birth wasn't any easier the second time around. He fell sound asleep in seconds.

Dusty awoke the next morning with his arm around Katie. They were no longer in the hospital room. He was back to where he'd left the night before. He again wanted to flip off someone who wasn't there, but didn't want to wake up Katie by screaming an obscenity.

After they were awake and dressed, he gave Katie a chance to back out of going to his parents' house, but she seemed just as determined as he was to help Ronald's wife and child.

The look on Katie's face every time they pulled up to his house never ceased to amaze him. "I told you it was a little big, babycakes."

"Like the Sears Tower is a little tall. I wish I'd dressed better."

"Don't be silly. You look fine. My parents are old money, but I would never rate them up there as snobby."

"It feels funny having only had two dates with you and I'm meeting them already."

"You don't have good 'meeting the parents' experiences?"

"No experiences at all, really. The only parents I met were of kids that I'd dated in high school and that's because I usually already knew them."

Dusty pulled into the garage then turned to her. "You'll be fine. Sit tight. I'll get your door." He hurried around and opened up the passenger door and offered her his hand.

Accepting it and standing up, she stared into his eyes. "What?" he asked.

"I don't know that anyone has ever done that for me before."

"Well, if there wasn't valet, I'd've done it at the restaurant."

"You may be too good for me, Mr. Andrews."

"Bullshit," he said, followed with a kiss.

"Is that the new age way to show your affection?" A woman's voice interrupted their kiss.

Dusty wrapped an arm around Katie and walked over to his mother.

"I forget about those 'hawk-ears' of yours."

"I was in the kitchen with May and I saw the car go by. Hello," she said as she extended her hand to Katie. "I'll claim the rotten child. I'm Norma."

"Pleased to meet you. I'm Katie."

Norma gave Dusty a kiss on the cheek. "Thanks for not bringing that horrible contraption and upsetting your father."

"I gave it away to a kid that really needed it." Dusty hoped admitting this now wouldn't affect his turning in the Beemer and getting both him and Katie a car in a few weeks.

"Good for you. Come inside, you two."

They walked to the kitchen where May was busy cooking. She greeted them both with warm hellos. "Dustin Charles. You don't bring girls home." She placed her hand on his forehead. "You feeling okay?"

He playfully smacked her hand away. "No one was worthy until now." Dusty turned to Katie and saw her blush. "Do I smell cooking what I think that is?"

"Of course. You knew I was going to make roast beast when I heard you were coming home."

Katie giggled. "Roast beast?"

"You never grow out of some sayings that the kids had," May admitted.

"You've been with them a long time?"

"Since before he and his sister were born."

"I don't think I told you I have an older sister, Dana," Dusty said. He was sure he only mentioned Alyson and didn't want Katie to slip and say her name.

"I don't think you have," Katie said, following along.

"How long have you two been dating?" Norma asked.

Katie turned to Dusty. He answered for her. "Not long, but we just clicked. You just know with some people, you know?"

Norma and May both exchanged a look and grinned. May spoke up. "All of you get out of my kitchen. Go in the sitting room. I'll be along in a second with some drinks and snacks."

They settled in what Dusty called "The White Room" when he was growing up. He was rarely allowed in it. "So what did you need to see me about, Dusty?"

"It's a very long story, but the Reader's Digest version is that I know of a young mother with a real piece of work for a husband. He's screwing half of Dinkytown and treats her like crap."

"And you're involved in this how?"

"I'm not really involved. I just see the guy come and go from a bar I've gone to a few times. I've seen him out back making out with someone, then he goes in and takes a call from his wife. When I saw Katie's roommate Courtney with him, I was a little fed up. Katie and I went to go visit her."

"And how did that go? Is that how you earned that butterfly band aid?"

"I was wondering how long it would be until you asked about that, but no."

"So you're stirring up trouble all over the place?"

"I didn't ask for this either. I didn't lay a hand on the guy. Can we get back to Gina?"

"Is that this young girl's name?"

"Yeah."

May walked in with teas and a tray of cheeses and crackers. "It's an orange tea that Dusty likes. If you don't like it, let me know," she said to Katie.

"Thanks. I'm sure it'll be fine."

"Oh, and May, nothing with cinnamon—ever. Okay?"

"Allergy, dear?"

"Dreadful," Katie replied.

"I'll remember that. Holler if you need anything else," she said to everyone as she walked out.

"So then," Norma started in again. "How did this Gina react to your news?"

"She already knew and was kind of upset at us for showing up." Dusty said.

"She already knew about his infidelities?"

"You could say that. It was after we walked away that she came back out to us. She all but said he was beating and raping her."

"She won't go to the police?"

"She's obviously scared to death of this Ronald."

"That could be a big problem removing her. They have to want to leave, Dusty."

"I know she'll go. We have to do it when he's not home and promise her she'll stay hidden."

"I know we have a room available at the shelter for her."

"Will he be able to find here there?" Katie asked.

"No one but the employees and women staying there know the address. You can't find it unless you're given the address by one of the residents. I won't feed you BS, kids. Women have been known to escape, just to go running back to the men they claim to be running from."

"Escape? It is like a prison?" Dusty asked.

"Not at all. We have lock in rules and such for their own safety. That and a lot of the women in there are drug users and try to get out and get a fix. We have zero tolerance for drug use. Usually if we can keep them safe and clean for a couple of weeks, they have a good chance of turning around.

There's a great number of women we've helped introduce back into the work force. Your father helps, too. His company has set up daycares in a few office buildings that cater to hiring these women."

Katie lit up, intrigued. "What kinds of jobs?"

"Everything, really. Of course, it's a lot of secretarial work, but there are sales positions and even on-the-job training offered for places like our law firms."

"Of course law firms," Dusty said, rolling his eyes.

"Even that end is a tough job, kiddo. So… What exactly do you want me to do?"

"How does it work? You go pick these girls up?"

"If she's willing to go, I can make the arrangements."

"Why wouldn't she?" Katie asked.

"Fear is the biggest factor. If she's been with him for a long time, she'll probably feel like that's all she deserves. She could have been abused as a child as well. It's a horrible cycle. If she won't go, we'd need a reason to believe the child is being abused before we can forcibly take him or her."

"She didn't mention that," Dusty said. "I didn't notice any marks on the kid. I think she would have said something since we were reaching out. I'm sure he's at work tomorrow at four for sure if not by ten. Can you go get her?"

Norma patted her son's leg. "Let me go make a call." She left the room.

Katie scooted closer to Dusty. "You really intrigue me, Dusty."

Again he shrugged. "It's just what's right."

"What if she won't go?"

"I think she will. She came after us, didn't she?"

"I hope so. For her and that baby's sake. You going to go over tomorrow with them?"

"I think I'll leave the professionals to their job. I just wanted to get the ball rolling."

She gave him a kiss. "I've never met anyone like you. You come from all of this, yet you are the most unselfish person I've ever met."

"Dana was spoiled enough for the two of us. I was just along for the ride. Speaking of ride." He stood when his dad walked into the room. "What happened to the Aston Martin?"

"You should know better than to ask that. Who's your friend?"

Dammit. His dad had never told him what happened to that damn car. "The love of my life, Katie." Dusty walked back to her. She was already standing and fidgeting nervously again.

His dad shook her hand and offered a pleasant, "Nice to meet you. You in law school, too?"

"Veterinary medicine actually."

"Nice match up. You may need a good lawyer in your field."

"I'm not sure there's animal malpractice."

"You'd be surprised." He walked over to the bar and poured himself a drink. "You want something stronger than May's tea, Katie?"

"No, thank you. This is fine."

"Son?"

"I really shouldn't. We have to drive back tonight, Dad. We came to talk to Mom about something. May's making a roast so we're staying for supper, but then we have to split."

"School all right?"

"Everything's fine." Dusty decided that conversation could wait a couple of weeks. He would have to keep an eye on that storm and be sure he and Katie came out again if he was still here. He wasn't going to miss that night of sex for anything.

Chapter Twenty-One

Dusty sat in *Puck You* the following day. It was four-twenty. He was worried Ronald wouldn't be in that day. Just as he got up to leave, Ronald hurried in, running his fingers through his hair and tucking in his shirt. The bartender immediately yelled at him for being late.

"You're not the boss," Ronald shouted as he flipped him off and continued to the back room.

Dusty walked outside and called his mother. "He's here. Go to the house."

"I think you're enjoying the cops and robbers aspect to this, Dusty," she said with a chuckle.

"I wouldn't want any of your people hurt. I've seen the dude in action. I hope you get her to go with you."

"I'll call you after we have her."

"Thanks, Mom."

As Dusty snapped his phone closed, he saw Katie walking over to him. "What are you doing here?"

"Are you kidding? I was dying to hear how it was going." She gave him a kiss that curled his toes. "I missed you last night."

"You're the one that insisted on going home."

"As much as I love your company, I still have to get to class, Dusty. We can't make a living having sex."

"We could forget the careers and try for porn stars."

"Quit it," she said with a laugh as she gently smacked the center of his chest.

"There's no news yet. He just got here. I called Mom and gave her the go-ahead."

"You don't think you should be there?"

"She'll know it was us. I think she'll leave with my mom. Trust me. I've dealt with that particular power of persuasion for years." He wrapped an arm around Katie and led them toward his car. He caught sight of someone in the alley and stopped to get a better look at her. Dusty thought maybe it was the girl he caught Ronald with in the alley before, but it wasn't. *Here's another one for the mix.* There was something about the way she stood there that made Dusty uncomfortable.

He took Katie by the shoulders and said, "Wait here a second."

Dusty approached the woman slowly. She didn't seem to know he was there. She stood against the wall with her eyes closed and a lit cigarette in her hand. Her coat hung open; today's weather didn't call for that. He saw scratches on her shoulder and noticed her hair was a mess. She wore black boots that went to her knees and a tight dress hiked a little too high. A scarf hung outside the wooden fence surrounding the dumpster. Dusty could only imagine what transpired in there. She and Ronald were in the same shape. Sex against a wall by a fenced in dumpster in thirty degrees in broad daylight. This took the cake.

"Are you okay?" Dusty asked as he got closer. Her eyes opened up a bit, but then she closed them right away. She was dressed like a street hooker or junkie. He'd never run into any of them around here, only driving through the shadier parts of Minneapolis on streets he knew better than to be on in the first place. "Miss?"

“Is she okay?” Katie asked as she approached him slowly, against his advice to stay put.

“She doesn’t look like it.”

Katie took a few steps closer to her. “Are you okay?”

She finally opened her eyes and took another drag of her cigarette. “I’ll be fine as soon as that jerk-off returns with the money he owes me.”

The woman slid to the ground, Katie rushed to her side. She tried looking into the girl’s eyes, but they had rolled up; there was nothing but white. “Shit, Dusty. Call 9-1-1.” She shrieked again, “Tell them to hurry!”

There was a lot of commotion outside of the bar while the girl was being loaded into the ambulance. Dusty saw Ronald watch what was going on and slink back inside after seeing who it was. There was almost smugness about his reaction. Again Dusty fought the urge to pound him into the pavement.

Dusty and Katie sat at the emergency room, waiting to hear the status of the girl they’d brought in. After several minutes of silence, Katie turned to Dusty. “Have you always been this much fun on a date?”

He stroked her hand. “I swear, finding a doped-up hooker is a new one for us.”

“What do you mean ‘for us?’”

“I mean a new one. I’m sorry. My mind is just in a blur. I swear these past few days are about as crazy as anything I’ve ever seen, babe.”

“Finally one I like,” she said as she gave him a soft kiss.

“Babe?”

“Yeah. You sure are odd with all those other names. I never met anyone that did that, either.” He smiled and gave her hand another squeeze. His mind was really racing as to what was going on. If this was the girl who had given Ronald the disease, was he too late? He had a feeling Courtney was okay, but what about Gina? Maybe this wasn't the first time he was with this girl. If he was such a ladies' man, why the hooker? His thoughts were interrupted by a nurse walking over to them.

"Are you the ones that brought that street girl in here?"

"We are," Dusty said, getting to his feet. "How is she?"

"We almost lost her."

"What happened?" He was worried Ronald had hurt her. "Was she beaten?"

"She had some scratches on her, but not bad ones. She had sex recently, there was no mistaking that. We're guessing things were a little rough, as girls in this profession often see."

"Why did she black out? Drugs?"

"We're waiting on the lab results to be certain, but according to the contents of her pockets, I don't think there is anything she wasn't currently on. You're not family, I really shouldn't be giving you any more information. Thanks for getting her to us, but you really should be going now." She turned to walk away but Dusty stopped her.

"Were there track marks from needles?" The nurse hesitated before she answered. "Yes."

"Will you run an AIDS test on her?"

"AIDS?" Katie cried, covering her mouth with her hand.

"Do you know a reason we need to? That really isn't standard procedure."

"We suspect someone she was with was also with a friend of ours. If there's a chance he's spreading it, yes, I think there is a good reason to test her. I'll see that the bill gets paid if there will be an issue. I need to know."

"I'll have to get a doctor to sign a consent, but I'll get it going."

"Rush it, please."

Katie began to shake. She sat back down, her hand still over her mouth. Dusty sat next to her and held her tight. “I’m sure Courtney isn’t stupid enough to go unprotected.”

“I’d like to think not. We have to tell her, Dusty.”

“We can wait for the results. There isn’t a reason to scare her just yet.”

Dusty’s phone rang. It was his mother. He walked over to the glass doors to take the call.

“We have her, Dusty. She’s tucked into her own room with her peanut. Cute little thing. Shy as heck, though. She’ll come around, I’m sure. They have great counselors on staff.”

“She give you a fight?”

“Not really. She seemed more scared that her husband would show up while we gathered her things. I said you were keeping an eye on him. She said to say thanks.”

“Maybe we can go say hi sometime.”

“That’s really not a good idea.”

“I suppose not. Look, Mom. Things got a lot hairier than I planned.”

“What now?”

“We found a hooker in the alley that numb nuts finished with a few minutes earlier. She was in bad shape. Don’t ask, but I need the results of a blood test really quick.”

“What are you involved in now?”

“It’s important, Mom. It’s for a friend.

“Where are you?”

“Still at the hospital.”

“I’ll be right there.”

“That’s not necessary.”

“Yes, it is. I’ll see you in twenty.”

Dusty’s mother showed up, taking over in her true fashion. Although he’d told her not to come, he was more than happy to hand control of the situation over to her. His parents were heavy donors to the hospital, not to mention the fact that his mother ran most of the charity events. She was well respected and when she said to jump, they jumped. After hearing there was nothing left to do but wait, Dusty and Katie went back to his place, stopping along the way for some take-out chicken.

"I can't help it, Dusty. My mind keeps going to what could have happened to Courtney if you didn't find out about him."

"I don't know, sweets. Remember what you said. She was probably smart enough to use protection."

"There are still accidents, though. I wanted you so bad I almost didn't stop for one our first time."

"Or third or fifth. I'm really thinking we need to go get some tests and establish a trust factor here and get you on the pill. I'm going to need stock in a condom company or get a loan from Dad."

Katie laughed. "I'm already on the pill. I wasn't going to take any chances, even though I was never very active."

He knew that, but had to play it up. "So we'll do the nineties thing and make a date for tests."

"Gee. Date number four to a lab. You are the hopeless romantic."

"I'll make it up to you. I swear."

"I'll let you, just not tonight. I want to spend tonight with Court, okay?

"Can't blame you. Dean wanted to go to a kegger. If you want to spend time with her, I'll go with him."

"It's so nice knowing some people with money try to make a difference. Your parents aren't what I would have expected when I saw that house and those cars. It really helps explain why you are the way you are, Dusty."

He leaned over and gave her a greasy-lipped kiss. "I think I'll keep you."

"I suppose you will."

After Dusty dropped Katie off, she couldn't get to Courtney fast enough. She promised Dusty she wouldn't scare her roommate unnecessarily, but she still needed to hold her tight. Katie fought tears at the thought of the remote possibility she could have lost her to a horrible disease.

Courtney giggled as she released from Katie's embrace. "What's with you, hon? I saw you yesterday."

"I missed you. You and Dean still all right?"

"We're hitting it off okay but you know…"

"I know what?"

"You know I'm not looking to settle down. I do enjoy his company, but I'm not going to go crazy here and getting all mushy, falling for the guy."

"The fact that you are even saying that makes me think you are."

"Get out of town. How long have you known me?"

"Dean and Courtney sitting in a tree. K—I—S—S—I—N—G."

"Are you four?" Courtney threw a pillow at her. "Knock it off."

"When you seeing him again?"

"I haven't set a date. I said I have a busy week."

"You do like him. You're playing hard to get."

"No, I'm busy. How often do I usually see you during the week?"

"I know. But you still find time to throw me out of here to…you know."

"Well, your little boyfriend took care of that now, didn't he?"

"You promise you won't go looking for Ronald again?" Katie begged.

"Of course not. The only thing I'd do for him would require me losing a good shoe."

"Why's that?"

"'Cause it would get lost up his ass."

Katie laughed. "Can I tell you something?"

"You can always tell me anything."

"Dusty's mom placed his wife in a shelter."

"Really? Why did she get involved?"

"He went to her for help. It's sort of what she does now. She quit practicing law a while ago and donates her time everywhere. They're loaded, by the way."

"Yeah, Dean told me. He said Dusty likes to live like a pauper, though. I never understood rich kids that do that."

"Well, it doesn't matter to me. I think I really like him, Court. I know it's early but I really am going to give him a shot."

"Then I'm happy for you. Just don't push your new lifestyle on me. A great date and some amazing sex doesn't have me ordering matching rings."

"I never said that. Geez, Court. It's only been a few days."

"Yeah, but I've never seen you this way. Next thing you know, you'll be moving in with the guy."

"And leave you? No way!"

"Right. Hey, it's your pick tonight. What do you want to watch?"

"*Turner and Hooch.* Duh."

It drove Katie crazy not to tell Courtney about the hooker, but she managed to keep her secret to herself. One day wasn't going to make a difference. *Right*?

After they were tucked in bed, Katie whispered. "Court?"

"What, hon?"

"You always use protection, right?"

"Hell, yes. You think I'm stupid?"

"No. I just wanted to check. We've all had our 'one too many drink' nights and I'm wondering if you ever slipped up."

"Do you think you're pregnant?"

"No. We've been safe. I just wondered…"

"'Cause I'm the resident whore."

"I never said that. Besides. You're not a whore. You're a slut. Whores get paid."

Courtney laughed. "You are a bitch, you know."

"One of the more endearing qualities of mine that makes you love me."

"Who ever said I love you?"

"You."

"Oh. I suppose so. I promise, Mother. I've always been safe."

"Thanks. I love you."

"Goodnight, princess."

Dusty woke up in a house he didn't recognize. He hollered, "Shit!" and hurried to a window. He was surprised when he found himself looking down on his cottage. "What the hell?" Remembering what Katie told him about one of her trips and him owning the main house, he went to his closet and stood in awe of the suit and tie collection he had. He took a few steps back, hoping to wake up out of this bad dream. After spotting his wallet and a business card holder on the nightstand, he took out a card. He saw his picture on it with a law firm that included his name in the title. "Dear God. I've died and gone to hell."

There was a calendar on the wall, but he had no idea what day it was. He took a watch out of a change dish. "Rolex. Shit." Discovering it was Saturday, he could only assume he didn't have to be at work.

After finally getting oriented, Dusty turned his thoughts to Katie. Why wasn't she with him? He went through a few drawers, looking for her clothes, but there wasn't anything. Next he went to the bathroom hoping to find signs of her. An extra toothbrush, lotions—hell, he'd be happy to see tampons fall of out the cabinet at this point. There was no sign of her at all. In frustration, he turned around and leaned hard against the sink. "What now, you damn codger?"

He thought of Katie's vet practice and hustled to the kitchen in search of a phone book. He opened it up to the yellow pages and found her clinic. Without hesitation, he called the number.

A familiar voice answered. "Barrow Animal Hospital. This is Karla. Can I help you?"

"Karla?"

"Yes. Who's this?"

"Dusty."

"Who?"

Shit. "Dusty. Dustin Andrews. Is Katie in today?"

"She is, but she's with a client. I'm sorry. We're really busy this morning and my mind is scrambled. What is your pet's name?"

"Uhhh…George." He heard her tap on a computer for a minute. "I don't see you in our file. You sure you brought him in before?"

"Hmm…must not have."

"You know Dr. Barrow, though?"

"Yeah. We…uh…go way back. Can you fit me in today?"

"I can squeeze you in right before we close. That's noon. Can you make it by then?"

"Can do. I appreciate it."

"What do I put you down for?"

"What do you mean?"

"What do we need to see George about? Is he sick?"

"Uh…no."

"If he needs neutering, we need to have him overnight. You can do that on Monday."

Dusty had to get in to see her so he quickly blurted out, "No, he's already lost 'the boys.'"

"Shots?"

"Yeah. That's it. His yearly things. Rabies or whatever and that panaleuka thing." He could hear her giggling. Katie had rattled off the various shots over the years. Dusty didn't have the memory for them.

"I'll get you in at 11:45. Annual shots don't take long. Bring in a stool sample if you can get a fresh one. It's more pleasant than using the wand on their little behinds."

"I'll try. Thanks, Karla."

"Have we met?"

"I thought so. Maybe she just mentioned your name in passing."

"Okey-dokey. See you then."

Dusty hung up, a little relieved to be able to see her, but a lot confused as to why the new change. He remembered more about what Katie told him when she went forward to a time when they weren't together. She managed to convince him that they knew each other in another time. This is when she had learned about Alyson. He suddenly feared for his sister. Without hesitating, he dialed her cell number. When she groggily answered, he hung up. He didn't know what to say. Immediately his phone rang.

He saw her name pop up on caller ID and cursed for not thinking to look for her name in his phone list first. "Hey, Alyson."

"Why did you call me and hang up?"

"Sorry. I dialed you by mistake. I thought I caught it before it rang."

"You sure you're okay?"

"I'm sure."

"You sound funny. You fighting with your dad again?"

"Not at all. I'm okay."

"You sure?"

"I swear."

"You want me to come over? We can do lunch." Come over? That's right. She was now living in the cities with a successful interior decorating business, thanks to a healthy loan from his mother.

"No. I have to go get a cat."

"A cat? You're not a fan of cats. What gives?"

"I just feel like some company around here lately."

"You're trying to impress a girl."

"No, I'm not."

"Why don't you buy a few houseplants first? If you don't kill those, then you can move on to the next stage."

"I have to get going, sis. Sorry I woke you. Maybe we can do lunch next weekend."

"All right. Call me. Love you."

"You too."

Crap. Now he had to go get a cat.

Dusty showered and dressed. He was glad to find a shelf of jeans in his closet and some plain t-shirts. The last thing he wanted to do was show up in a suit. He went to the closest Target and picked up cat food, a bowl, food, a pet carrier, a litter box, and some toys. On his way home, he cruised the strip where he'd found their cat, Blue, but had no luck. *Of course not, numbnut. The year isn't right.* After he reached home and got everything settled, he hurried to the animal shelter to find a cat. He was hoping to find one that looked like theirs, what Katie called a blue cream, but there wern't any. He checked his watch and noted the time. Everyone was busy but he needed to hurry things along.

Dusty went up to the counter and put two one-hundred dollar bills on it in front of the cashier. "I saw a calico back there that I'd like to get and make an extra donation. Can I have you put it in here for me?" He held up the carrier. "I'm running late for a meeting."

She raised an eyebrow. “You’re running late for a meeting but you had to stop and get a cat? Is it going to be stuck in the car while you do this meeting?”

“No. Don’t be silly. I have enough time to run it home. My daughter is really upset. Hers was hit by a car last week. I promised I get her one today but I got called away. Can you do this? Please?” He threw another bill on the counter. “It would mean the world to me.”

“You’re supposed to fill out some paperwork. People usually want a little history when they adopt.”

“As long as it’s good with kids, I’m fine. Can I sign it and you copy my driver’s license? I promise it’ll have a good home.”

She sized him up for a moment then picked up a walkie-talkie.

“Dawn? Bring up the calico in number 10. There’s a little girl calling for a new kitty.”

Dusty smiled wide. “Thank you.” He handed her another fifty when she gave him his license back. “Get your staff some pizza or something on me. I appreciate this.”

She accepted it with a smile. “Thank you.” She walked the carrier to the back, then retrieved the cat’s records from a filing cabinet behind her. She put them in an envelope and handed it to Dusty after having him fill out a form. “All the shot info is there. Age and what-not, too. Take a second to check the shot records and be sure to follow up. This one is fixed and de- clawed already. Enjoy your cat.”

“We will. Thank you.”

Chapter Twenty-Two

Dusty hurried off to Katie's clinic. He didn't have time to look at everything now. He knew it wouldn't hurt the cat to get its shots early if it wasn't quite due. "Sorry, buddy. You're going to the V-E-T, but she's going to be your mother so it's all good." A meow was his response. "You're welcome."

When he walked in the door, Karla greeted him with the pleasant smile she always had. He took note of her eyes. They were a shade of almost purple he had never seen before. Every time he saw her, she had a different shade of contacts in.

"You must be Dustin."

"That's right."

"That's George, I assume," she said as she peeked in the carrier. The cat was curled up in back, head buried in its paws.

"That's him."

She handed him a sheet of paper on a clip board. "I'll need to start a file for you. Can you fill this out for me please?"

"Sure." He took it and sat down. When he got to age of the cat and last shots, he wished he brought in the paperwork from the animal shelter. Since he'd told Karla he needed to do his yearly shots, Dusty fudged a date close to a year ago. They said it was fixed and declawed so he put in that information, too.

He stood and handed it to Karla. "The tech will call you in—in a moment."

"Thanks."

In less than five minutes, Katie's voice boomed over the speakerphone. "Can you bring the next client in? Paula is in back with Mrs. Jenkins. Scooter needed some fluids."

"Sure thing, Doc B."

She stood and motioned to Dusty. "Follow me."

They walked through the door; Katie's back was to them as she drew some shots. "You need me to stay and help?" Karla asked.

"I'll be fine. Thanks, though."

"Chart is on the table," she said before walking out. Katie put the shots down and turned around. She walked over and outstretched her hands. "Dr. Barrow. Nice to meet you."

"Dusty. Sorry, Dustin Andrews."

She hesitated as she looked him over. "You told Karla I knew you? Sorry, I can't seem to place the face."

"We've run into each other here and there. Actually, you deserted me once outside a bar in Dinkytown."

"Really? I'm sorry. I don't remember that at all."

He shrugged. "It was a long time ago."

She regarded him for a while, searching for the truth in his statement.

"All right. Let's get a look at your little boy here."

Dusty put the cage on the table and opened up the door. He was thankful the cat perked up and walked right out. Katie tilted her head and smiled at him. He thought he scored bonus points for the pretty calico.

"So, this is George."

"Yes. He's a beauty, isn't he?"

"How long have you had *him*," she said, with an emphasis on him.

"Oh… a year or so."

She gave the cat a quick exam, then quickly flipped through the chart he filled out. "You say he's five."

"That's about right. I inherited him when a friend moved." Again Dusty applauded himself for his fast thinking. She went to the counter and picked up the shots. She placed caps on the syringes and returned them to the refrigerator. "What's the matter?" Dusty asked. "He not healthy enough for shots?"

She crossed her arms. "First of all, George is a girl. Hasn't anyone ever told you the calico rule?"

Crap. How could he forget that? "No. I mean, yes. I guess I forgot and they must have never checked. I went by what they told me. If he was neutered, there'd be no evidence. Right? No nuggets, so to speak."

She returned to the exam table, picked the cat up, and cuddled with her. "You didn't last in the shelter long, Felecia. I'm glad to see you have a home." She gave the cat a kiss and returned her to the carrier then turned to Dusty. "I've known Felecia since she was a kitten. I spayed and declawed her last year. Her owners had to move into an apartment and were heartbroken they couldn't take her. Her shots were done last week before they turned her in, hoping to give her a better chance at a good home. They'll be happy to hear she's found one. Unless of course this was just some ploy to come into my clinic. I can't think of one good reason why that would be, Mr. Andrews. Would you care to enlighten me?"

"What are the chances of you knowing the cat, huh?" he said, trying to pull off the boyish grin that usually let him get away with almost anything.

"I'm waiting," she said as she crossed her arms again and leaned against the counter.

"I saw your picture in the yellow pages and remembered the night from college. You were outside of Dicky's with your roommate. It was the night before your birthday."

"How in the hell do you remember that?"

He shrugged. "I never forget a beautiful face." His eyes went to the calendar on the wall. It was a huge tear away, day-at-a-time calendar. The date finally registered. "Today is your birthday. I thought I'd try for another chance."

Her arms flopped to her side. "You're unbelievable. You adopted this poor cat to get a date?" She looked at his chart again. "You're a lawyer. You must have gotten this conniving in school. Another good reason I steered clear of the other campus." She angrily took the paper off the clipboard and crumbled it up. "Get out of my office."

He hurried to her and held her hands. "Don't get pissed. You can't bust my chops for trying. Come on. How about you don't hold being a lawyer against me and I hold you against me instead?"

That earned him a slap. Katie called for Karla. The door quickly opened up. "Yeah, Doc. B?"

"See Mr. Andrews and Felecia out."

"I thought his cat was George?"

"He was mistaken."

"Wait!" Karla said, excited. "Our Felecia?" She peeked into the cage and spoke to the cat. "Hi, honey! Welcome back!" She seemed to sense the tension in the room. "Crap. What gives?"

"See him out and don't start a file. Unfortunately for us, we won't be seeing Felecia anymore."

Karla picked up the carrier. "Follow me, sir."

"Wait a second, Katie. I'm sorry. Just give me a chance."

"Are you going to keep her or will you take her back to the shelter?"

"I'm keeping her. Does that get me a date tonight?"

"It's my birthday. You think I don't have a date? I happen to be dating a very nice chiropractor."

"Wilson? Are you shitting me?"

"You know him?"

"Hell, yeah, I know him. I know him well enough to say you ain't the only one he's seeing."

"Ain't? Win many trials with that vocabulary?"

"Come on, Katie. Let's go talk. There are some things I need to tell you."

"Get out of my exam room. Now!" She harshly strode the few paces to her office, off the exam room, and slammed the door.

"Come on, sir," Karla said. "You best split when she loses her top like that." When they were at the door, Karla turned to him. "You really got Felecia just to try to get a date?"

"Sort of."

"You promise you'll take care of her and not take her back to the shelter?"

"I will. I gave them three hundred dollars for her. You bet I will."

"Gee whiz. You're cute enough. You're loaded. What gives? Things can't be that bad out there."

"Your boss has always owned my heart. You haven't seen the last of me."

"I wouldn't advise showing up again. When her mind is made up, it's made up."

"I don't think so."

"Good luck to you then." She held the door as he walked out, then locked it behind him

After getting the cat settled in his home, Dusty returned to the phonebook to look up Dr. Wilson Gregory. The thought of him being with Katie all but made smoke come out his ears. He couldn't believe in a time where he and Katie didn't exist as a couple. He called Wilson's office, but they had already closed at noon as well. He looked up his private residence and found the address. He left for the chiropractor's home without a plan of what he would do when he reached it.

When there was no answer at the door, Dusty walked around to the back. He found Wilson and a companion by the pool. Wilson was giving a woman, whose top had been unfastened, a back rub. After noticing Dusty, he approached him. "Can I help you with something?"

"Actually, yes. Is there somewhere we can talk in private?"

Wilson squinted. "What's this about?"

"I'd really rather do this inside," Dusty said as he shook his head toward the woman.

"Follow me."

They entered the kitchen through the patio door. "Can I get you a drink?"

"Not so sure if you want to offer me a drink when you hear what I have to say. But I'll take a beer if you're feeling gracious."

Wilson removed a bottle on Leiney's out of the refrigerator and handed it to Dusty. "So what gives?"

"I take it that lady friend of yours out there is not the one you have a date with tonight."

"What's that to you? That's none of your business."

"It's my business all right."

"You a private dick or something?"

Ohhh. That's a good one. "Yes. Doc Barrow is a little frustrated with your extracurricular activities."

"Aw, man. How'd she find out?"

Dusty held his arms wide open. "You aren't the most discreet, my friend. In fact, you haven't changed any since college."

"College?" Again he squinted his eyes at Dusty. "You don't look familiar."

"I saw you a few times at *Puck You*. I overheard you bragging about having a few women on hold at all times."

"I was the stud even back then, wasn't I?" He perked up like a proud rooster, instead of being ashamed.

"Mostly I thought you were full of shit. In any case, you can guess your date tonight is cancelled."

"Dammit!" he ran his hand down his face. "I really liked this one."

"So why cheat on her?"

"If she put out, I wouldn't have to now, would I?"

"You're not sleeping with her?" This news made Dusty very happy.

"That woman has had a nickel between her knees for two months now. She has to know I can't wait forever."

"Well, you're free of her now." Dusty pointed outside. "And there's a line forming already."

"Should I call her or something?"

"Definitely not. She's pretty upset."

"Shit. No chance I can buy you out? You know. Double what she's paying you or something?"

"Sorry, my friend. I have standards. Wish I could help you. Really."

"It was worth a shot."

"Hey. This may sound funny, but where were you taking her? I could use a good reservation tonight. I have a date."

"*Chez Pauls*. Six-thirty. Help yourself."

"Thanks, pal." Dusty placed the beer on the counter then extended his hand. "Thanks for the beer. Sorry about this. It's just my job. Nothing personal, you know."

"Pffft. Plenty of fish in the sea that want a piece of this," he said as he grabbed his crotch.

Dusty had to look away to keep from laughing. He never understood the men that did that. After he reached the gate, he quickly snapped a picture of Wilson as he resumed his backrub of the woman, whose top was now lying beside her. He felt bad for a second, but he felt the maneuver was fitting of his new private eye status. *The job suited him.*

He pulled up at Katie's at six sharp, wearing the best dress suit and tie he could find in his closet. He knew she wouldn't be impressed with Armani but hell, he looked good in it if he did say so himself.

Katie opened the door happy enough, but the smile quickly faded when she saw Dusty. She tried to slam the door, but he put his foot out, stopping it.

"Move your foot," she barked.

"No can do, sweetheart. I need a minute of your time."

"I don't owe you anything. What are you doing at my house?"

"I don't take no for an answer."

"I already told you I have a date."

"That, my dear lady, has been cancelled." He opened his phone and held it up to her, showing her the picture he took of Wilson.

She quickly seized it out of his hands. "When was this taken?"

"Around one."

"How did you…why…" She closed the phone and pressed it hard to his chest. "Get out of here, would you?" She tried to close the door again, but ended up slamming it on his foot. This time Dusty fell into the house and held his foot as if in pain. He lay on his back moaning.

"Oh my God! Are you okay?" She dropped to her knees and held his foot in her hands, ready to remove his shoe.

Dusty sat up and took her hands. "You don't actually call me God until we've had sex, but that's okay. I don't mind."

"You pig!" she said as she stood. He followed her up. "Get out of my house before I call the cops."

"And what are the charges? I find you incredibly attractive and decided I can't live without you and would like to get to know you? I want to take you to *Chez Pauls* for dinner. Oh no! Not that!" He bellowed out the door. "Quick! Someone call 9-1-1!"

Katie looked as if she was holding back a laugh. "It's called stalking. Now get out."

He took a step closer to her and leaned in so their noses almost touched. "One date. I swear I'm harmless, Katie. Give me the chance you didn't give me all those years ago." He took her hand and brought it to his lips for a kiss. He could feel her quiver and loved that he could have that effect on her still. Even if it was technically the first time they were meeting. Again. Whatever.

After a brief pause she asked, "Why did I tell you no that night?"

"You said I was cute but too young for you."

"Were you in high school or something?"

"I was in college. I'm just graced with young looks. Graced in every sense of the word, except when I ask you out."

"You tried more than once?"

"Technically, no."

"Can you define technically?"

"I can. Over dinner."

"Did you keep Felecia or did you take her back to the shelter?"

"George is adjusting well to her new home."

"You're going to change her name to George?"

"She likes it."

Katie finally let her laugh go. "One dinner, no dessert, no coffee, and you're out of here."

"Deal."

Katie rolled over and pressed her back into Dusty's chest. They had finished a great first date and every rule Katie laid out hadn't stuck. They returned to his place after dinner, dessert and coffee, commencing in sex shortly thereafter. He wrapped an arm around her and pulled her close. "You're incredible," he said with a kiss to the back of her head. "I also happen to like the way we fit."

"Not too bad yourself," she said with a moan. She reached back and ran her hand down his back and thigh.

"Don't kill me for asking, but how come you didn't sleep with Wilson?"

"It never felt right. I kept waiting to be attracted to him, but it never happened. Even drunk I turned him away."

Dusty laughed. "You did have to get drunk to go out with him." He said it a little too matter-of-factly, but Katie never caught it.

"No. I had a few drinks the first time we hooked up, but I still couldn't go through with it. He seemed nice enough, so I wanted to give him a chance. Something was missing." She turned back around to face him. "How did you know I never slept with him?"

"He sort of complained about it this afternoon."

"That asshole." She went to sit up but he gently pulled her back down.

"This wasn't a quest to see if I could boldly go where he hadn't, Katie. I meant what I said to you over dinner. I've watched you from afar off and on. My only goal was to have you."

"So now you've had me. What now?"

"Have you again and again for about the next eighty years."

She laughed. "Do I get the wedding invitations out?"

"I'm open next Saturday."

"You're a nut job.'

"A nut job that is madly in love with you."

"Whoa." Katie sat up.

"What?"

"Love? After one dinner and sex?"

"Great sex. I'm pretty sure the neighbors will refer to me as God from this day forward."

She gently slapped at his chest. "Even after I pulled the pillow over my face?"

He chuckled. "'Fraid so, cupcake."

"Argh. That proves it. I can't date someone that uses pet names like that."

"Bet you can and do."

She flopped back down. "I don't usually do this."

"I know."

"You really pissed me off. I don't know how you got me here after that stunt you pulled."

"You like the way I prepare caviar."

She leaned over and gave him a gentle kiss. He kept her there, turning it into something that lasted much longer. Within another moment, round two began. Dusty again wondered why he was brought forward to this time, but right now he didn't care too much.

Chapter Twenty-Three

It was seven the next morning when the two of them began to stir.

Katie gave Dusty a quick kiss. "Mind if I hop in the shower?" Dusty only grunted in response. She was finishing rinsing off when hands reached from behind, cupping her breasts. She jumped and let out a soft scream that turned into a laugh. "Dammit, Dusty. You scared the crap out of me."

"Sorry, my sweet. I missed you." She spun around and he gently kissed her lips. "You staying for a while?"

"I think I'm letting you make me breakfast this morning."

"Wise decision," he said as he kissed down her neck.

"Food, Dusty."

"Damn," he said with another kiss. "I do believe I can scrounge up enough to make eggs benedict."

"Seriously?"

"You bet, doll face."

"Gah. Never mind. If you can't can it with those names, I'll drive through *McDonalds*."

"No, you won't." He kissed her again and stepped back out. "I put a pair of pajamas out for you. As much as I love that dress, I don't think you need to lounge around in it today."

"Oh, I'm staying today?"

"Of course you are. I make a mean cup of coffee. Before I went to your house yesterday, I made sure that there wasn't a drop of cinnamon in anything in this house."

The water for the shower shut off. She opened the sliding glass door and quickly removed the towel he placed on the rack for her and covered herself. "How do you know about that?"

Crap. "You mentioned it last night."

"No, I didn't."

"You did, too. Over dessert."

"No, Dusty. I didn't. And even if I did, you said you took care of it before you came to my house."

Shit. "Maybe Wilson told me?"

"Wrong. He didn't know either. What the hell is this?" she shouted. "Goddammnit! I just had sex with a psycho stalker." She began to pace the floor of the bathroom. "Please put a towel on for heaven's sake."

He rushed to her side. "I'm not a psycho stalker. Please stop freaking out."

"Towel!" she again shouted, motioning to his lower half.

He reached in the cabinet and removed a towel, then wrapped it around himself.

"Then explain it, Dusty."

"Can I explain it over breakfast? I'm starved."

"Talk."

"I'll explain over cooking. How's that? You have to let me finish and you have to eat before you split."

"No deal."

"That's the only deal you're getting." He walked to the bedroom and picked up her dress and shoes. "You'll get this back after we've eaten."

"What makes you think I won't go home in your pajamas and my coat?"

"I drove you here."

"Shit!"

"Come on, Katie. One meal."

"Last time you said that, we had sex."

"I accept."

"Dusty!"

"Okay," he said, holding his hands up while he still held her items. "Truce. Just come down when you're ready. There's a hair dryer under the vanity."

"Leave me my clothes."

"That's not part of the deal."

Dusty watched as Katie walked down the stairs in his pajamas. They were at least four times too big for her, but she looked as cute as hell. He returned his attention to the stove. After a few minutes he swore he heard Katie talking. He turned down the Canadian bacon and walked into the living room. She closed the sliding glass door right as he reached her.

"Who were you talking to?"

"Your handyman."

"Who?"

"Your handyman. Frank something."

"What?" Dusty hurried past her and walked outside without so much as a shirt on. He found Frank around the corner. "What the hell are you doing?"

"Fixing this gutter. I don't think they did it right last time. I don't want Katie slipping again."

"That's not what I mean. Why the hell am I here? This makes no sense at all to throw me into a future where I'm doing nothing but keeping my proctologist busy, looking for my head up my ass."

"Speaking of head up your ass...How many lawyers—"

"Quit it. This isn't funny. Why are you putting me through this?"

"Do you remember when Katie went to your future? The 'you' that told her about Alyson?"

"Of course. Well, I don't remember it, but I remember her telling me about it."

"Did you think that was fun for her?"

"Of course not, but at least that served a purpose."

"Who said this isn't serving a purpose?"

"What good is it, then?"

"I'm enjoying the shit out of it. Now get back in before you catch a cold. It's about fifteen degrees out here, jackass." Frank turned to walk away. Again Dusty flipped him off with both fingers.

"I see that."

"I don't give a shit!"

"Dusty?"

Dusty turned around to find Katie standing there with a tilt to her head. "Why are you swearing at and flipping off that nice old man?"

"He's not what you think."

"Apparently, neither are you." She turned away and went back in the house.

"Wait a second," he called out, hurrying after her.

"Go put a shirt on."

"You love my chest."

"Gee, lawyer. Ego much? I could hang my coat on your nipples. You're freezing. Go put a shirt on."

He pulled a sweatshirt out of a wooden chest by the front door and quickly pulled it over his head. "Look. Let's try this again."

"No. I want to get dressed and I want you to take me home."

"After we eat." He returned to the kitchen and flipped the Canadian bacon. Katie opened up his pantry. "What are you looking for?"

"Chocolate."

He glanced at the calendar. "Yeah, I suppose you're due in a few days."

Hands on her hips she said angrily, "Excuse me?"

"Every month, you chow down on a whole bag of chocolate two days before your period. I keep saying I want to buy stock in Hershey."

"You're no big guesser of the secrets there, Andrews. Every woman indulges in chocolate around that time of the month."

He walked over to her. "Maybe, but you get this one little pimple every month. Right here." He pointed just past the corner of her mouth. "You cuss like a sailor every time and swear you're never eating chocolate again."

She swatted his hand away. "How do you know that?"

"Because you've done it every month for the past seven years. Well, except for when you were pregnant."

"Now I was pregnant?"

"Twice."

"I've never had an abortion. How dare you!" she turned to walk away, but he blocked her way.

"No. That's not what I mean. I shouldn't get ahead of myself. Let's go back to what you know."

"I don't want to. You're creeping me out." She walked out of the kitchen. Dusty turned the stove off and walked into the living room with her.

"You had sex on your twenty-fifth birthday."

"Ooohhhh, big guess there, buddy. What was his name?"

"Shit. I know this one."

"Right. Let me go." She walked to the door.

"I know him, just give me a second. Asshole clobbered me twice."

She spun around. "There's a surprise. You probably didn't have it coming at all."

"Sure I did. I won you away from him."

"You're insane." She reached the bowl on the table by the front door and picked up a set of keys, then put on her heels. "I'm driving myself back. You can come get your car later." She pulled on her coat and opened the door. Before she closed the door he hollered, "Rex Hemingsen!" Only a few seconds passed before she knocked on the door. He opened it up and smiled.

"Why do you know that?"

"If you'd listen to me, you'd understand. We don't belong here, Katie. That sweet old man out there is messing with my head. I've already won you over. We already have a life together. I don't have a clue why he insists on torturing me. I'm pretty sure I've already saved Courtney, so I don't understand why I'm here."

"Courtney? My Courtney?"

"Yes. Your roommate Courtney."

"She killed herself a year ago. What the hell are you talking about 'you saved her?'"

"Holy fuck." Dusty leaned against the wall and slid down. He buried his head in his arms. Deep down he felt this wasn't their final fate, but he still couldn't help getting completely distraught at hearing the news.

Katie kneeled and placed a hand on his back. "You all right?" He shook his head no. "I'm sorry. Maybe I shouldn't have blurted it out like that. She—"

"Tried to beat AIDS to the punch. I know." He lifted his head up and blinked away the tears that filled them. "I'm sorry. You shouldn't have had to live through this again."

"What do you mean 'again?'"

"Jesus, Katie. I'm so sorry." He pulled her close and buried his head in her neck. He was unsuccessful at keeping the tears at bay. A few sobs broke out and Katie held him tight.

When Dusty's mini-melt down was over, Katie sat beside him with her back against the wall as well. Dusty laced her fingers in his. "I'm sorry."

"Don't be. I don't know how you were so close to her, but I didn't know you."

He let out a loud sigh. "You were much better at this than I am."

"Better at what?"

"Explaining whatever the hell it is that we do."

"Now, I understand the whole lawyer thing. Only lawyers and politicians could say so much and never make a point. I haven't understood anything since I woke up this morning. You were so sweet last night. You literally charmed my pants right off. I never allow that, especially after our sketchy start. But now, you're talking nonsense. You keep throwing things at me like we had a past together. I don't get it, Dusty."

He pulled her hand to his lips and gave it a long kiss. He never grew tired of kissing any part of her body. "Now I understand how you felt."

"How I felt when?"

"When you were going through this."

She let out a long sigh. "You're doing it again."

"I'm sorry." He finally looked up at her. "Hear me out, okay?"

"Okay."

"I mean really. You have to search deep down and know what I'm telling you is the truth."

"I'll do my best." Her eyes stared hard at his, nervously going from one eye to the other.

"I know things about you because we've been together for a long time, Katie. When you turned thirty, you started time traveling back to our past. It's a long story, but you ended up staying with me when I was twenty-one and you were twenty-five." She went to speak, but he put his finger over her mouth. "Let me finish. That guy you were talking to isn't a handyman. Somehow he's behind this. He was there for you when you needed an ear. We never knew the part he played. You thought he was some kind of angel helping you out. There wasn't anyone you could talk to about what you were going through. You thought Courtney would have you locked up, so that only left me and him. I wanted in your pants no matter what you said or what crazy story you fed me, so that left him."

"But I don't know him."

"Yet. He was sweet to you, Katie. He's a bastard for me. He thinks I was selfish for making you stay with me when I was twenty-one, and maybe I was, but you seemed happy." He gazed hard into her eyes. "Are you happy now, Katie? I mean really happy?"

"I thought I was."

"You kept forcing yourself to go out with Wilson, trying to like him but it wasn't happening. Why?"

"I don't know. He wasn't *the one*, I suppose."

"You're gorgeous. You should be beating men away with a stick."

"I'm not all that, Dusty. Maybe I'm not a mutt, but no one looks at me the way you do. There were always my studies, then I went straight into business for myself. I never made time for a social life."

"But are you happy?"

"I don't know what you want to hear. Do I feel complete? I suppose not. Thirty came and went and I thought maybe I'd have a kid or two by now. I'm okay with my life. I guess it isn't my time."

"I want to hear you say you're not complete. I need you to say it. Otherwise, I was wrong for being so selfish and keeping you in your past. If that's the case, then I'll be stuck in this blasted future without you. I can take it, if for some reason that damn codger chooses now to punish me, but we have two great kids, babe. Losing you would be one thing, but I couldn't live not knowing what will happen to them."

"Kids? You said I was pregnant and I didn't get that. We have kids now in this past of ours?" Katie stood. "I really feel for you, Dusty. I really do. You get a kewpie doll for having the most intriguing way of trying to win a second date. But you know what? You already had me. Why pull this shit?"

Dusty stood and put his hands on her shoulders. "It's not shit, Katie. What'll it take to convince you?"

"All right, hotshot. What do we have?"

"What do you mean?"

"Kids? Girls? Boys? Twins? What?"

"A girl and a boy."

"And their names?"

"Our daughter Alyson came first. It's spelled with a 'y.'"

"I suppose this is because of my name?"

"No. We named her after my best friend, who is also my half-sister. You saved her life, Katie, but that's for another talk. Our son is Alexander."

She gasped and covered her mouth with her hand again.

"You named him after a favorite uncle of yours. He died when you were sixteen. You promised your aunt you would name a son after him."

Katie's hand went to her eyes. As she covered them, she swayed.

Dusty closed the gap between them just as she collapsed into him. He picked her up and walked her to the couch. After he laid her down, he placed a hand on her cheek. "I'm sorry. Maybe I should have made sure you were sitting before I sprung that one on you. It's funny how something like our kids' names is what convinces us of what we're doing."

"What's that?"

"You told me of how you convinced the older me you were telling the truth because of our daughter Alyson's name." She still looked a little green. "How you doin', cupcake?"

Katie's eyes went wide. "Cupcake?"

"I know. You're not a fan."

"No. It's not that. You've done this to me before."

"Call you cupcake? Tons of times."

"No. I fainted at the coffee shop years ago. You were there when I woke up. You called me cupcake. Now I remember you."

A broad smile spread over Dusty's face. "That's happened twice that I know of. Once when you returned to me and once when I returned to you. I'd love to know your version."

"I overdid a run. I took off with a hangover and an empty stomach. You were at the door when I walked in and caught me as I passed out."

"That's how it goes. How did you get away without me bugging you for a date?"

"Oh, you bugged me, all right. I was too stubborn and hightailed it out of there. I was embarrassed as hell. Secretly I had hoped to see you again, but it never happened."

"This is very strange. The more I do this, the more I'm convinced I'm going to strangle that old fart next time I see him."

Katie laughed. "Can I get you anything?"

"You promised me Eggs Benedict."

"Coming right up, buttercup." He stood up and turned to walk away, but she caught his hand. "What is it?"

"I really put up with years of you calling me those names?"

He leaned down and gave her a strong kiss. "I'm incredibly hot in bed. You overlook the little things."

Katie and Dusty talked more over breakfast. Dusty could tell she was still apprehensive about the whole idea, but she seemed to be accepting it.

"I know I think I'm a fool for believing this, but I can't explain everything that you know any other way."

"Trust me, sweetness, I wish I was full of shit. I really felt for you going through this, but now…"

"But now what?"

"I think I need to buy you more jewelry."

She laughed as she stood, then walked over to his chair. Now on his lap, she wrapped her arms around his neck. "I have a better solution for right now."

"There's my girl."

"I'm beginning to think I'm the nympho you say I am. I don't know what it is you do to me. "

"Why do you think I married you?"

"Stop it. It takes two to tango, you know."

"And I like the way you dance, baby."

Again they made love on the couch. Just as they finished, the front door slammed shut.

A woman's voice called out, "Dusty?"

"Oh shit!" Dusty quickly pulled a comforter over them.

The woman kept talking as she walked in. "Will you get that goddamn gutter fixed. I parked over by your tenant's place and I almost broke my ass again!" She stopped when she saw Dusty's head pop over the back of the couch. "Oh geez! Shit, I'm so sorry!" The woman quickly covered her eyes and ran into the kitchen. "I'm sorry!"

Dusty sat up and handed Katie her pajama top. "I'm sorry, babe," he said with a laugh.

"This isn't funny, Dusty. Do I even want to know who that is?" She said as she pulled her shirt on with a huff.

"You get jealous of her every time you see her."

"Shouldn't I?" she said, glaring at him.

"No. Not when it's my sister." He gave her a kiss on her forehead and stood, pulling his pajama bottoms on.

Alyson shouted from the kitchen. "Oohh… hollandaise! You done in there or should I attempt to whip up a bene myself?"

"Don't you dare! You'll burn my house down. Gimme a sec." He leaned over the back of the couch and kissed Katie again. "Come meet her. You two get along great."

Katie grabbed his arm. "Wait. Does she know?"

"In our time, yes. Now—no. It's bad enough telling you. I don't want to try with her. I don't think we'll be here long enough to worry about it."

"What do you mean?"

Again Alyson shouted from the kitchen. "Dusty. Come on. I'm starving here. You had me worried to death about you, and now you're boffing your brains out. No offense in there."

"None taken," Katie hollered back, grinning at Dusty.

"Come meet her." He walked into the kitchen, took a dishtowel off the counter and whipped Alyson in the ass. "You witch. Since when do you pop in without calling?"

"I love you, too, shithead." Alyson lowered her voice. "So…spill it. She someone I should bother getting to know?"

"You could say that."

"Dustin Charles. You're blushing. And for God's sake, put a shirt on."

Katie walked in with the sweatshirt he was wearing earlier. "I had to ask him already today, too." She handed it to him then leaned into his side.

"Alyson, this is Katie."

The girls shook hands and exchanged hellos.

"Sorry to barge in like this. I didn't know what to make of Dusty's call yesterday and I thought something was up. I don't need to stay. I can go visit friends."

"No. Stay," Katie said. "You can tell me how rotten your brother is, so I know what I'm up against."

The girls drank coffee at the counter while Dusty made Alyson breakfast. Dusty loved the way Alyson told the stories of their childhood. When they were younger, he always treated her with kindness and friendship, even when others tried to exclude her. Dusty never accepted an invitation to a party that didn't include Alyson. Neither one of them dated much in high school since everyone thought they were a couple. No one else knew they were brother and sister, that suited them both fine.

"You're not giving me any dirt here, Alyson. You were supposed to tell me how rotten he is."

"Sorry. Can't help you there. I really don't know why he's single. Maybe it's the lawyer thing." Alyson ducked the flying potholder. "Why didn't you ever stand up to your dad, Dusty?"

"Maybe because I needed someone to watch my back while I did it and she was never there." He winked at Katie. That was one story he'd covered. With everything that came out, he was seeing how they truly needed each other through every stage of their lives. He dropped the plate of food in front of her. "OJ?"

"No, thanks. Coffee's fine."

Dusty returned to the coffee pot and froze as he gripped its handle. He let go and spun around. "Why are you here, Alyson?"

"I told you. Your call worried me."

"No. I mean why are you here? Without Katie saving you…you would've been dead right now."

"What? What the hell are you talking about? Katie saving me?"

"You remember. Before you moved to Fargo. We got in that fight by the lake."

"Yeah, and that crazy chick that barrel-assed across the lake on the snowmobile interrupted us when she crashed, then proceeded to tell me how great Fargo was. You helped her—"

"That was still you!" Dusty said as he walked around and gave Katie a tight hug that pulled her off the chair.

"I'm gonna be sick."

Dusty sat her back down. "No, you're not, babe. See! This is some kind of twisted fate." He held both cheeks and gave her a hard kiss on the lips.

"That was you guys?" Katie asked, in a sort of shock.

Dusty again took her hands. "You're mine. You must submit to the fact."

"One of you want to tell me what's going on? That was you, Katie?"

"It was."

"What were you doing?"

"I needed some space that day. I think my mom got pissed at my belly ring or something. I took out the snowmobile when I wasn't supposed to. I remember having a hard time finding the keys. They were really pissed that I crashed it. I was grounded for a month."

"You drove like an animal across thin ice. I remember that much," Alyson said.

"I was really pissed." She looked up at Dusty. "What did you mean, I saved Alyson?"

"Yeah, Dust. What gives?"

"Shit. I wasn't going to go here. Eat up, sis. I don't think you'll want to after you hear what I have to tell you."

Chapter Twenty-Four

By the time Dusty finished the story, both girls were in tears and a tight embrace. Being best friends since practically birth, Dusty could read every one of Alyson's facial expressions. She had gone from the 'biting her lower lip waiting for the punch line' expression to the wide eyed 'holy shit you're not kidding around' look.

"So that check that I received from the Small Business Association to get me started with my business came from your mother?"

"I guess so. I'm finding out some things are meant to be no matter what."

"Like what?" Katie asked.

"Like you yacking your brains out over some cinnamon effect."

"Really?"

"I can't tell you how many times you've revisited a *Chez Pauls* meal."

"I can't help it, Dust," Alyson said. "I'm really creeped out here. To think I was dead in some other future of yours." Alyson shivered and wrapped her arms around herself. "So this Courtney? Are you still going to go fix that?"

"I thought I did. Honestly, I don't know what I'm doing here now. It doesn't make any sense other than that damn geezer messing with me."

"What's with him anyway? You think he's God? You know…I'm picturing a George Burns type character here. Holy crap. You really did get a cat."

Dusty's new addition had just walked into the room and distracted Alyson. He picked her up. "This is George. I'm glad you finally decided to come out from under the bed."

"He adopted her to try to pick me up. You should hear some of the things he's tried," Katie said with a laugh.

"Hey. I win you over every time, missy."

"George? The cat's a female, asshole," Alyson blurted out.

"Am I the only one on the planet that doesn't know that?"

"Apparently," the girls said together.

"In all honesty," Katie continued. "I have met two male calicoes in my practice days. They exist, they're just rare and, of course, sterile."

"Of course," Dusty said, mocking her. "Back to Frank. There's no way that bastard is God." He put the cat by her food bowl and joined the girls again.

"Well, what then? An angel trying to get his wings?" Alyson asked.

"That's funny. Katie used to ask the same thing. That asshole ain't no angel either."

"Ain't? How's that book coming, writer boy?"

"In my day, done and published. Here— I bet it's stuffed in a drawer."

"You wrote a book?" Katie asked.

"You encouraged me to finish it. I guess that's why I assume it's not done. It's not some great work of non-fiction that changes the world or anything, so that has nothing to do with these trips. It's just a sci-fi novel."

"So we're at square one with this Frank," Alyson said.

"He's the key to this mess somehow. I love him to death for having Katie save you and if I can end up where I need to be and save Courtney, I'll kiss his wrinkly old ass. But everything else is making me insane."

"So there's nothing you can do now?"

"I don't think so. If I go back, then this 'now' won't exist." Again he focused his attention on Katie. "That's what I was getting at earlier, babe. I don't think I'll be here tomorrow when I wake up."

"So where does that leave me?"

"I honestly don't know. I never studied these things. It's not like there are facts to follow on the subject. We watched every movie ever made—humorous and otherwise. I thought we were done until I went to the coffee shop."

"Sunriders off campus?"

"Yeah. That's when he showed up again."

"So you went looking for him."

"I guess I did."

"Is that the only place he shows up?" Alyson asked.

"No. He was outside not long ago and he's been to the ice rink."

"So let's go ice skating!" Alyson stood up, suddenly excited.

"Why? You think he'll show up?" Katie asked.

"Maybe he will. Since we're here doing nothing, we might as well go have a good time. I'd also like to ask him a question or two." Alyson said.

"About all of this?"

"That and I'd like to know if Robbie is ever going to ask me to marry him."

Dusty became serious. "Do I like this Robbie?"

"The you now does."

"Okay, then. I trust me." He walked over to Katie. "You game for some skating, sweetness?"

"I haven't in years. Go easy on me, would you?"

"Of course."

"Liar. Dusty used to be a hell of a hockey player."

"Used to? I pffft in your general direction."

"You haven't been on the ice since college, law boy."

"Be prepared to bask in my awesomeness, sis."

The three of them clowned around at the outdoor ice rink for an hour. They skated in a line with Dusty in the middle for the most part. The girls weren't too sure of themselves and Dusty would never admit he was a bit rusty. He never dreamed he'd be as unsteady as he was in the beginning. After several trips around, he was finally feeling like he needed to cut loose. He let go of the girls and picked up speed. After making it a few laps around alone, he pulled off a perfect hockey slide stop. The girls mock-cheered him on and he took his bows. He got going again and decided to go backwards. His second time around, a small child no more than four, came darting in front of him. Dusty tried to turn fast and put a skate down to slow himself, but instead it brought him to a screeching halt. The force of the stop sent him backwards into the wall and flipped him over the side. Katie and Alyson skated as fast as they could to him. Katie crawled over the half wall, Dusty was out cold.

Dusty bolted awake and grabbed the back of his head. He was expecting a lump from his fall, but there was nothing. Confused as hell once again, he took in his surroundings. He was back in his cottage and on his couch. Jumping to his feet, he swore and again flipped a double bird to an elderly man who wasn't there. He walked to his bedroom, finding Dean asleep on the bed.

"I'm back to the night after some kegger? Perfect."

"Huh?" Dean asked, picking his head up.

"Nothing. Go back to sleep. It's only seven. Sorry."

"Dick." Dean turned over and pulled a pillow over his head.

Pleased he wasn't feeling hung over, Dusty headed for the shower. "No consequences from what was probably an all-night bender. Score."

Dean picked his head up again. "What?"

"Sorry."

"Shithead."

Dusty chuckled and closed the bathroom door. A check in the mirror revealed a healing cut over his eye, confirming he was "when" he thought. After the shower, he made coffee and waited until eight to call Katie. She answered, sounding groggy.

"Sorry, sugar bear. Did I wake you?"

"Who is this?"

For a moment Dusty was worried, but then he realized she was giving him grief over the new name he threw into the mix. "Your sex god. You were expecting someone else?"

"No. Just hoping for someone with enough sense to stick to a decent term of endearment."

"Cookie face?"

"I'm hanging up."

"No, don't. I'll quit. Why are you whispering?"

"Court is still asleep."

"You guys pull a late nighter?"

"Sort of. I'm sure it wasn't the caliber of your kegger, though."

"I feel great this morning. Poor Dean looks like death. When can I see you today?"

"When do you want me?"

"I always want you. I'd rather have had you here last night in my bed instead of riding the couch and waking up, looking at Dean."

"You big baby. You lived. Have you heard from your mom?"

"Not yet. She usually knows better than to call too early. I'll give her a holler then come get you."

"Meet you downstairs in thirty minutes?"

"Sounds good."

Katie got out of bed and crawled in with Courtney. She snuggled up close until her best friend stirred.

"What?" Courtney moaned.

"I wanted to say good morning before I take off with Dusty."

"Do you have to go *lesbo* to do it?"

Katie giggled and hugged her tight. "I had fun last night. I just had to say I love you and see you later." She climbed out of bed. Instead of going back to sleep, Courtney sat up.

"What's up with you?"

"What do you mean?"

"We're close and all, but you're really acting strange. Something is up. Don't even tell me it's not."

Katie opened her mouth to lie, but she couldn't do it. "All right. Don't freak out."

"About what?"

"Ronald."

"I'm not returning his calls. What more do you want?"

"It's not that I want anything. Dusty kind of found him with another girl."

"So. We knew that."

"This was different."

"Just spit it out dammit, Barrow."

"She was a hooker."

"What?" she screamed, tossing her blanket aside. "What the hell, Katie?"

"We found her just before she blacked out. There were a lot of drugs on her. They're testing her for AIDS."

"Oh, my God." Courtney fell back hard onto her bed. "Why didn't you tell me this last night?"

"I didn't want to worry you. What if she's negative? I didn't want to worry you for nothing. Maybe this girl was a one-time thing. If that's the case, you don't have anything to worry about. You promised you never went without a condom with him."

"I swear I haven't."

"Then you don't have to worry at all."

"Then explain to me why I feel dirty as hell?"

Katie sat next to her, pulling Courtney upright "We all freak out on the 'what ifs.' Shit, Court, I almost forgot with Dusty, we were so crazy for each other. You're the doctor in the house. I know you know better. I'll go with you if you want to get a test done. We'll go together. Dusty and I want to, anyway."

"You're that serious about this kid?"

"Yes, I am. He's a lot more mature than his age. I really like him. Let me have this."

Courtney wrapped her arms around Katie. "I'm happy if you're happy." She leaned back, "But I'm pissed off you didn't say anything last night. Let's get dressed and go to the clinic. I can't go back to bed now, you bitch."

Katie kissed her cheek. "You know, I actually prefer that to half of the names Dusty calls me. I'll call him back and tell him we have a special date today. Do I have him drag Dean's ass out of bed? Dusty said he was in bad shape."

"Hell, no. Not unless we have to. We've been safe, too. If there was reason to suspect, I'd make him come along."

"Maybe he wants to anyway."

"I said no, Katie. We're not as serious as you two. We're far from claiming the 'one partner' thing and going without a condom. I think you're an idiot for thinking at this stage that you're ready for it."

"I'm not going to argue with you about it."

"I'm sorry to snap, hon. I'm still edgy about this."

"That's okay. Get dressed. I'll let you borrow my cow scarf again."

Katie had a cow-print scarf with udders for fringes. Courtney loved to borrow it when she needed to piss off a vegan, or sometimes just be a goof. Today was a good day to try to get a smile where they could.

The girls were waiting inside the glass doors downstairs when Dusty pulled up. It had started to snow lightly.

"Good morning, beautiful women of mine." He gave Katie a kiss and turned back to Courtney, playfully waiting for one. He was rewarded with a slap to the back of his head.

"Thanks for letting me know about the hooker, dick."

"I didn't want to worry you unnecessarily."

"Did you hear back from your mom about the results?"

"She said she'd call as soon as she heard. They don't usually get test results this fast, but she's really hustling them."

"You sure the clinic is even open on Sunday?"

"Yup. Mom told me it was."

"You told your mother what we were doing?" Katie shrieked.

"I asked about it so I could get my friend in if need be."

"Oh."

Dusty grinned and touched her cheek. "You're blushing, babe."

She smacked his hand away. "Let's go tell my dad we're having sex and see how well you fare."

"Pass."

Peeking into the rearview mirror, Dusty saw Courtney staring in a daze out the window. "You okay back there?"

"Hardly. Six years of medical school down the drain for a few romps with a cheating jerk."

"You don't know that."

"Really? You think they'll let a doctor with AIDS practice medicine? Would you want me treating your bleeding wound?"

"You already did."

"Shit!" Courtney leaned her head against the window. "Is that why you're going in?"

"Didn't even occur to me. Katie and I already decided this." He reached back and placed his hand on her knee. "I know you're fine. Even if this hooker is positive, that doesn't mean you are. Maybe Ronald was never with her before. You said you used condoms anyway. You're fine."

Courtney remained quiet for the rest of the drive. Dusty's mind went to what Katie had said. It was after she moved out that Courtney slipped up. He knew she had to be fine and wished he could take her worry away. He whispered to Katie, "I thought you weren't going to say anything and worry her."

"She knew something was up. I can't keep secrets from her."

"Nope." Courtney said from the back. "And you can't whisper for shit either."

They had their blood drawn and were on their way back to the car when Dusty's phone rang. He said he was going to pull the car up so he could answer it in privacy. It was his mother.

"Hey, Mom. What's the good news?"

"I wish it were good news. The girl was positive, Dusty. It's the clinic's duty to try to get the names of all the partners of the person whose test results are positive. She's not giving any names but since you suspect this Ronald was with her, they'll want to notify him. I've already asked them to take blood from Gina at the shelter."

"Shit. My friend is gonna freak."

"Did you get her to the clinic?"

"We're leaving now. Can you pull some weight here and get her results rushed?"

"You feel comfortable giving me her name?"

Dusty looked over at the girls as he unlocked the car. "I know you'll be discreet. Stillman. Courtney Stillman. Would you call me as soon as you hear?"

"I will. Same as before. This will cost you some volunteer hours, you know."

"You can throw Katie and me at the animal shelter some weekend. She'd probably enjoy that."

"Or four."

"Whatever you want, Mom. I owe you."

"Yes, you do."

"You going to send someone over to talk to Ronald?"

"They usually call. The clinic can only warn them and strongly suggest they come in. We can't force them. It's your word against his and he'll probably deny it."

"Can't you send Dad over with a cop with some bullshit paper saying he'll be charged with attempted murder for spreading it if he doesn't get checked out?"

"I don't think that would fly. You know your father doesn't like to get involved in my charities, except from his wallet."

"Then I'll handle this."

"How are you going to handle it?"

"I'll get him to the clinic."

"What are you going to do?"

"Just strongly suggest he goes."

"I don't like this, but you do what you have to. You have one day to give me a status, otherwise they're going to call him."

"I'll get him in, Mom. Thanks for everything—again."

"I hate the situation, but I love the spark and compassion you have for your friends. I really like that Katie. You bringing her over again soon?"

"In a couple weeks I will. I have to run, though."

"Bye, Dusty. I love you."

"Love you, too. Thanks again, Mom." Dusty pulled up to the curb and the girls climbed in as he hung up.

"Was that your mom?"

"Yeah, but she doesn't know anything yet." He didn't want to break the news to them. Knowing Courtney was okay, he figured it was best to stall and give her good news later. "I have something I remembered I have to do. You guys want me to pick up some food before I drop you back off?"

"I thought you wanted me over?" Katie said.

"Of course I do, but I have to take care of something first. I'll cook tonight. Okay?"

"That's fine."

"Fine-fine or woman-fine?"

"It's really fine, Dusty."

"Court? You and Dean want to come over tonight?"

"No, thanks. I'm going to hermit for a while if it's all the same with you."

"I know you're fine, Court. I wish you'd cheer up."

"Well, you can forget that for a few days until we hear back." She crossed her arms and turned away, making it clear she was done discussing it. Dusty wasn't going to tell her his mom was rushing the tests. She'd probably get upset at that, too.

"If you wouldn't mind driving through Burger King, I could use a gut bomb to hold me over," Katie said.

"Sure, babe."

Chapter Twenty-Five

After dropping the girls off, he went straight back to his place and woke up Dean by kicking the bottom of his feet. "Wake up, numbnuts. I need your help."

"What could you possibly have to do on a Sunday, assface?"

"I need you to write me up a fake Criminal Law letter."

"What for?"

"I need a dude to go in and take an AIDS test. You have to make it sound like he has to go or he'll get arrested for attempted murder."

"Assault with his dick as a deadly weapon? What are you smoking?"

"It's not that far-fetched. If he knows he has it and doesn't do anything about it, he's essentially going to murder people eventually."

"Why pick on this guy?"

"I have my reasons."

"Why don't you type it?"

"'Cause I'm not taking Criminal Law, you are. I want it worded right."

"You worried about this guy not buyin' it?"

"I don't think he's all that much for brains. I want it to look good enough, in case the cops get involved."

"Cops? What the hell are you getting into?"

"The dude needs to go in. I'll tell you more if I have to. You're on a need to know basis."

"Hundred bucks an hour. I'll try to keep it at an hour."

Dusty kicked him again. "You asshole. You'd charge your own mother."

"For legal advice—you betcha."

"The clock starts now. Go." Dusty whipped the covers off. "Jesus! You could have slept in your underwear, jerk."

Once the letter was done, Dusty put his suit on. "Where are you going?" Dean asked.

"To drive you to your place so you can get yours on, too."

"You dragging my ass to church?"

"Not enough holy water in the world to drown your sins. You're going with me to drag this dude to the clinic for his test."

"And we have to do this looking like the Men in Black, why?"

"I want to look official. The guy is going to be a jerk. I need a little back up here."

"So let me call my brother."

"Jason? You think he'd help?"

"He loves a good smack down. He'll meet us there if he's not on duty."

"What's he going to cost me?"

Dean shrugged. "Case of beer."

"It's a deal. Call him."

Dean's brother was a fireman and built like a brick shit house. It hadn't occurred to Dusty to ask for someone else but if Dean thought he'd go, Dusty welcomed the extra muscle.

They met Jason an hour and a half later, right down the street from Ronald's house. Dusty filled him in. As he talked, he sized Jason up. He had a couple inches on both of them and at least fifty extra pounds of solid mass.

"You think this guy will get rough?" Jason asked.

"I don't know. I've seen him in action on a regular basis and he's a dick. If I go demanding he go in for a test he doesn't want to take, it will more than likely get ugly."

Jason punched a fist into his hand. "Good. Wait, though, I can't have blood spraying if you think he has AIDS."

"I am honestly not sure if he does. He was just with this hooker a day ago. We seriously need to rule it out."

"All right. I'll try to watch the blood drawing punches."

"That would be smart. Look, Jase, I appreciate the help, but what I'm doing isn't the most legal thing on the planet. If it gets ugly, there no stopping this douche bag from pressing charges. You sure you want in?"

"Hell, yeah. Besides, what are you two lawyer wannabees gonna do to him? Paper cut him to death?"

Dean gave his brother a shove and in return he was placed in a headlock.

"You ladies ready to go?" Dusty asked.

Jason released Dean and said, "Let's hit it."

They drove down the block in Jason's car. It was a friend's Buick. He borrowed it, thinking it was 'under-cover cop' looking. The three of them exiting the vehicle attracted the attention of a neighbor carrying in groceries. They straightened their shoulders and walked up the steps to the porch.

Ronald answered the door with a beer in his hand. "What do you want? You damn Jehovah Witnesses or what?"

Dusty stepped forward and handed him a letter. He honestly couldn't remember if he should worry about being recognized or not. He didn't think he would be, dressed this way, even if Ronald would have remembered him from the sports bar. "You're required to come with us down to the clinic and get a blood test."

"Blood test for what? Someone else claiming I'm the father of their kid? I always wrap the thing. That's crap." He reached for the letter, crumpled it and threw it behind them.

"It's an AIDS test, sir. You'll need to come with us." Dean said as he picked the paper back up.

"AIDS? Bullshit. No way. I'm telling you. I wrap the thing. I'm not as stupid as you look. I even wrap it with my wife 'cause I can't trust the skank and I don't want no more kids."

Jason stepped forward. "This isn't a suggestion. A woman you were known to be with tested positive. You'll need to come with us."

"Who?"

"A Candy Knowles."

"I don't know anyone by that name."

"She's a hooker. Probably gave you another name."

"I don't need no hooker."

"We know you were with her outside of your work yesterday."

"Bitch is lying."

"We have an eye witness."

"Then she's lying. Fuck off." He tried to slam the door, but Jason stopped it with his hand. He shoved it open, took Ronald by the collar, threw him hard against the wall, then held him there firmly by his neck.

"You can get your coat or I'll cuff you and drag your ass in the car. Capiche?"

Ronald didn't put up any more of a fight so Jason let him go.

"Let me see that paper."

Dean handed it to him. He breezed through it, clearly not understanding the legal jargon Dean had used. "You're saying I can be accused of murder if someone claims I had sex with them and they turn up with this AIDS?"

"Only if you test positive. If you come with us and take the test and if it's negative, you're in the clear. If you're as careful as you say you are, then it shouldn't be an issue."

"I'm telling you—I'm safe."

Dusty asked, "Was this the first time with this hooker?"

"Yes, it was. I didn't even know she was a hooker. I don't need to pay no hookers. I told you that."

"She said you owed her money."

"She's a liar."

Dusty glanced at Dean with a look of frustration. The guy was a real piece of work if nothing else. "That's neither here nor there. You need to come with us. Now."

"Am I under arrest?"

"You will be if you don't come willingly."

"How long will it take?"

"You got a date?" Jason asked, looking at the beer. There was no answer from him.

Dusty stepped in, took Ronald's coat off a hook and handed it to him. "Let's go."

Ronald pulled the coat on, then his boots. After a sideways glance, he bolted across the porch and jumped down the small flight of steps. Jason took off after him and caught him a few houses away, tackling him in a snow bank. "Nice try, shithead." He walked Ronald back to the car with one arm wrenched behind his back. Dean held the door while Jason stuffed him in the car, then climbed in after him. Dusty drove while Dean took the passenger seat rather than the other side of Ronald. His brother's shoulders were wide and he took up more than his share of the back seat. He didn't want to sit that close to the creep.

The women at the clinic stopped what they were doing as they watched the fashion in which their next walk-in was brought in. They didn't ask questions as he was escorted into the chair to have his blood drawn. Dusty spoke to the woman at the counter, whom he recognized from the other appointments.

"This is with the others. You're to call Norma Andrews with the rush results."

She leaned in and whispered. "I'm not supposed to do that without the client's consent."

"But you'll make an exception for my mother and the hundreds of thousands she donates to your little clinic here."

The woman straightened back up. "I suppose I can make this exception."

"Thank you."

Ronald was out in fifteen minutes, then they were on their way back to his place. No one spoke as they drove. Dusty let Jason take the lead. He figured silence was part of the intimidation process. He stopped at Ronald's driveway and waited for him to get out.

"That's it?" he asked.

"That's it. The clinic will be in touch with you about the results. We suspect you'll be more careful from now on."

"I already told you I was. This was a bullshit waste of my time."

"I strongly advise you to watch where you stick it from here on out."

Ronald slammed the door shut.

Dusty started to pull away but Ronald smacked the side of the car twice. Dusty hit the brakes and rolled down his window. "You need something?"

"You the same people that took my wife?"

"No. But I'm aware of the situation."

"Can I talk with her?"

"It's her decision to call you, when and if she's ready."

"Thanks for nothing, pricks!"

Dusty squealed away from the curb.

"Well. That wasn't as fun as I hoped," Jason said once they'd reached Dusty's car.

"Thanks for the muscle, anyway," Dusty said as he handed him a fifty. "I think just having you there was enough of a deterrent to make him behave."

He pushed the money back at Dusty. "Buy me a drink sometime. We'll call it even."

"You got it."

After he pulled away Dean said, "Can I go finish my nap now?"

"Sure."

"Where's my hundred?"

"You're really going to charge me?"

"I know you got money from your mom. Don't give me shit."

Dusty peeled away another fifty and handed it to him. "Thanks."

"Just get my ass home, sweetheart. I don't know how you don't have a hangover today after last night."

"I guess it's just the adrenalin of what I needed to do."

"That was the dude Court was seeing, wasn't it?"

"Yeah. She didn't want you to know. She's pretty shook up."

"Hell. We're safe. Besides, the guy was an ass, but I think he was scared enough of Jason not to lie. I don't think he was with that hooker before. That puts her in the clear. You going to tell her?"

"No. The girls don't need to know we were any more involved in this. When her results come back negative, which should be tomorrow, everything will be back to normal."

As he drove home, Dusty hoped beyond hope that this did the trick. Maybe now that the scare was out in the open, Ronald never returned to that hooker again, never slipped up, and there was no chance he'd infect Courtney even if she and Dean didn't work out.

After dropping off Dean, Dusty called Katie and again apologized for having to drop her back off at the dorm. "I'm on my way home. Can I come get you?"

"Of course. If it's too much driving for you, I can get Court's car."

"I'm fine. Half an hour?"

"I'll be waiting. Hey, heard from your mom yet?"

"Uh…no. She said something was off and the results wouldn't be in until tomorrow."

"Damn. I'll let Court know. Thanks for trying."

"Tell her I'll call if anything changes."

"Thanks, Dusty. See you in a bit."

A half hour later, when Katie got in the car, Dusty leaned over and hugged her tight. He kissed her possessively for several minutes before putting the car in gear.

"Gee. You really did miss me last night."

"You have no idea."

"Can I ask what you had to do this afternoon? You're awfully dressed up."

Dusty put the car back in park. "I never could lie to you."

"Never? In the couple days we've been together you've had opportunity to lie already?"

His head dropped back to the headrest. "I so want to tell you everything…again."

"Is this about Courtney?"

"Some of it."

"You did get the results back."

"We did on the girl, but I know Court is okay."

"How? Our results couldn't have come back yet."

"We saw the guy today and took him in."

"We who?"

"Can we do this back at my place?"

"Why? You afraid I won't want to go with you once you say whatever it is you're having a hard time spitting out?"

"You shouldn't get pissed. Freaked out maybe, but not pissed. I'm dying to get out of this monkey suit."

"You're scaring me, Dusty."

He took her hand. "I'm sorry. There's no need to be worried. Really. Can we go? I promise everything is okay."

"Every ounce of me wants to trust you."

"Then do. I swear everything is okay now." He leaned over and gave her a kiss on the cheek. "I promise."

"All right. I don't know what it is with you, but I trust you."

He gave her another quick kiss then pulled away from the curb.

Once they arrived at his place, he changed into sweats pants. He walked out into the living room and was about to pull a shirt on when Katie said, "Stop." She walked over and ran her hands over his chest then kissed the center of it. "Okay. I'm done."

He grinned. "I told you—you love my chest."

"When?"

"Uh… maybe in my dreams last night." He pulled his shirt on, then took her hand. "Come keep me company while I cook." He dragged her along to the kitchen, then picked her up and placed her on the counter. They shared a long kiss before he broke away. "How about dessert first?"

"How about you finish telling me what you started to say in the car first?"

He stared at her for a second then said. "All right. Let me get water started."

"What are you making me?"

"Incredibly horny?" When she only crossed her arms, he responded, "Lasagna."

"Ooooh. Nice. You may cook as you explain."

"You're all heart." He picked up a large pot and filled it with water, then turned on the burner.

"You know, if you add salt, it'll boil faster."

"You going to do this?"

"Sorry." She waved her hand as if shooing him away. "Carry on."

He opened the cabinet above the stove and pulled out the salt. "You want hamburger or a five cheese?"

"Go crazy."

"Good call." He took out a frying pan then removed a package of meat from the refrigerator. "I bought this yesterday. Don't worry."

"You forget about food in your fridge a lot?"

He shrugged. "It happens." He had already forgotten this wasn't the Katie that found the Chinese food weeks old in his fridge. Taking a peek back in there, he saw the containers she probably found a couple weeks from now and chuckled. "What's so funny?"

"I see something I should probably toss out."

"Do it before you forget."

"I will later." He had no intention of it. Dropping the burger in the pan, he took a spatula to it while he resumed his story. "I went to take Ronald into the clinic after I dropped you off."

"That's your big secret? You could have told me that. Did he give you trouble?"

"A little. We took Dean's brother for muscle, though."

"Dean's brother? You told Dean?"

"I didn't want to, but he figured it out. It was easy enough after hearing the dude's name. I needed him to help with a letter I drafted to the jerk and yeah, I wanted someone else along. I didn't know how crazy this guy was going to get. Dean didn't even say anything until it was over. He wanted to help."

"Court's gonna be pissed."

"He's fine with it. I really think the dude was telling the truth about the hooker. He was only with her that day. Courtney is in the clear. Besides, you're the one that told her when you shouldn't have." Dusty heard her hop off the counter. When he turned around, she was walking into the living room. "Shit!" He turned down the heat on the meat and went after her. "I'm sorry. I'm not trying to start a fight. I just wish she wasn't told and upset about it in the first place."

"Well, I couldn't lie to her."

"It's okay." Dusty pulled her to his chest. "I don't want us fighting over this. I'm trying to take care of everything and maybe I'm not doing it so well. I know what she means to you. That's all this is about, babe."

"I don't understand your obsession with this. You hardly know me yet you're dead set on Courtney's health and love life."

"Everything fell into place funny. That's all. It was by chance I saw them together, then I met you and her, then I found out about him. Finding the girl in the alley was a freaky coincidence. You were with me there. It can't be explained away by anything but chance or fate for all of us."

"You said your mom called with the results from that girl."

"Yes. I didn't want to upset you two. She was positive."

Katie gasped. "But we need to tell Court!"

"No. Let's wait on her results. I know she's fine."

"How do you know that?"

"I believe this was the first time he was with this girl. Court will be in the clear."

"I don't know, Dusty."

"They both swear up and down they are safe partners. I give her that much credit. Let the test come back then we'll tell her. Maybe the scare will be a good one and she'll really be extra careful from now on."

Katie leaned into him. "I need a hug."

"You got it."

Dusty and Katie returned to the kitchen, assembling the lasagna when everything was cooked and ready. They play fought over how much cheese to use. Katie always added more after Dusty stopped with each layer.

"You're a fiend," he said with a laugh.

"I've never met a cheese I didn't like."

He knew the answer, but he asked anyway. "Brie?"

"I love Brie."

"I'll have to buy a wheel of it and some champagne for our next date."

"Don't forget the strawberries."

"Ooh…you are a pro at this."

She hopped back up on the counter and curled her finger at him, calling him over. He got as close as he could to her and pulled her closer to him so their hips met.

"Dessert time?" he asked. She only nodded a yes. "You want me to throw the lasagna in first?" She shook her head no.

Dusty hated the fluffy rugs his mother bought him for his kitchen—until now. What started off on the counter ended up on the floor with the struggle of removing Katie's jeans. Again the hunger and anticipation took over their lovemaking. It never ceased to amaze Dusty how he could never get enough of Katie. With the wanting so great, it was over too quickly for both of them. Dusty picked Katie up and carried her to the bedroom.

"Sorry. I have no control when it comes to you," he said.

"I do believe I started this one."

He kissed both cheeks then her lips. "I love how you've never held back what you wanted."

She rested her head on her hand. "You always talk like we've been together for so much longer than we have. I think I like that."

"It doesn't scare you that I'm rushing things?"

"It did a little. Does, I guess, but there is just something about you. I can't put my finger on it, though."

"How about a whole hand?" He took her hand and placed it low on his stomach. She slid it down further. "Ready again?"

"I'm always ready for you."

"You younger men and your stamina."

He laughed. "If you ask my mom, it's an Andrews' thing. She always teased that Gramps would be having sex on his hospital deathbed."

"He one of those Hugh Hefner-young woman on his arms types?"

"Nope. He and my grandmother have been married for sixty-three years."

"Wow. Horny and loyal. Two of my favorite qualities in a man."

"You're not his type."

Katie laughed then reached around to his behind and pulled Dusty closer to her. "Maybe not. But I'm glad I'm yours."

After a much slower round two, the satisfied couple returned to the kitchen to get their creation into the oven. Dusty turned to Katie. "Well, now we have an hour wait and we've already done all the fun stuff there is to do in the house."

"Why don't we put in a movie?"

"Sounds good. Go pick one. I'll get a fire going."

As they cuddled by the TV, Dusty again felt at peace. He was certain everything was going to be okay and this was his last night here. It was hard for him to concentrate on the movie—not that he needed to since it was one they watched over two dozen times together. His thoughts kept going to what would happen when he made it back to his present day. Would he get the flood of memories and a nosebleed like Katie? Would she remember this now as their life? He gave her a squeeze, again feeling the electricity of love he felt when they were close. Never would he have imagined his life this insane or that he would be so happy. He fell asleep as content as he ever had and hoped to wake up in his normal time.

Katie shook Dusty awake. He bolted upright, afraid of where he would be. He was grateful to smell lasagna and see his small table set for two.

"Sorry I fell asleep, baby."

"That's okay. I almost did, too, until I heard the timer go off."

"How about we call it an early night?"

"That's what I thought, but I do want to go home again."

"You sure? I have time in the morning to get you back if you have an early class."

"I really think I should be with Court. I know you have to understand. She wanted breathing room today, but I'd really like to be there for her tonight. Okay?"

"Of course." He motioned to the table. "Let's see what you did to my arteries with all that cheese." Not that he was worried. Dusty was smiling inside. He'd be gone tonight and just as with the kegger and no hangover, he was sure to be gone tomorrow and have no consequences from eating a double helping of over-cheesed lasagna.

Chapter Twenty-Six

Katie walked into the dorm room quietly. It was only eight, but the room was dark. Her thoughts were that Courtney changed her mind and went out instead of lying there in bed, but as upset as she was, there was no telling what she'd do. She was surprised to find her sitting on the Papa-san chair, staring out the window.

"Hey," Katie said softly. She wasn't sure if Courtney heard the door, she didn't want to scare her.

"Hey."

"You okay?"

"Just thinkin'."

"You care to share?"

"It's nothing in particular." Courtney's phone was vibrating on her desk. Katie walked over to answer it for her. "Don't. It's Dean again."

"Why are you not talking to Dean?"

"I don't want to talk to anyone, Katie. Dean's a nice guy. He doesn't need a tramp like me killing him in his prime."

"Stop it, Court! You're not a tramp and you're not ruining anyone's life." She knelt down in front of her. "I'm not supposed to say anything, but I can't take you like this. Dusty talked to Ronald today."

"Why?"

"Because he was worried about you and wanted some answers. The guy swore he was only with this hooker the one time. Even if she's positive, you wouldn't have it."

"But if he was with her, he was probably with others."

"But you said you were careful."

"Of course I was, but my luck I'd be in that .001 percent chance of condoms not working."

"I know you're fine. Trust me. It was just a scare and a good reminder for all of us to be more careful."

"You mean me. You've taken the test plunge and are ready to commit to Dusty already, for cryin' out loud."

"I didn't think I was. He's so sure of us, it rubbed off on me. I want to give it a shot. I'm tired of dating buffoons. Just because I'm ready doesn't mean you're supposed to be. We've said a thousand times that our lives are too busy for one guy. Don't get mad at yourself over my choices."

Courtney put her head on her knees. "You'll move out soon. I know it."

"I won't. I swear. Unless you're ready for me to go, I'm not going anywhere."

"So you are thinking about it?"

"We haven't talked about it, no. But it's a nightly battle in my head to return here to you. And guess who keeps winning?" Courtney threw her arms around Katie and had the good cry she must have been fighting all day. Katie joined in with no delay.

Dusty was parked in front of Katie's dorm room entrance after school the next day. He was happy to catch the two of them walking toward him together. When he woke up this morning still here, he was surprised. He thought he was done and he'd get to go home. Maybe part of his reward for fixing things was being able to breaking the news to them. "Hey. I thought you two shared goofy schedules and never met."

"Today was a fluke. My teacher dropped her uterus," Courtney said with a straight face.

Dusty laughed. "What's the punch line?"

"No punch line. It literally dropped. She's had eight kids. Shit just happens. Makes me want to switch to OB/GYN. Not. What are you doing here?"

He reached in his car and pulled out a bottle of champagne. "I'm toasting the lot of negative HIV test subjects."

Courtney jumped up, hugged him, and hung from his neck. He handed Katie the bottle and wrapped his arms around Courtney, holding her there. When he let her down, she wiped a tear from her eye. "Thanks, Dusty."

"My pleasure. Dean's negative too, if you're wondering. When we took shithead in, he went in, too."

"What do you mean?"

He turned to Katie. "I was sure you told her last night."

"You told me not to so I didn't. Well…most of it."

"Tell me what?"

"We dragged Ronald in yesterday for a test. We didn't think he'd go of his own free will."

"We?" She glared at Katie.

"Not me. He went with…"

"Dean? You took Dean?"

"He wanted to help. I needed backup with this guy. He was a real piece of work. I didn't tell him, he figured it out. Don't get pissed. He wasn't worried about you having it; he wanted to be able to tell you he was clean."

"Right." She turned to walk away but Dusty stopped her.

"Stop it, Court. It wasn't about you. With your medical background, you probably know better than anyone that it doesn't show up this fast. Ronald was negative too, but that doesn't completely clear him with the hooker. He swears he was only with her the once so you're okay. As far as it goes for him, he could still test positive in as much as six months down the road. Dean did it *for* you—not *because* of you."

She jerked her arm free and walked away. "I want to be alone."

"Court…don't." But it was no use.

Katie leaned into Dusty. "She'll calm down. I'll take you up on staying at your place tonight, though."

"Good call."

Dusty walked around to the passenger side of the car and opened Katie's door. *Crap. Looks like I may be here for a while yet.*

Katie hung up with Courtney at nine. She wanted to call and say goodnight. "She was short with me, but I think she's all right," she explained to Dusty. "I think she liked Dean more than she was letting on."

"She still pissed at me?"

"Oh yeah. There was mention of a feminine exam tool and your ass."

"Ouch."

"Did you talk to Dean?"

"A little. He really doesn't give a shit about what happened. They took their precautions. He really likes her and is kind of bummed. Said she hasn't been returning his calls. I told him she's been glum about the whole thing and probably just needs time."

"I hope he doesn't give up."

Dusty walked over and wrapped his arms around her. He tugged at his pajama top that she wore. "As much as I love seeing you in my stuff, we should bring some of your clothes over here."

"That will really make her flip. She's already worried I'm going to move in here."

"I hope you do soon."

"Dusty. It's too early for that. I really need to give Court some time to get used to the idea of us. We've been together a long time."

"You have to part eventually. She was talking about going to Seattle soon."

"We'll deal with that when we have to, okay? I don't want to complicate things."

"All right. I trust your judgment. As long as I can have you to myself here and there, I suppose I'll live."

"I still have to fit in studying, you know. I don't know why I never see a book or anything open around here."

"I'm a fast learner," he said before placing his lips on hers and laying her down on the bed.

Dusty woke up to the sound of knocking on a door. He felt a weight on his chest and was beyond thrilled to discover it was his sleeping son. Looking around, he discovered that he was back in his living room. He gave his son a tight squeeze, relieved to finally be home. Sliding carefully off the couch so he wouldn't wake Alex, Dusty walked over to the door with his son still sound asleep on his shoulder. The face that greeted him when he opened the door surprised him.

"Gina?"

"Hey, Dusty," she said at a soft tone when her eyes lowered to the sleeping baby.

Dusty was tongue-tied at the sight of her. The last time he saw her, she was nothing more than a scared child. Now she looked like grown woman. Her hair was pulled back in a neat bun, she had just a touch of makeup on, and was dressed very professionally. *What the hell did he miss?* Looking down, he noticed she was four or five months pregnant. He smiled at her. "Look at you!" He leaned over and kissed her cheek.

"Geez, Dusty. You saw me last week at the office. Have I popped out that much?"

"No," he said with a chuckle. "There's just something about a pregnant woman. You look great." His mind raced. *What office?*

"Is Katie home?"

He was just about to say, "No, she's in Seattle," when Katie came up behind him.

"Hi, Gina. Is that the paperwork there?"

Dusty's attention went to a portfolio in her hands.

"Sure is. I typed up the last of it this morning."

"That rotten boss of yours making you work on a Saturday," Katie said, shaking her head.

"It's not his fault. I wanted to get them finished up so you had plenty of time to look them over before your meeting Tuesday."

"You work too hard."

"I love my job. What can I say?" She rubbed her stomach as she talked. "Dean is very good to me."

Dusty's head was spinning. *Was Dean her boss or her husband? Both? What the hell was going on? Did the shelter get her a job where Dean worked now? Where's Courtney?* This was too much input at once.

Little Alyson came running over. "Gina!" She flew up into her arms.

"Careful, peanut," Katie said to her. "Mind the baby in her belly. You shouldn't do that anymore for a while."

"It's okay," Gina said as she hugged Ali tight.

"How about Daddy?" Dusty asked his daughter as he bent down. He had missed her hugs over the past couple of days. "Mind your brother, though," he said in a whisper.

Dusty noticed Katie looking at him funny for the way he held onto Ali. He reluctantly released her and stood back up.

She returned her attention to Gina. "You have a good rest of your day. Thanks for bringing the paperwork over."

"My pleasure. See you guys later."

Dusty said his goodbyes as well and closed the door. "What are those?"

Katie dropped them to her side as if she was frustrated with his question. "Are you still asleep? The partnership papers for the clinic."

"Oh, right. Sorry. She did wake me out of a sound sleep."

"You seem a little off. Let me put him down. Here, take these," she said as she handed him the papers. "I'll take him." After her son was settled in her arms, Katie turned to Dusty. "Are you sure you're all right?"

"I'm fine. Just tired, I guess."

Katie was hesitant but went upstairs to put Alex in bed. As soon as she was gone, Dusty dove into the papers. After scanning then briefly, he saw they were for making Steve Hickey a full partner at the animal hospital. Steve had worked there since Katie took maternity leave with Alyson years ago. This was long overdue. The date on the paperwork showed that this had happened a few months ago. Dusty wasn't happy to finally realize he wasn't back for good. If he was, Katie would be in Seattle. *What now, dammit?*

He put the papers down and went out on the front porch. The neighborhood looked the same, but something was missing and he couldn't put his finger on it. It finally occurred to him. The "for sale" sign was gone from the house next door. He jumped when he heard, "Hey, butt munch. You have a second?"

He turned around to see Dean leaning on the fence in between their houses.

"Uh…sure." *Holy crap, Dean lives next door?*

Dusty walked over and met Dean at the fence. "I picked up that damn new dishwasher. Will you help me drag it in?"

"Sure. Cost you a beer."

"Duh."

The guys got the dishwasher in place. Dusty was under the sink connecting the hoses. He was dying to know what was going on. Trying to think of how to word his questions carefully, he finally tried to approach the subject of Gina.

"Gina is sure looking good."

"She get those papers to Katie today?"

"Just left."

"I told her not to go in today, but I can't keep her out of there. She really loves the work."

"That's too bad. I rescued her from one dirtball and she ends up with another." Dusty chuckled as Dean kicked his feet.

"She's really taken with this legal stuff. I wouldn't be surprised if she goes to school herself. That's one little lady that isn't going to stay a secretary for long."

Dusty still didn't have the answers he wanted. He tried to pry some more. "So, married life is treating her well this time around?"

Dean squatted down. "What the hell are you smokin'? Freeman say something to you?"

"Freeman?"

"Freeman. My partner, her husband, the father of her kid? Geez, Dusty. You have play dough between your ears or what?"

"Sorry, man. I was napping with Alex when she showed up. I must still be half asleep. She looked happy, that's all I was saying. I guess I was dreaming about that day we hauled her dickhead ex to the clinic."

"Shit." Dean chuckled. "Of all days to get reminiscent about. Hey, you have to go see your car, man. The paint job came out totally cherry."

"Love to. Holler and see if he wants to have a beer when we're done here. Hey…thanks again for doing those papers for Katie."

"Thanks, my ass. I'm billing you."

Dusty laughed and returned to the pipes. "A man who had been caught embezzling millions from his employer went to a lawyer seeking defense. He didn't want to go to jail. But his lawyer told him, 'Don't worry. You'll never have to go to jail with all that money.' And the lawyer was right. When the man was sent to prison, he didn't have a dime."

"Douche." Dean stood and again kicked Dusty's feet.

Dusty heard the door close and Dean hollered, "Hey, babe. Let me help you with those." After bags rattling and unmistakable kissing sounds, Dusty peeked out from under the sink and smiled. "Hey, Court."

When the long day was over, Dusty went to bed cuddling with Katie. He caught a glimpse of how life was supposed to be and he wanted it. Now he knew why he hadn't left yet. Katie spun around and faced him.

"You would tell me if something was up, wouldn't you?"

"Of course. Why?"

"You weren't yourself today."

"Which me do you think I was?"

"Don't tease me like that, Dusty. That's not something I ever want to go through again."

"You're telling me. Don't worry, babe. If I ever see 'he who should not be mentioned,' I'll kick his ass."

"Don't you dare touch that sweet man."

If you only knew. "All right, pumpkin. I promise. If one of us has to go again, I'll do it."

Katie laughed hard. "Yeah, right. You'd probably crash and burn at picking me up again."

Dammit! She is physic! "Not a chance. You know you'd fall for me all over again."

She gave him a kiss. “I suppose you’re right. You going to do me or what?”

“You never have to ask me twice.”

Falling asleep happy for the first time in almost a week, Dusty let out a content moan before he drifted off.

Chapter Twenty-Seven

The next day brought Dusty awake again in his college home, but at least Katie was by his side. They hurried through getting dressed and pouring coffee in travel mugs. Dusty dropped her off, planning for another day of skipping class. He hoped this wasn't his new fate. He couldn't figure out what else he had to do and why he needed to be here. Looking for Frank was out of the question. Dusty was at peace with figuring this out for himself. His day was spent with killing some time at the outdoor rink. After being frustrated with the shape of his older self on the ice, he vowed to put some time in every year and start the kids ice skating next year for sure.

Dusty called his mother for a follow up on Gina. He was glad to hear she was happy where she was, tested negative, and had already started training for a new job. After grocery shopping and getting some movies, his day was already wasted. He decided to go to the dorm and wait for Katie.

After knocking on the door, he tried the knob. He didn't expect anyone to be in. He was surprised when he walked in and saw Courtney putting on makeup. "Hey. You still pissed at me?"

"You're not on my favorite people list, but you can come in."

"Where are you going? Date with Dean?"

"No. I'm going out with a new student. He just transferred here. He has the cutest accent. You know what they say about Italians." She chuckled and returned to her blush.

"I thought things were going so good with Dean. What happened?"

"Nothing happened. You didn't really think I was going to stick to one guy, did you? I know Katie has taught you better than that about me."

"Court…" Dusty flopped backwards onto Katie's bed. "You liked him."

"I'm going to take that intern offer in Seattle. You and Katie are hitting it off so great…I know I'm going to lose her soon." She let out a heavy sigh. "It doesn't matter how I feel about Dean. I can't start something that I'll only have to end soon anyway. I thought about it a lot last night while I was here alone."

He rushed over. "Don't move to Seattle, Court. You'd hate it there. It does nothing but rain."

"As opposed to the snow?"

"But it's gray all the time. You'd hate that. Don't you do the tanning bed thing for winter depression? At least we get sun sometimes."

"Dusty… I know you mean well, but that's where my job is. Will be. I'll cope."

"But what about Dean? Come on. He's my best friend. I know he likes you. Katie talks of nothing but living next door to each other, you guys having kids together…."

"You know I'd love that if this was a perfect world, but I have to go. It's a great start for my career. It's not like Dean has proposed or even professed his undying love for me. It's only been a few dates, for cryin' out loud, Dusty. We don't move as quickly as you two. I can't stay, give up a great opportunity, and spend all my time avoiding the guy if it doesn't work out."

"You like him though. Don't you?"

"For as much as I know on the subject. I guess I do. Did. I don't know. Look at my track record, hon. Shit. I could have killed the guy. Then what? He's a great guy. He'll find someone soon. Someone that really deserves him. I'm sure he wants someone a little more deserving of wearing white on their wedding day, anyway."

"Oh, bullshit! Who can really wear white these days?"

"My cousin Izzy."

"No shit?"

"I shit you not. Both of them were. I didn't think that was possible anymore, either."

"Yeah, well, you didn't think dry counties existed until I told you over dinner about camping in Kentucky either. Come on, Court. You going to tuck your tail and run because you're afraid you're not good enough? I call bullshit again. Why don't you let him decide for himself what he wants?"

Courtney put down her brush and placed her hands on Dusty's shoulders. "You know I love you for Katie. You're a great guy, Dusty. It's only been a short while, but you two really seem to click. The sound of the two of us living next door to each other with our kids running around is appealing and of course would be a dream come true, but it's not realistic."

Dusty held on to Courtney's hands. "What about the internship at the hospital here that you were talking about? Did that fall through or something? Why the rush to take off for Washington?"

"They haven't responded yet."

"*Yet*. See. Give it a chance. Don't accept Seattle's offer yet. Please?"

"What is with you about this? Sheesh. I promise. I'll give it a few days. But I'm still going out with this kid. He promised me *Chez Pauls*." Dusty moaned. "You know she didn't throw up because of the food."

"I know, but she says she tastes it the second time around every time she hears that name."

Courtney put her hands down and gave Dusty a kiss on the cheek. "I really like you, you know. You're perfect for Katie. Really. Just let me do what has worked for *me* so far." Courtney walked to the door and blew him a kiss, then waved goodbye. "Lock up when you leave."

Dusty grumbled. "Dammit." He pulled out his cell phone and called Katie. When she answered he said, "You're taking me out to dinner tonight, babycakes," instead of hello.

"Sure, my love. Where to?"

"*Chez Pauls*."

"I know you didn't just say that, Dusty."

"Sorry, we have to. Where are you?"

"I was dropped off at your place. I thought I'd save you the drive today. Where are you?"

"Your place waiting for you."

"Crap."

"The back door isn't locked. Go in. I won't be long."

"You going to tell me why I have to go to *Chez Pauls* again?"

"I'm making Dean go, too."

"Uh oh. Let me guess. Courtney is going there with someone else."

"You got it. I just said goodbye to her on her way out."

"Who is the date with? She seemed pretty down about dating at all."

"Some new kid. An exchange student."

"Dammit. She's pushing Dean away."

"That's my thought. I'm not letting her win this."

"She can out-stubborn a mule, Dusty. You've already seen her temper, and that was nothing. I really don't know that you want to get involved here."

"Yes, I do. If I don't, I'll never get home."

"You have to go somewhere before you come here?"

"No. Sorry. That's not what I meant. I'm leaving now. I'll see you in a few minutes."

"Hey! Bring me my black pants and heels since you're there. Pick out a top you like."

"You're telling me to go through your things?"

"Nothing to see, dreamboat. Have a party in my closet."

"Dreamboat? Am I rubbing off on you?"

"Hopefully later."

"Good God almighty, I'm hopelessly in love with you."

"If you hurry, you can join me in the shower."

"Leaving now." He shut his phone and hurried though the clothes, picking out a nice blue silky top he hadn't seen her in before.

Dusty called Dean on the way home. "Katie and I want to take you to dinner for your help with that Ronald jerk."

"You don't need to do that."

"I know, but she wants to."

"Courtney goin'?"

"She has something going on tonight and can't come."

"I think I've been dumped, dude. She isn't returning my calls."

"She's had a rough time with this and needed some space. She'll come around. Don't stand my girl up, okay? You have someone on back up you can call so you don't feel like a third wheel?"

"There's always Tina. We've passed the awkward *not dating anymore* stage and are pretty good friends. She'd like a nice treat. You shelling out the big bucks again?"

"You know it."

"All right. I'll meet you there. What time?"

"Seven."

"Sounds good."

Dusty and Dean pulled up behind each other at the valet. Katie wasn't the happiest about Dean having a date along, but she was pleasant enough to his friend.

As they walked in to the restaurant, Courtney spotted them immediately. Dusty caught her looking away. After everyone took their seats, he walked over to her, tall and proud, and gave her a kiss on the cheek. "Hey, Court. I forgot you were going to be here." He reached his hand out to her date. "Dustin. Nice to meet you."

"Rodney. Nice to meet you, too." Dusty was surprised at the lack of an accent.

"You guys order yet?" Dusty asked. "Want to join us? I'm sure we can get a bigger table." He swore he could see smoke coming out of Courtney's ears. He patted Rodney on the back. "That's okay. I understand if you want to be alone."

"Courtney?" Rodney said. "I'd love to sit with your friends and meet them, but it's your call."

Forcing a smile, she shoved her chair back. "That would be great. I'll let the waiter know."

"Sit, Court. I've got it." Dusty hurried over to the table. "I found a friend of ours. They're going to join us. I have to get them to give us a bigger table."

Dean stood and said through bared teeth, "I'll go with you." Once they were away from the table, Dean elbowed him. "What the hell are you doing? You knew she'd be here?"

"No. I had no idea. She made a new friend, though. It's only polite to invite them over."

"You're a dick."

"Love you, too." He turned to the maître d' and explained that they needed a bigger table. It wasn't a busy night so he was happy to accommodate the request. Dusty got everyone settled, seating Courtney next to Dean and their dates to the other sides of them. He introduced everyone to Rodney. "How do you and Courtney know each other?" Dusty asked. "You a new student?"

"Student? Hell no." Courtney turned away, obviously embarrassed. She was lying about who this was. Dusty was intrigued.

"What brings you to our neck of the woods? Can't be the gorgeous weather."

Rodney took Courtney's hand and held it up. "Isn't it obvious? She's the greatest, isn't she?"

"That she is." Dusty waved the waiter over. "Can we get two bottles of *Perrier Jouet* please?"

"Dusty!" Katie scolded. "That's expensive!"

"I don't care. I'm using Dad's card. Besides, we should celebrate that Court found such a great guy and welcome her new friend to the area." Rodney let out a laugh. "I'm not a new friend. I've been in Minneapolis for a week of meetings and having nothing but deli sandwiches breakfast, lunch, and dinner. I told them to piss off and escaped tonight. I wanted a nice meal with my favorite cousin."

"Cousin," Dusty said as if it were the most interesting thing he ever heard. "That's great." He asked him what he did for work and the two carried on.

Dean stole the chance to lean over to Courtney. "Your phone lost or something?"

"No, Dean. I've just had a lot on my mind."

"You could have answered and told me that. I'm not a Neanderthal. I would have understood, Court."

"I'm sorry. It's not like you took any time filling my sheets." She motioned her eyes to Tina.

"She's just a friend."

"Sure she is." Courtney stood up. "I'm going to the powder room. Katie?"

Katie stood up. "I'll go. Tina?"

"I'm fine. Thanks."

Courtney figured Katie had to ask to be polite, but she was glad Tina declined. As soon as they walked in the room, Courtney blew up. "What is this shit, Katie? Can't I have one night alone?"

"Don't get pissed at me. I had no idea. Dusty said he wanted to take Dean out for dinner. I thought it was strange to come here again so soon, but I went along with it."

"Does he want to rub this Tina in my face or what?"

"They're just friends. Do you even care? Dusty said Dean told him you weren't returning his calls. I suspected as much, but I thought you'd come around and get over yourself already."

"Excuse me?"

"You heard me, Court. We've all been worried at one time or another that we were a little cavalier in our sex lives. You didn't screw up, so just get over it already. I can't take this 'woe-is-me' shit any longer. Dusty wants me to move in with him and I don't want to because of you. If you don't snap out of it soon, I will."

"Don't let me stop you, princess."

Katie stormed out of the bathroom. When Courtney joined them at the table, no one would have known there had been a tiff.

Katie turned to Dean. "Will you order for me again? I love hearing you speak French."

"Sure. You want the same thing?"

"Something seafood. Surprise me."

"You got it."

Tina put down her menu. "Do me, too."

Courtney rolled her eyes and turned to her cousin. "What do you like, Rod?"

Dean liked that Dusty managed to keep conversation flowing throughout dinner, giving everyone proper attention and their turn at a story or two. He felt awkward sitting next to Courtney. He wanted to do so much more than just be polite. It was increasingly difficult to stop trying to touch her. The desire to stroke her arm or take her hand was getting tougher and tougher.

After they finished their meals, the piano player announced he was going to take a short break. Dean turned to Dusty, Dusty shook his head no. He figured Dusty wasn't in the mood to play. He was doing a good job at keeping track of what was going on at the table. Dean watched Tina and Rodney all night. They seemed to be hitting it off. *So much for an afterthought of making Courtney jealous.*

Not heeding Dusty's wishes, Dean went over to the maître d'. He returned with the host behind him. "We would love if you wanted to get up and play a song or two. As long as you keep it to an older musical number. Can you do any of those?"

"I have a few I can do," Dusty said, standing up and promptly punching Dean in the arm. Dean whispered something to Dusty and he nodded in agreement. Tina loved to dance and Dean knew it. When Dusty played a slow Chopin waltz number, Dean encouraged Tina to take Rodney up. "The girl loves to waltz. Take her for a spin."

"You don't mind?"

"Hell, no. We're just friends. Go ahead."

Next, as ordered, Dusty did a number suitable for a tango. It would be all over for poor Rodney. No man could resist a tango. It was too perfect that there were a dozen roses on the piano to complete the scene. He watched as Tina placed one between her teeth. *Always the show girl.* Rodney didn't do too badly trying to keep up. Dean finally dared to lean into to Courtney.

"They make a cute couple."

"Shut up."

"Come on, Court. Stop with the cold fish act. Let's go somewhere and talk."

"I don't want to." She crossed her arms and focused her attention on Rodney and Tina dancing, as the rest of the people at their tables were doing.

Dusty's last song was "Misty." Dean had requested this for another reason. After giving it a few notes to sink in, he stood and took Courtney's hand, not giving her a chance to turn him down. He stole a quick glance at Katie who had picked up her napkin and dabbed at her eye. If he knew the story about Courtney and the song, he was sure Katie did.

He held Courtney tight as they slow danced. Her head stayed buried tight into his chest. Dean knew it was her favorite song, even though it was hard for her to listen to. Although they only had a few dates, he'd already heard the story about her childhood friend named Misty. She died of leukemia when they were only twelve. Her mother played the song for her over and over on their old record player. It was that heartbreaking incident that made Courtney decide to become a doctor. She never wanted someone to suffer as Misty had or even suffer as she had in losing a dear friend.

As soon as the song was over, Courtney ran from the dance floor and took off outside without her coat. Rodney started to go after her, but Dean stopped him. "I'll go to her. We'll be right back. The song gets to her." He shouted to Dusty. "Didn't I tell you not to play that when she was around?"

Dean was grateful Dusty followed along and apologized. "Sorry, dude. I totally forgot. Should I go get her?"

"I got her. Be right back."

Dean hurried outside after stopping for their coats. He saw his keys hanging on a peg in the valet booth and handed the guy there a ten for them. "I'll find it in the lot." Scanning the street, he found Courtney on the corner in front of the parking ramp. She didn't seem to know what to do. He rushed over to her and wrapped her coat around her shoulders. "It's freezing. Let's go back."

"Not yet. I feel like an ass."

"Then let's go sit in my car. I got my keys."

Once they were in the garage, he hit the button on his fob to start the car and saw the lights flash in the last stall. The overhead light was burned out. It would have been hard to see otherwise. They crawled in the back seat together.

"I'm sorry that asshole played that song. I'll deck him later for you."

"It's not his fault. It's a beautiful song. I'll cry until the day I die when I hear it. Sorry I ran off."

"That's okay. I wanted you alone anyway. You've been driving me crazy all night." Dean raised her chin and kissed her. She fought him at first, then began to kiss him more aggressively back.

She finally broke apart. "I'm sorry I didn't answer when you called."

"That's okay. I should have stormed over and put an end to the bullshit myself, instead of letting Dusty play his games."

"I knew it!" she screamed but Dean pressed his lips to her again, silencing her. He leaned her back in the seat and ran his hand up her thigh under her dress. She greedily unbuttoned his belt then quickly stopped.

"We can't do this, Dean."

"Sure we can. The light is burned out."

"No, I mean, we can't. I don't have anything on me. My purse is in the restaurant. You have any on you?"

"No. We don't need them, Court. We're both negative." He kissed her with a wild tongue, anxious to taste every bit of her. His hands worked at her dress, pulling it higher and positioning his hands across the band of her thong.

She stopped him again. “But what about—”

“You’re on the pill and you had your period last week. You’re not getting pregnant.”

“We can’t, dammit!” She sat up and pulled her dress back down.

“You’re not afraid of the sex. You’re afraid of liking it. You’re afraid of loving me the way I already love you.”

“That’s not true.”

“The hell it’s not. You’re pushing me away. This whole Ronald thing was the excuse you wanted to keep your distance.” He took both her hands in his. “Don’t do it, Court. Don’t move to Seattle, either. I’m asking you to give us a chance and stay here. Take the internship here and give me a shot.”

Her eyes finally met his. “You love me?”

“I know you think Dusty and Katie are crazy, but it does happen that fast. Yes, I do love you already. I have a few years on Dusty so don’t give me that for an excuse.” He leaned in for another kiss and she eagerly accepted him.

Leaning back, she pulled him back on top of her. “Do me, lover.”

When he entered her, they both let out moans of ecstasy. Courtney cried, “Holy crap. I feel like I’m a virgin all over again.”

“You have no idea…ooh man...how good this feels. You’re so warm…so…oh holy mother…” Dean could only whimper shamelessly after that while Courtney joined in with obscenities of her own. The two of them climaxed together in only minutes. Dean finally managed a “Holy shit,” after catching his breath. “What the hell have we been doing before?”

“I don’t know, but I do like this,” Courtney said as she pulled him in for another long kiss. After taking a few minutes to compose themselves, they walked back into the restaurant holding hands. Everyone was back at the table. Rodney and Tina were now sitting next to each other.

"Everything okay?" Dusty asked Courtney.

"Just fine. We're going to split." She turned to Rodney. "Sorry, cousin. You think you can get Tina back home?"

"Sure thing."

"You don't mind, right?" Dean asked Tina. She grinned. "Not at all. It's fine."

Katie stood and hugged Courtney goodbye. She ran her hands down the back of her friend's hair. "You have fucking hair, hon." She winked and kissed them both goodnight.

Dusty shook Dean's hand then he hugged Courtney tight. "You can kill me later, sweetie."

"Not on your life. Thanks for giving my head a view other than the inside of my ass."

"Unlike your boyfriend there, no charge." He kissed her on the cheek.

The waiter walked over, leaving the check on the table. "You were done here, sir, correct?"

Dusty let out a heavy breath. "God, I hope so."

Chapter Twenty-Eight

Dusty woke up to the phone ringing. He slapped around on the nightstand until his hand found it. He lay back flat on his pillow and mumbled a groggy hello.

"Dusty. Help me."

He bolted upright. "Courtney?" He turned to his right. He was surprised to find Kaityln there. Wasn't she with Courtney? Confused, he asked, "What is it?"

"It's time. Dean isn't due home until this afternoon."

"Dean? It's time?" he repeated, still not sure what was going on.

There was banging on the front door. "This isn't funny, Dustin Charles. I don't have my key on me. Open up the damn door."

"You're outside?"

"Hurry up. I'm freezing!"

He shot out of bed. Kaitlyn sat up and asked, "Who was on the phone?"

"Courtney."

She was suddenly alert. "It's time?"

"So she says," he answered, still unsure as to what that meant. "She's here."

"Ohmygod." Katie rushed passed him. Dusty hurried behind her. They'd almost reached the door when they heard a scream. Hurrying past Katie now, Dusty moved her aside and opened the door. Courtney stood there in a nightshirt, no pants, snow boots and a winter coat. There was a puddle under her.

"Shit. My water just broke."

Dusty smiled as he reached for her hand. "Come in and sit. I'll go get the car warmed up and take you in."

"I'll call Mrs. Nelson to come stay with the kids," Katie said as she hurried to the phone.

As Dusty paced the maternity waiting room, he tried to piece together what happened. His last stunt must have worked. *Dean and Courtney stayed together!* Dean came flying through the door an hour after they arrived. "Am I too late?"

"Not yet, buddy. Get in there!"

Dean flew through the double doors that Dusty pointed to. Dusty saw a nurse escort him to the room. The birth was probably too close to suit him up in scrubs. Part of Dusty wished he could go in, but mostly he was glad he couldn't. Getting Katie through her delivery of Alyson in the car was one thing; that had happened too fast to even think. They had Alexander in the hospital; Katie had called him every name in the book and a few she'd invented. He was certain their baby-making days were over.

He was about to go back to the chairs when he saw a nurse walking out of the room. "Talk about good timing," he said to himself, thinking it was over and Dean just made it in time. When he saw an orderly carrying Katie out, he rushed through the door.

"What happened?"

"Her nose started to bleed and she passed out."

"No!" cried Dusty as he caught up. He wanted to take her from the orderly, but he assured Dusty he had her. The next birthing room was available so they went in there.

"Has this happened before?" the nurse asked.

"Years ago. They never found the cause and figured it was a fluke." He took one of her hands in his and gently stroked her face with the other. "Babe? You okay?"

The nurse slipped an oxygen mask on her. "I'm going to get the doc. He may want to start an IV."

"Do whatever you need to," Dusty said in a rush. It finally occurred to him, he did this to her. Was she getting a flood of the new memories he just gave her? Why wasn't it happening to him instead?

Katie's eyes opened slowly. A tear began to run down her cheek.

The nurse stopped. "You okay, honey?"

"I think so."

"I'm going to get the doc anyway. Be back in a flash."

After the nurse left, Dusty pressed his lips to Katie's forehead. "I'm so sorry, babe. Are you hurting?" She shook her head no and he stood upright again.

"You're a bastard," she said, softly. "Why didn't you tell me you went back?"

"I just got back to 'now' this morning. It's not like Courtney gave me a chance to tell you."

Katie winced. "I love you. You saved her."

He grinned wide. "Tit for tat, doll face. I owed you one. Did you see it all?"

"I think so. I can't believe I fell for a fumbling, mumbling goon."

"It would seem I have a gift when it comes to winning you over. You're a sucker, sugar. I wonder if I'll get to catch up on all the memories of them living next door."

"I could punch you in the nose and see if that starts it."

"Punch away."

She managed a smile. "Did you at least give Frank my love?"

"For what? That geezer didn't do shit for me besides leave me stranded in our past and send me to a different future for no reason."

"I beg to differ."

The two of them turned around to the sound of the familiar voice.

"You two will never figure it out, will you?"

"Frank!" Katie said with excitement. She wanted to get up but Dusty held her down.

"Give yourself a minute, baby." He turned back to Frank. "What do you mean by that?"

"First of all, you had to repeat what Katie went through. All of it. All or nothing, you punk ass kid. I do believe you said you'd plant your lips on my wrinkly ass if this turned out. Pucker up."

Dusty rolled his eyes. "Why did I have to relive Alyson's birth?"

"I was sick of you beating yourself up for choosing the route you did. You couldn't have changed anything, and it wasn't worth fretting over. She's happy, healthy, and perfect. I've also come to realize my kids are my proudest moments, and I didn't mind seeing that again as much as I thought."

"So you *were* there that night. Wait. *Your* kids?"

Frank removed his glasses, then a toupee, and then finally his moustache. Dusty and Kaitlyn were frozen in shock with the face that looked back at them. "I had to find out beyond a doubt that Katie wanted to relive those years. I was feeling that I'd been selfish. I guess this proved it once and for all."

"You're…." Again, Dusty couldn't find his words.

"Yes. You, you jackass." He smiled and moseyed over to Katie. "How you doin', cupcake?"

"I can't believe I didn't know it was you."

"You were a little preoccupied with the pickle you were in." He bent down and kissed her cheek.

Katie laughed. "You never said that our whole lives. Why do you say it now?"

"I got it from Alyson. Funny how that works, isn't it?" He winked at her and turned to the younger Dusty. "Don't make me come back again. I have great-grandchildren to occupy." Again he returned his attention to Katie. "When you're thirty-seven and I forget our anniversary, go easy on me, okay?" He gave Dusty a salute and walked out the door. Before Dusty could run after himself, the nurse and doctor rushed into the room. He wanted to stay at Katie's side more than kick the crap out of himself.

A quick exam showed she was fine. The doctor wanted to do a CT scan, but Katie assured him it wasn't necessary and refused.

"Just lie here until you feel better," the doctor said before they left.

Dean walked into the room. "You all right, Katie? I was worried sick but it was too close to leave Court alone."

"I'm fine. Just too much excitement, I think. Well?"

"It's a girl!"

Dusty helped Katie sit up. Dean walked over and gave her a strong hug.

"How's our little mama doing?" Dusty asked.

"Doing great. Hey, Dust. Was that your grandpa leaving here? Dude looked just like you."

Before he could answer, Dusty's nose began to bleed. Katie hollered his name and rushed to his side. Dean took his arm and helped him into a chair. He leaned his head back as Katie reached for the box of tissues. Dusty held one hand to his nose and another to his pounding forehead. "Goddammit, Katie. This shit hurts."

She gave his shoulder a squeeze. "Like a sonofabitch."

He dropped his head between his knees, for fear he was going to black out.

"What is going on with you two?" Dean asked. "I know you're not doing drugs. You rode Court and me like mad until we quit pot altogether. There's no way you're snorting anything."

"It's just a sympathy nosebleed for you, buddy. How many names did Court call you?"

"Sixteen and a few that made me want to check for a 666 tattoo on the back of her head. You sure you're all right?"

Dusty still held his head between his legs. "I'm fine. Go to your wife. We'll be in after a minute."

Dean turned to Katie. She nodded for him to go as she rubbed the base of Dusty's neck. "It'll just be another minute."

"Fuck me," Dusty mumbled.

"Later." She leaned down and kissed where she was rubbing, then continued with her massage. "Learning much?"

"Just that we've gotten to keep our best friends next door to us almost our whole married lives."

"We got to go to Hawaii again for their wedding, too."

"I see that. I also see we have a time share now."

"That was you and Dean, not me, my love."

"Yeah. I'm getting a woody here reliving the 'thank you' you gave me."

She leaned his head back and kissed his lips under the tissue. "Let's see the baby and say bye to Court and go home and get the kids."

"Let's leave them at Mrs. Nelson's for another hour."

Katie laughed. "We really shouldn't keep abusing her for sex time."

"Like she or they care."

"True enough." She sat on his lap and ran her fingers through his hair.

"What are you doing?"

"Did you see yourself? I need to run my fingers through your hair while I can."

He gave her a kiss. “I bet you’re still as gorgeous as you are today.”

“Sweet talker.” She kissed him again. “I wonder where you came up with that name.”

“Frank Collins? I don’t have the foggiest idea.”

She stood. “Come on, I want to see Court and the baby. You okay?”

He took the tissue away. The nosebleed had stopped. “I suppose so.” He stood. “Oh. When your client with Felecia moves, we have to adopt her.” Katie stared into his eyes. “I didn’t get that memory. What did you do?”

“I’ll fill you in later.”

They walked hand in hand to the door. Dusty stopped at the baby pictures that lined the wall. “Was this your birthing room for Alex?”

Katie looked around. “I’m not sure. Looks the same as the one Court’s in. Why?”

He pointed to one of the pictures. “The only baby with his arms sticking straight over his head is kind of hard to miss.”

Katie squealed as she touched the picture. “I always wondered if I carried him funny and that’s why he does that.” She gasped and cupped her hand over her mouth.

“What’s wrong, babe?” She pointed to the pictures of the two children surrounding Alex.

“Well, that answers that,” Dusty said as he held Katie by the waist and led her out of the room. Under each child was their first name only. To the left of Alex was Frank and to the right was Collin.

About the Author

June, who prefers to go by Bug, was born in Philadelphia but moved to Maui, Hawaii, when she was four. She met her "Prince Charming" on Kauai and is currently living "Happily Ever After" in Minnesota. Her son and daughter are her greatest accomplishments. She takes pride in embarrassing them every chance she gets.

Visit http://www.junekramin.com_for more releases.

Time Travel Trilogy:

Dustin Time
Dustin's Turn
Dustin's Novel

Romantic Suspense/Thriller:

Double Mocha, Heavy on Your Phone Number
Hunter's Find
Amanda's Return
I Got Your Back, Hailey
I've Also Got Your Front, Hailey
More Hailey coming soon!

Romance:

Come and Talk to Me
Money Didn't Buy Her Love
Devon's Change of Heart (Money Didn't Buy Her Love II)
I'll Try to Behave Myself

Contemporary Fiction

The Green Flash at Sunset
Baby, Just Say Yes

More to come!

Visit http://www.beforehappilyeverafter.com_for her middle grade fantasy series written under the pseudonym of Ann T. Bugg.

Made in the USA
San Bernardino, CA
02 August 2016